MOON OF COBRE

MOON OF COBRE

WILLIAM R. COX

SAGEBRUSH
Large Print Westerns

First published in Great Britain by ISIS Publishing Ltd.
First published in the United States by Bantam Books

Published in Large Print 2005 by ISIS Publishing Ltd.,
7 Centremead, Osney Mead, Oxford OX2 0ES,
United Kingdom,
by arrangement with
Golden West Literary Agency

British Library Cataloguing in Publication Data
Cox, William Robert, 1901–
    Moon of Cobre. – Large print ed. –
    (Sagebrush Western series)
    1. Western stories
    2. Large type books
    I. Title
    813.5'4 [F]

ISBN 0–7531–7306–9 (hb)

Printed and bound in Great Britain by
T. J. International Ltd., Padstow, Cornwall

Book One

THE CRIME

CHAPTER
ONE

Ben Hancock rose at eleven, his usual hour. The shades were drawn against the sun over the town of Cobre and it was hot in the room. Since, when at home, he slept nude, he washed carefully at the basin before donning clean cotton underwear and a linen shirt and his work clothing of dark, tailored trousers, tight-fitting in the legs, and the striped gray and black vest which was his trademark and upon which the polished star proclaimed his position as marshal. He tugged on handmade boots, grunting a little. Then he drew the curtains and surveyed the street, Buxton Street, the main stem.

Clouds stretched above, the sun was high and the street was quiet, or at least without untoward noise. Hal Wayne's four-span freight wagon was rumbling toward the Mogollons with supplies for the mines and kitty-corner across the street Linda Darr was watching for his morning greeting. He waved and she smiled and went back into her shop.

Hancock put on his roll-crown Stetson and went down the stairs to the office-jailhouse-kitchen of adobe which was his personal domain. There were no prisoners today, which was Friday. He made himself a skillet of bacon and eggs and picked up the newspaper

Dan Melvin left for him each day. The coffee was still warm from last night.

The headline read: Marshal Banishes Gambler from Texas.

Dan Melvin did not like Texans. There was another story, a dispatch from the East, captioned Treaty With Korea, which went on to say that President Arthur's representatives had signed an agreement of peace, amity, commerce and navigation with Korea, but did not give the location of that nation. Hancock made a mental note to ask Melvin where it was and turned his bacon. He liked to keep up with things now that he was a substantial citizen, and the editor of the *Copper Bulletin* was a great source of information. There had been a time, a more violent time, when the young Ben Hancock had not cared about such matters. He sipped the harsh black coffee, thinking a bit of old times, of those who had died and those, of smaller number, who had survived.

One of the survivors was overdue in Cobre right now; Luke Post, a friend. A man did not have many friends in this world, Hancock ruminated. It was good to tie to one who could be trusted. Now that times were good and there was a chance to cash in, a friend deserved a break; also Luke was always in a position to come up with ready capital.

The eggs sat like yellow-white twins in the grease, then turned brown at the edges. Hancock ladled the fat over the yolks to set them, moved the pan to the back of the stove. At that moment there was a commotion on Buxton Street.

Hancock sighed and went quickly through the office and to the door, pausing, blinking a little in the sunlight, a tall man, slightly stooped, clean-shaven in a day of beards, tanned and slender. People were coming out of their places of business, pedestrians were gaping. Linda Darr was in the window of her shop, looking toward Hancock, suppressing a grin even as she registered disapproval. There were three young girls, arm in arm, walking down the center of the street.

They wore mother hubbards. The small one in the middle had belted her robe tight to her tiny waist. They were smoking cigarettes and singing an indistinguishable melody. They were drunk, or they were muddled by drugs, or both. They were escapees from Mrs. Jay's house down on Maine Street and in the distance the pimp could be seen hurrying toward them.

Hancock debated. The pimp would beat them when he had dragged them home, but in the meantime there would be a scene. There was only one course open to him. He walked out and blocked the path of the three maids.

Daisy, the small one, looked up at him and sang, "Here's old marshal, my love, my love; come to give us all a shove . . ."

He said, "Now, darlin', you know better than this."

She said, "You should know what I know, you are my true love, my turtledove."

He said, "You needn't tell the world, Daisy, you'll get us both in trouble."

The young lady on the right hooted, "She's tellin' the truth, you always ask for her . . ."

5

Hancock cut her off. "Now, girls, Chompy's right behind you. Better you should come with me for awhile than have him on you, huh?"

Daisy said, "Chompy, Chompy, the hell with Chompy." She was extremely pretty and younger than she admitted. "I'll cut his heart out if he touches us."

Hancock sniffed. "Youall been smokin' that Mex weed. Now, come on, a rest will do you good."

The pimp, a sullen-faced young bully, walked widdershins in the background, undecided. Hancock gave him a look and made a gesture. Chompy retreated to the boardwalk.

Daisy said, "I don't mind, really. I don't mind." She turned to the others. "Do you girls mind?"

They considered. They were country girls, from some bleak ranch run down by misuse or from the mines where the living was worse. Daisy, the stranger not long from some place east of Cobre, was their leader in mischief. They giggled.

Hancock said, "You've already spoiled my breakfast. Now go ahead there."

He shepherded them into the building. The first two went resignedly, stolidly, easily stupefied by any display of authority. He detained the third for a moment, looking into her round, fringed eyes.

He said, "You go in the kitchen, Daisy."

"Maybe I will, maybe I won't."

"Daisy!" He stared hard at her.

She returned his gaze without flinching, then shrugged and went obediently into the kitchen. He opened a great oaken door with iron hinges which led into the jail. There were three single cells for serious offenders and a tank for Saturday night drunks. He put the two whores in the tank and they sat on the floor and mooned at him, smiling silly grins, trusting him.

The one called Cora said without guile, "You goin' to give Daisy a bounce, Marshal?"

"Just behave yourself, both of you." It was like admonishing schoolchildren. He went back into the office, to find Chompy lingering uncertainly in the doorway. Hancock told him, "Tell Mrs. Jay I won't fine them this time. And you keep your hands off them, understand?"

Chompy was a breed, with a low brow and greasy hair. "They need beatin', you know that."

"I don't know any such thing. Furthermore, I don't want to hear any of it."

"I got to keep 'em in line. Mrs. Jay depends on me to keep 'em in line."

"I said no beatings. Now get the hell out of here. You want to do something, stop them getting that Mexican weed."

"I can't find it. I dunno where they get it. You right, Marshal, a couple of them things and they start climbin' the walls. It's no good for Mrs. Jay's business."

"The town is getting down on youall. You tell her I'll be down to see her."

"She's got the only house in town," said Chompy reasonably. "We do what we can. You got to have a house."

"You've got to keep it quiet and decent."

7

"That damn railroad," Chompy complained. "Everybody's scared crapless about whether Cobre gets the damn railroad."

"True," said Hancock. "Includin' me. You savvy?"

Chompy swallowed. "I savvy." He departed, going north on Buxton Street. Hancock watched him turn down Pass Avenue toward Mrs. Jay's, then went into the kitchen.

The bacon was crisp but the eggs were congealed. Daisy had put it all on a platter and sat at the table, legs crossed, arms folded, staring into space. Hancock cut into a loaf of sourdough bread.

"You want something to eat?" he asked.

"No, thank you." The voice was distant, cool, without feeling but well placed.

He sat down and looked at her. "You're not high on that peyote or marijuana or whatever it's called. You're just having a ball, raisin' hell as usual."

"Is that so?"

"You tell me." He picked at the unappetizing breakfast, nibbling bits of bacon, dipping the bread into the eggs. She looked at him, half smiling without mirth. She was on the edge of beauty but there was something awry with her. He said again, "Tell me."

"Ha!"

"I'll never understand," Hancock complained. "You come from some place back East. I been there, I recognize things like your voice, the way you talk. When you do talk."

"Ho!"

"Oh, you talk, all right." He lowered his voice. "When the door is closed and it's dark upstairs in that room you say things. And you laugh. And you carry on some."

Now she stirred. "I'm a whore. All whores are actresses."

"You don't know a damn thing about whores. You're new at this. You enjoy it."

"That's a lie!"

"I've known whores all my life," he told her.

"And you're going to marry Linda Darr? Ha!"

"Contrary, that's you. Just plain ornery. But there's some reason for it. I want to know." She was so young and so tough she seemed invulnerable, but he knew better since he had lain with her so often. It was a problem that battered at him. He did not like mysteries, he was a forthright man. He had come to the time of life where reason was preponderant.

"I don't want you to know," she said calmly. "I'm Daisy, you see. Daisies don't tell."

"You keep sayin' that. Look, I know I can't change you, do anything for you, we been through all that. I just want to know what makes you tick, so I can look out for you."

"Just put me in the cell with the others. I've been up all night. I'm quite weary, Marshal."

He said helplessly, "Oh, sure. Put you in with the others. Like you belong with them. Why, you even got Mrs. Jay worried. I misdoubt that ever happened before. The way you carry on, knockin' things about, stirrin' up the others, you'd think she would get rid of you. But she only worries."

"She needs me." One rounded shoulder lifted the mother hubbard, she recrossed her legs. She obviously was naked beneath the thin covering. "If you want me in your bed, Marshal, why don't you say so?"

"Crazy. You're plumb crazy sometimes."

"Ha! You must like crazy, you always ask for me, never for any of the others." Now she laughed on a low, somehow dangerous note. "Why, Marshal, the world is insane. You and the law and this little town and the railroad and the Buxtons and the preacher who comes sneaking into my room when his wife won't have him and the mineowner with his funny ideas about what to do in bed, you think this isn't craziness?"

"Could be," he said. "But I'm wondering. How come you to know so much about craziness? Where are you from? Who is your mother and father?"

Now she froze. "Ha!"

"You know what happens to whores? You know? Course you don't know. Damn it, I've seen old whores die in jail, right here in Cobre."

"Ha! I'll never make an old whore." She got up and moved toward the door, swaying her hips. "Marshal, can't I please go to jail?"

"I could send you home," he said. "I'd be glad to see you got fixed up and pay your fare and all."

She turned and stared at him. "Home?"

"To your folks. Or to any place where you'd be all right."

For a moment she hesitated, her eyes widening like a child who has been proffered a sweet. Then she said, "Marshal, I'll go to hell my own way. In a basket or a hearse. But don't say 'home' to me. Not ever. Not ever again."

There was no mistaking the vehement finality of her tone, nor the hatred and lost innocence of her, nor the fire burning in her. He got up, feeling old and inadequate, and led her through the big door and into the cell area. The other two whores were sound asleep. Cora was sucking her thumb. He unlocked the door and allowed Daisy to join them. She lay down on a bunk and seemed to be immediately slumbrous.

He went back and locked the big door and hung up the key and went into the kitchen and scoured the dish, the pan, the other utensils — the insects of southwestern New Mexico were infamous — and tried to dismiss the pretty little whore from his mind. He should be satisfied with the world today but he was not, she had spoiled the edges of things.

He went into his office and sat behind the scarred heavy table with two drawers which served as his desk. There were dodgers on the walls and a calendar with a snow scene and a gunrack holding rifles and shotguns. There were three bucket chairs and a small potbellied stove polished and somnolent for summertime. His revolver and belt hung on a wooden peg and each hour gathered a bit of dust from the street and he knew he should cleanse it. Instead, he went out and walked north on Buxton Street.

Across from his office at Jersey Street and Buxton was Abe Getz's Dry Goods Emporium, then two dwellings, then the Wells Fargo office. He walked across to speak with Speedy Jackson, who handled the telegraph wire and ran the freight and passenger business and knew all that happened, sometimes even before it took place. Speedy was small and thin and very sporty, bow string tie, striped shirt, green eyeshade as badge of office.

"Some folks burnin' up the wires, believe me." He spoke out of the corner of his mouth, confidentially. "The railroad, the railroad. I say damn the smelly, noisy damn railroad."

"Why, they'll have you running the telegraph office at the station," Hancock said. "It'll be right nice for you."

"Like hell. I come here to get away from trains. Hate 'em, they stink." Jackson altered his tone, became reproachful. "I seen you pickin' up the gals. Too bad."

"They're asleep and happy as beavers."

"Not Daisy. Don't tell me Daisy's happy."

"I wouldn't know about her." He evaded the subject. "Anything new from Santa Fe?"

"Just the same damn thing, railroad, railroad, railroad."

"Got a pal coming in on the stage. Luke Post," Hancock said. "Look after him, huh? I'm ridin' out a spell."

He went past Mueller's General Store and crossed Alamo Avenue and waved at Smokey Moriarty, the aged fire chief. Cobre had really grown up since he had come here to act as marshal five years ago. He came to the Chinaman's laundry, went down the alley to the rear, next door to Lawyer Finnegan's office.

He went through a door, parted a hanging bamboo portiere. The odor of tobacco and opium was overpowering. He yelled, "Hey, Ching Hoo," and retreated to the alley.

There was a furious fantan game going on in the back room and Hancock knew it but no one took any interest, since it was a foreigny business and had nothing to do with local affairs excepting when violence broke out, in which case Hancock knew what to do. Ching Hoo was an old man with a long, skinny mustache, a great hand-rubber and diplomat.

"You got any of the old stuff left?" Hancock asked.

"For my friend." Ching Hoo bowed low.

"Send six pints over to my place pronto. Neddy will be there."

Ching Hoo said, "Mebbe I no got six, though."

"Six of the best. I've got a pardner coming in," said Hancock. "Don't disappoint me, now."

"You velly good to me. I am humble servant. Six."

"That's what I said. A half dozen. Six." It was a small enough graft, he thought, going back onto Buxton Street. The still was in the yard, between the law offices and Smokey Moriarty's house on School Street, which ran parallel to Buxton. Everyone knew it was there but they also knew that Ching Hoo aged his whiskey in some peculiar manner of his own, and that it was better than anything that could be supplied by Madison's or the Mex places or the general store's brand of eastern stuff. Cobre was willing to wink at federal law under any circumstances and Ching Hoo made a nice dollar selling to the more prosperous citizens.

On Buxton Street two drunken soldiers from Fort Bayard were arguing in loud tones. Hancock went close and listened.

"I tell you, New York's the place," said a red-haired infantryman.

"Chicago," said a horse soldier. "Crap on New York."

"New York," said the redhead and aimed a punch at his companion.

Hancock reached out and caught them each by the collar and brought them sharply together. They cried out in pain and struggled, trying to kick at him. He rammed their skulls against the wall of the law offices until they were babbling incoherently for mercy. He turned them loose and said, a bit out of breath, "Dammit, get back to the fort. It's too early to be drunk in Cobre, don't you know that?"

They cursed him in an undertone, but made for their horses at the nearby rack. He waited until they had, with some difficulty, mounted and started on the east road to Bayard, then he went across Buxton Street, thought of entering the elaborate establishment of Jim Madison, booze, gambling and rooms upstairs, very fancy, the best place in town, decided against it. He had already decided not to go down the alley past Madison's to Mrs. Jay's to speak about the girls. He went instead into the livery stable and blacksmith shop of Jeb Truman.

The wide, bushy-bearded smithy was hammering on an anvil, shaping the ends of a broken whiffletree. It was off a Candlestick wagon which waited lopsided in the yard. Young Neddy Truman, the spittin' image of his father, waved a hand and his father stopped pounding.

Hancock said, "I'd like for Neddy to spell me awhile. I got to ride out, thought I'd take your buckboard."

"You want the roan?" asked Neddy. "He's rested."

"The roan'll be fine," said Hancock and the boy went to hitch up the rig.

Jeb Truman said, "Nice day, Marshal."

"It is that."

"People still ravin' about the rails?"

"Some people."

"I got some land on the right o'way, too," said Truman. "But I dunno. This hell hole of a town, you think the railroad people will come through here?"

"No more of a hole than Centro," said Hancock. "It's six of one, half dozen of t'other."

"Them hoors," said Truman. "I keep tellin' Neddy, I catch him with them hoors again I'll kill him."

"You just happen to live near them. Why don't you build over on School Street or some place?"

"I got my business here, I live here." Truman was dogged. "Let them hoors move."

It was true that the Truman property ran from Buxton through to the short block, Texas Street, which alone separated him from Mrs. Jay's place. His dwelling was only one empty lot removed from the palace of joy. From thence, Maine Street did an oblique turn to the

Mexican section of Cobre. It was the north end of the town, far removed from the more elite establishments of the south end and Jeb Truman was ever bitter about this, feeling himself looked down upon by the banker, the butcher and the candlestick-maker.

"Jeb, you're a good man," Hancock told him. "But you are as stubborn as your best mule. Either you live with your business or you move to the other side of town and live like you think you want to live."

"That's what Ma keeps saying. I swan, you and Ma and Neddy. All alike. Can't see things. I was here first, wasn't I? Why can't the damn hoors move?"

"They don't want them on the other side of town, not any more than you want them here."

Truman said, "Raisin' tarnation hell all night. Howlin' and paradin' past the windows nekkid."

"Keep your shades drawn." This was an old story, Hancock had been through it many times.

"Let them keep their damn shades drawed," roared Jeb. Behind him his son made signs, the rig was ready.

Hancock said, "Jeb, I do believe you stay up nights peekin' out your window just to see what's goin' on at Mrs. Jay's."

He ducked the swing of Truman's maul and skipped outdoors, laughing. The smithy was half in earnest, half in jest, he knew. The son was a goodhearted, good-natured, healthy boy of twenty, strong as two oxen. They got into the buckboard and drove back to the marshal's office through increasing traffic.

Neddy said, "Good thing Pop didn't ask about who you got in the hoosegow or he wouldn't've let me come."

Hancock dug in his pocket for keys. "See you don't get caught in the cell with them, now. I'm trustin' you."

"Oh, I won't get caught," said Neddy. "And I do thank you for the chance — I mean the job."

"The town pays for deputies when I need them," said Hancock. "Don't thank me — and make damn sure you're not caught."

He waited until Neddy brought him a rifle and his gun belt and some ammunition, which he put on the seat alongside him. The buckboard was a special, well braced and springy contraption, comfortable on the open road. He drove down to Broadway at the south end of town, turned west to the courthouse at the head of the avenue, then south again on Gary Road. There were mountains all about him, the ever-changing, ever-present clouds formed a brave series of shapes and pictures for his delight. The grama grass grew belly-high on the plain. This was a wide valley or a high plain, whichever one chose to consider it. Cattle grazed within a mile of town, but to the southwest were copper and silver mines. It was conglomerate country; even the Apaches were whimsical, sometimes quiet enough, biding their time before again coming out to devastate unwary outlying habitations. It was strong and rough and beautiful country, poppies growing wild along the edges of the road, mesquite intermingling with green grass, yucca standing high in scattered array like a broken battalion in a war scene.

17

This was Candlestick, but just prior to reaching its border were the plots Hancock owned. He had bought them on a tip, a strip of them, one acre wide, and those he could not swing himself he had purchased in the name of Luke Post, who had sent the money posthaste. He could see them from the road and he lifted a hand in fond salute.

A career on the frontier plying his trade of lawman had brought him little. He was thirty-five and it was time to think of settling down. It was time either to go the way of others he had known, shooting and drinking and whoring, or to marry and raise a family. It came to that.

He had been a boy in Texas, a drover with Luke Post, going up the trail to Kansas in the earlier days, learning what could be learned from the rough men and the good men and the medium men. Luke had taken to cards and made it big in Denver. Hancock had taken to lawing in Dodge for awhile, then the other places as the rails came, making westward, shuffling the cattle business, watching over the cowboy towns to their little deaths. He had gone back to Texas, always moving when the commerce came in and the solid citizens took over. Now he had come to leaving his guns in the office, walking the street like the patrolmen he had seen on his one big bust in New York with Luke.

This was the way of Cobre, founded on cattle and mining, struggling to be a respectable rail center. The railroad would mean the end of the rough stuff, the end of Ching Hoo and possibly of Mrs. Jay and certainly of such as Jed Buxton and the wild bunch of riders who worked Candlestick. The miles of Buxton fence, starting here south of Hancock's property, would not be affected, Matt Buxton's beef would simply be driven to town instead of to the railhead. Not that Matt Buxton worried, he no longer had to fret about money. Matt's fence stretched for twelve miles along the Gary Trail, Matt's cows were fat and sassy, Matt himself was fat and sassy.

Well, Hancock would have money also when the rails came. The Judge and Banker Clark and Abe Getz and all the rest were planning on the railroad, it was as good as built right into Cobre. If the situation just remained normal so that the big-money people could retain their trust in the town's future, everything would be all right.

The horse slowed down for a steep grade. Hancock let the reins loose, stretched his legs. It was a good country to settle in, he thought. He had been born in the Southwest, he knew it all, the desert, the mountains, the high plains. He was part of it and it was part of him. Everyone knew him despite his long absences, he was Pat Hancock's son, one of the old families. Even the new people, the farmers and bankers and storekeepers and mining people, knew that Pat Hancock had been killed by Cochise's Apaches, some said by Cochise himself, as if that was a big honor.

There was a chance he might run for sheriff. Elias Buchanan was getting old and had never been a real town buster. Buck was a politician, first and last, and the meeting to which Hancock was now making his way was political. The old sheriff had a lot of things on his mind, mainly, as everyone else, the railroad.

19

At the top of the rise the ground was rocky, with the poppies defying the stony soil and the yucca brave but scarce. Two miles south was the swinging gate to Candlestick, where the meeting was to be held. There was a break in the barbed wire just below the promontory on which Hancock pulled in to blow the hired horse.

Hancock reached for his gun belt, donned it. The cut ends of the wire were shiny, brand-new. They had been made not long ago. There were tracks, also fresh and new.

He pulled the buckboard off the road and tied it to a sapling. He took the rifle and crossed to the break in the fence. He hunkered down and examined the tracks.

There were three ponies, unshod. Then there was a horse, a big animal with a broken shoe on its left front hoof. It was plain enough that three Apaches were stalking Candlestick beef. It happened all the time, it had nothing to do with warfare on a large scale, the braves were hungry and their women wanted meat for a stew.

If it had not been for the track of the horse he might have gone to the ranch for help. If he had good sense, he thought, he would do that right now. But the big horse was probably ridden by a white man and since Sheriff Buchanan was expected for the conference at Candlestick it might well be he who had chased in after the Apaches.

Hancock debated, walking in the tracks. There was a rocky knoll of some height to his right. He climbed it, careful of the way he went, avoiding loose stones. A yucca grew bravely and there was some sparse buffalo grass atop the little hill. The pasture was beyond but he could not get a view of it. He was obliged to go farther to see what was going on. The silence was oppressive, he began to sweat, knowing Apaches, knowing the aging, somewhat clumsy sheriff.

It would have been better to let the Indians take the beef. Matt Buxton could well spare a steer or two. They needed it or they would not have come in this close — or they were young braves daring each other, making a brave deed of their thieving.

There were people, maybe a majority of people, who claimed the Apaches were not human, that they were varmints to be extinguished before the country could be safe. It was true that they were "The People" and would not meekly surrender no matter how chivvied and oppressed by the military, indeed often turned to whip a troop to bits. They would have to be decimated and chained and guarded before it was all over and even then, he thought, it would be no cinch to keep them in order. But, after all, this had been their land. He had sympathy for them.

He came down off the knoll and just then there was the flat crack of a gun and then a yell which was half a moan. Hancock ran back up the hill, the sweat now pouring from him, his ears aching with the sounds he knew were coming. It was Buchanan, all right, by the voice. The high, keening scream could be the sheriff also, as the Apaches closed in on their wounded prey.

There was no use going in alone and on foot. It was too late, Hancock knew very well. He levered a shell into place and took out his revolver and placed it beside him on the hilltop in case the Remington should jam. He heard the scream again, but the Apaches were in a hurry and the torture would not be prolonged.

After awhile the three of them came down around the hill, riding slowly, defiantly, slaughtered beef in coarse sacks across the rumps of their ponies. They were very young. One of them yipped and waved a bloody piece of hair. Another gave their peculiar, keening war cry. The one in the lead was grinning; he was scarcely more than a boy.

Hancock shot the boy through the body. Then he threw down on the second rider, the one with Buchanan's scalp. The Apache fell over backward, slid down the tail of the pony, which bolted. The third got off a shot from an old musket. Hancock felt the wind of it as he shot the Indian point-blank, through the left side of the chest.

The first Indian was trying to crawl to where his rifle lay. He had a knife in his hand. Blood streamed from his belly but he still crawled. Hancock shot him through the head.

"Settin' ducks," he muttered, wiping away the sweat. "A hell of a thing. Like shootin' fish in a barrel."

Still, there was the sheriff. He scrambled down from the promontory and went past the Indians, cautious, making sure all were dead, knowing how hard they died in battle. There was another slope, which had cut off his view of the meadow. The grass was so high that the bellies of the cattle were hidden by it. Flies buzzed and a buzzard circled.

They always knew, the black birds, he thought, picking up the tracks again and following through the thick, tall grass. They were on the spot as soon as the deed was done. They were circling to pick out the initial repast of what promised to be a great day for buzzards.

The big horse was munching at roots. Buchanan lay stretched out on his back. He had worn his hair bushy and thick and now he was bloody-bald.

They had hit him in the shoulder to knock him off the old roan horse. Then they had stuck an arrow in each eye and sliced away at his testicles and then they had scalped him. Buchanan was not young, he had probably died quickly, before he knew all that happened, Hancock hoped. The Apaches were young and they had their beef and they were in a hurry or it would have been worse.

There was nothing more he could do. He went back along the way he had come. He walked past the dead Indians to the road. He felt old and weary. He untied the horse and snapped the reins and drove on to the gate over which the Candlestick brand was simulated on a weathered signboard. He drove up the well-worn road to the main house. He was still sweating and the inside of his mouth was dry.

Matt Buxton had built the best and biggest and most comfortable ranch house in New Mexico, or at least he so boasted, for his wife Virgie. The couple were childless. The house was a byword in the entire Southwest. Brick had been brought from rail's end, fine glass from San Francisco, tile from Mexico. It was Spanish style, with the patio in the center, two stories high, with a cheerful red roof. Instead of palmetto there were pines from the high plains.

Beyond was the bunkhouse, in the same fashion, but spartan, as befitted the station of the riders, and indeed exceeding their fondest desires, since running water was provided from the stream that ran burbling all the way from the Gila River to the west. Even Matt Buxton's tough home guard appreciated running water, Hancock knew.

The stable was imposing, unlike most ranch barns, a place to store hay for the Morgans and other fine horses, a place for milch cows, and nearby a pen for hogs and a white-washed chicken house. One of Matt's favorite penalties for disobedience was to set his hands to work cleaning that chicken run. The corral was close at hand and it was here that action was taking place as Hancock drew rein and descended, his knees, annoyingly, buckling a little as he moved toward the imposing, bulky figure of the owner of Candlestick.

The men were yelling, and beyond the spectators and the rail fence Jed Buxton could be seen, atop a bucking, flailing young buckskin, a wild one, it appeared. Jed was high-waisted and wide-shouldered, he took after his mother, and he could twist a bronch with the best of them, Hancock conceded — which was about all he was good for.

The home guard lined the fence, ordinary enough cowboys, made tough mainly because Matt was tough and Jed was mean; Kit Larson, Dave Pitts, Muley Ward and Sandy Farr. These were what some people believed to be the guns of Candlestick, although they had other titles and indeed Larson was foreman of the ranch, a rawboned man of great physical strength and tenaciousness of character. All were loyal first to Matt, then to the brother. Now they were howling encouragement to the buckskin, in the fashion of the time and place, maligning the rider. Matt paused, staring at Hancock; a fat man, of medium height, with a strong jaw and narrow eyes and long apelike arms ending in huge hands.

"You seen a ghost, Ben?"

Hancock said, "Worse."

"Better come in and have one." Matt turned, leading the way through a gate and then through his office and into the patio, where it was cool and water tinkled and the Chinaman named Hip Toy was smiling and producing, as though by magic, a tray with a bottle and fine glasses from some place in Europe. Hancock remembered the architect who had done all this at Matt's behest, a slim man from Philadelphia, who spoke with a slight lisp but seemed to know all the good things, the material things to make a rich man feel secure in his castle.

They sat at a tiled table and Matt, always sensitive, asked quietly, "Something real bad?"

"Over on your west meadow," said Hancock. He took a drink of the good liquor. "Gettin' old, Matt. Haven't seen a dead friend in too long, maybe. Three 'Paches got one of your steers — and Elias."

"Buchanan?" Matt's eyebrows shot up toward his lowering hairline. "What the hell?"

"Yes, what the hell? Buck didn't have any sense, we know that. Thought Indians were dumb animals. He went in after them and they stuck arrows in his eyes for luck."

"The bastards." Matt waited, expectant but not questioning.

"I was a few minutes too late. Reckon that's what is bothering me. Just a couple minutes, maybe not that if I'd gone dumb-head into the pasture. Took high gun on 'em."

"How many?"

"Only three."

"You got 'em?"

"There's a mess in your field," said Hancock. "Better get it cleaned up, there's buzzards already."

"Hip Toy," said Matt, not taking his eyes from Hancock. "Send the boys with a wagon and some shovels to the south pasture. Bury the Injuns, bring in the sheriff."

Hancock took another drink. "Damn, it made me sick. Things have been so quiet, a man forgets how it was. Damn Buck for going in there alone."

"Bad luck," said Matt. He poured himself a second libation. "You on your way here to meet him, too. This changes things, Ben. It changes everything we was to talk about."

Hancock shook his head. "I hate to think on it."

"Poor Buck gets a funeral instead of another term in office. Nice man, Buck. Not a strong man, but he had his own kinda guts." The fat man ruminated. "You're shook. But you got to know it, you'll be sheriff."

It was true. Had it been in the back of his mind all the time, lurking behind the shock and disgust and horror? Had he realized it the moment he heard the first shots?

He said, "Hadn't thought of that. Naturally."

Matt Buxton said, "You will. It's the logical way. County seat is Cobre. You the only lawman. Who else?"

"I don't know. Somebody will run. It's a good job. Taxes, all that, fees for certificates." Hancock heard himself talking calmly, and it helped. "But if you and the town say so, then I reckon it's me all right."

"Town's got the votes."

"You've got the say-so." Hancock finished the drink.

"I say so," said Matt without inflection. He could swing the county vote and influence the town vote. He could do about anything he wanted in this country. He had been early in the land, he had come up from Texas with a herd and had marked the grama grass and had returned with wife and his little brother Jed and had conquered all — drought, Indians, mining interests, rustlers, hoof-and-mouth disease, storms from the mountains; and he had built this empire.

"I'm grateful, Matt," Hancock said.

"Don't suppose you'd care to eat right now."

"No, I couldn't right now," he said. "Sorry. I liked old Buck." He paused, then added, "And I haven't had to kill a man in some time. It was never one of the things I cared about, you know that."

"You was a good law officer," said Matt. "And Injuns ain't rightly people, you got to figure."

"They breathe, they walk around, they have feelings. I've always wondered about Indians. Never knew too much about them, not the real ones, the ones like those up yonder in the hills."

"Nobody knows about 'em," said Matt. "They don't want you to know about 'em."

"Could be." Hancock finished his drink. "Never thought I'd be squeamish. Town livin', it softens you up."

"Sure you won't stay?"

There was a sound behind them and Jed Buxton came through the gate, dusting his boots, looking as always neat and clean and expensive. He wore only handmade clothing, even on the range, it was said. He was fifteen years younger than his brother and beneath his mustache his lip trembled a little, giving the lie to his swagger.

"You find 'em?" asked Matt.

"Sure. The boys are cleanin' up." Jed spoke to Hancock. "You sure did make a mess, didn't you?"

"Partly. Partly it was the 'Paches." It was hard to conceal his dislike for the spoiled brat of the Buxton family.

Jed reached for the whiskey decanter. Matt unobtrusively put his hand over it, spoke to his brother.

"Bothered you, did it? Don't start up, now."

The strangely unjointed face darkened, Jed blurted, "Sure you didn't do in ole Buck to get his job, Marshal?"

Hancock, already on his feet for departure, felt his throat contract. His right hand went to his gun butt, he fought for control.

Matt said gently, "Now, now. That ain't funny, Jed. You just upset, that's all."

He interposed his bulk between them, taking Hancock by the elbow, steering him toward the patio gate. When they were outside he said, "I know you been havin' trouble with Jed in town. I know how he is."

"Do you, Matt? Do you think you know?"

"He's wild." Matt Buxton wiped a hand across his face, a bit bewildered. Then he toughened up. "He never had a ma or a pa. Only me. I was real busy, Ben. It's my fault he's like he is."

In the face of what he knew was a plea, Hancock relaxed, removing himself from Matt's grasp. "He's going to catch it, some day. Well, we're all upset. I'll take care of notifying Buck's family. See you in town."

"Tomorrow's the ball. They won't call it off. Buck don't — didn't — live in Cobre. Truth, he didn't have too many friends, real friends," said Buxton. "You know that. He was — kinda — my man."

"I know. See you, then." Hancock got into the buckboard. He clucked to the horse and retraced his route along the private road. He was angry at Jed, he was usually angry at Jed. Buck, he thought, had certainly been Buxton's man, he had dwelt on Buxton property, he was seldom among the people he represented excepting in the line of duty. And now, would Ben Hancock be otherwise than Buxton's man?

A wagon came in view, Larson driving, the others riding behind. They were headed for town and the undertaking establishment of Con Boyd. They had wrapped the body in a tarp. Hancock waved curtly and went past them, urging the horse. He hoped Luke Post had arrived on the stage as planned. He needed to sit down and talk to a friend, someone he could trust.

He was aware, then, of hunger. Four men dead, but a man has to eat, he thought, a hell of a world. A few hours ago it had seemed simple enough. Now — it was lousy, a puking place, the world which contained deadly Indians and sonsofbitches like Jed Buxton and victims like Buck Buchanan.

Maybe he should have stayed in the East. He remembered Laurie Pomfret with a sudden shock of loss. He had been young then, and Luke had been young, and nothing daunted them. Laurie had been a revelation to him, a woman widowed and with a child, still a girl, already somewhat famous as a singer in the expensive halls, a chanteuse they called her, a beautiful girl with a hearty laugh and a fine feeling for a western visitor. She had taught him many things — not least the joys of cleanliness and bodily care . . . He must have been in love with her.

Yet he had left with Luke, returned to the Southwest. She had been, after all, no virgin, and he had bedded her — and this, in his simple lexicon of those days, meant that they could never marry. His wife must be pure, an angelic character, knowing no other man, a worshipper of himself, forbidding all others. A stupid belief, he now knew, a callow interpretation of things he had heard and read and been led to believe. He had been a damned fool of the first water. Linda Darr was no part of Laurie Pomfret. Linda Darr was the best New Mexico could afford him now, but at her best she was a faint carbon of lively, vital, lovely Laurie, the New York girl.

But he would probably marry Linda. That was the way things worked out, a man at thirty-five had to be wise, there were few attractive women in the country, there were a dozen reasons why he would marry Linda Darr.

CHAPTER
TWO

The moon tucked itself behind a cloud bank and rain fell on Lordsburg, dripping from the harness of the horses drawing the stagecoach, running from the hatbrims of the driver and the shotgun. Brakes squealed and a man came from the doorway of the hotel with a large umbrella, hurrying, hand outstretched. Within the stage the woman moaned and put a hand on the latch, saying, "Not another mile tonight, Brewster. I can't do it, you understand?"

"Quite, madam." A burly man got out on the street side, speaking to the driver, asking for the luggage. There were four huge cases.

The hotel clerk was saying, "Mrs. Van Orden, we had your telegram. Everything is waiting for you. Welcome to Lordsburg, ma'am."

"Thank you." Her voice was musical, carefully placed, polite, not quite formal. She placed a dainty booted foot upon the step and leaned on the proffered hand, ducking under the umbrella with grace, so that her perfume wafted up to the shotgun, causing him to cough into a horny hand.

"Bye, Miz Van Orden," he croaked. "Real nice drivin' with you. Sorry you ain't goin' to Cobre with us."

"Thank you, you've been wonderful," she called as the coach splashed away in the sudden puddles. She hugged the clerk's arm, picking her way across the boards, her traveling skirt of dust-covered serge held high above ankles that brought a whistle from somewhere in the dark. She laughed, liking that, liking all the rough men who had ogled her so openly but politely for all the miles of the bumpy, wearying, interminable journey westward.

The lobby was gloomy, ill-lit. Two men lounged in chairs, one with a newspaper, his gray sombrero pulled down on the bridge of his nose, a man all in gray, down to stitched gray boots. His clothing was extremely neat, his trousers properly rounded like a stovepipe. He was watching, of course.

She looked neither left nor right, going to the foot of the stairs. Brewster, in tweeds and stout British low-cut boots and gaiters and a hard hat, came with the four cases, imperturbable, bearing his burden with dignity and enormous strength, pausing a moment for instructions.

"If you'll sign, please," said the clerk, folding the umbrella, scurrying behind the desk.

She walked four steps, found the pen, gazed at it for a moment, then wrote, "Mrs. Laurie Pomfret Van Orden, London, England." She tilted back her bonnet, loosening the ribbon beneath her chin, glancing around, chin high, eyes bright. It had been said in London, Paris, Rome, Madrid that she was a beautiful woman. She was thirty-five now and was anxious for this to remain true. There was a sheen to her, as on an expensive gem.

The man in gray also lifted his head. His eyes were deepset and hungry, he was quite handsome in a chiseled, formal manner, cheekbones and nose prominent. His glance met hers and held, each recognizing something special in the other, but when it appeared that he would speak she turned and followed Brewster up the stairway, the clerk following with a key.

The chamber was spacious, "Best in the house — in New Mexico," the clerk bragged, accepting a gold coin, staring at it in amazement, hesitating, then pocketing it. A Mexican woman appeared, as ordered in the telegram, with hot water, and a coffin-shaped tin tub was carried in by two boys who stared round-eyed at the grand lady. Brewster distributed more money, everyone bowed out. Laurie followed the clerk to the door and spoke quietly.

"The man in gray, who might he be?"

In a whisper, the clerk replied, "You wouldn't want to know him, ma'am. That's Cole Strand."

"Should I know the name?"

"No, ma'am. He's a gunner."

"A gunner? In the military?"

"Nothing like it. He's a killer, a hired gunslinger, downed a dozen men we know about."

She raised a perfect brow. "And why is he not in jail?"

"Well, he's quick. He don't murder anybody. He just calls them out."

"A duel?"

"You might say. Only with Strand, who's got a chance?"

"You mean he calls his man out and the man cannot win?"

"That's about it."

"And this is not against — oh yes, I remember now. Someone told me, years ago. Yes. I remember." She nodded and went back into the room and closed the door. "Ben Hancock. He went away, Brewster."

"I don't quite understand, madam." Brewster's face was flushed from the steam of the very hot water. He was pouring scented oil into the tub.

"The one who went away." She began to remove her outer clothing. She sat down and attacked her buttoned boots wearily, sadly. "A western man."

"Quite, madam." Brewster was unconcerned with the past, trying the temperature of the water. "A bath will do it for you, madam."

She said, "You are a wonder, my friend. My late husband was right. You are the greatest legacy I could have."

"It's a pleasure, madam." He knelt, a bulky figure, to unfasten the other boot. When he arose he said, "And now I'll be having my own bath, if you please."

"Do you think she is really there? In Cobre?" Her eyes were bright, but then they darkened and she asked faintly, "Do you think she's forgiven me?"

"I couldn't say," Brewster said softly. "I never knew her."

"All my fault," she said, rocking her body back and forth. "I left her behind. And then I married Donald and should have sent for her. I knew of the strange thing within her. A wildness, a heartbreaking way she had of staring into space. She didn't know about her father, of course. It was — in her. The life I led, she must have hated it. Then I left her, with that French governess."

"Let us hope she is in Cobre."

"Those Pinkertons, they have been wrong so often."

"Let us hope," he repeated, going to the door.

"All the money and what is it worth? Nothing."

"It pays for hiring the detectives," he suggested.

She managed a smile for him. "Brewster, what would I do without you? They do not breed your kind in this United States. You are wonderful, wonderful."

Expressionless he said, "Thank you, madam," and bowed himself out.

She shed the rest of her garments, leaving them in a heap on the floor. She slid into the tub, taking with her a bar of scented soap. She had never been one to regard her body as anything more than useful, she did not examine it now, working up lather, letting her mind ride back, facing the facts, as she had always faced them.

All her own fault, she repeated, as a litany. Once she had blamed others, but the years had brought recognition of things within herself which were responsible for all the trouble. Karma, the strange Hindu had said in England, bringing it upon yourself either now or in another incarnation. By your own actions, he had said.

As a child in Newark in New Jersey, she had been spoiled by her parents, by the teachers at Miss Craig's school, by the voice teacher at the conservatory. She remembered herself, a fair child in pantaloons, walking through Military Park beneath the huge old oaks, her bearded, tall father holding her hand, talking to her, telling her that her voice was God's gift, that she should use it for the common weal, that she did not need money, there was plenty, that life could be kind to her only if she were kindly toward others. A fine man, Dr. Sidney Pomfret, he was of a wealthy family who had come to America during colonial days. Everyone loved Dr. Pomfret. No one knew he drank applejack from the moment he got up until he fell asleep at midnight.

Her mother had been beautiful, but the drinking, indulged in at first to keep her husband company, later to bolster her failing health, had finished her early. So it happened that the money ran out about the time fifteen-year-old Laurie eloped with the coachman, Jack Grimm, who beat her and tried to sell her on the streets of New York, and she pregnant at the time. Dr. Pomfret had delivered the baby, had altered the birth certificate to suit future laws by naming it Maureen Pomfret, and then had died quietly in his bed.

And Jack had died, too, trying to hold up a New Jersey train in emulation of the James Gang of Missouri, for whom he had always had great admiration — Jack Grimm, a handsome, filthy, evil young man — the father of her child.

But that had been later, much later. It was in the waning time of the war that she had gone to New York and made her first appearance at a concert for which she had paid herself, from her depleted inheritance.

Fortunately she chose for her finish a song called "The Battle Hymn Of The Republic." Max Goldman heard her, put her before vast audiences at no charge, at rallies, in the music halls. She became "The Songbird Of The North," and when the strife ended she was an established performer.

She could then rid herself of the aging Goldman and begin to enjoy life. She made money and she spent it. She took lovers and left them. Scarred by her unwise marriage, she was careful to make no permanent associations.

It had been a great life, she admitted, soaping her abundant bosom. If she had only spent more time with the baby, things would have been fine. If she had, possibly, tried harder to hold onto the young westerner, Ben Hancock . . .

He was the only man who had come close to becoming dear to her, she thought. His simplicity, his naivete, his maleness had broken down barriers. He had been delightful with Maureen, then a baby. He had been very young, no older than herself — and he had explained honestly and truthfully that he could not marry her and had better take leave while the going was good. And she had agreed.

Now she did not know. She wondered if he were dead. Had a gunman like Cole Strand called him out to shoot him? She had heard from time to time of his friend, Luke Post, who had been in New York with him. Luke, a high gambler, owner of race horses, had come East more than once, but she had never sought him out, sensing that he had not approved of her, that he may have been the one who warned Ben against her.

And then had come Donald Van Orden, a blond, elderly, gentle Britisher, and she had married him. He had been nervous when around Maureen, and she had been forced to leave the girl in New York while she toured Europe, meeting lords and ladies and counts and countesses and yogi and a king and a queen, singing for all of them, drinking wine and dancing all night, her complaisant husband tagging at her high heels. But Donald had died of it, the pace had ruined his heart. It was like losing a cousin or an uncle, she reflected, rinsing the soap from herself. The water was becoming tepid and the room temperature lower as the rain beat down upon the roof and streamed across the windows. She arose and reached for the towel, her own towel from Scotland, thick and comforting.

There was a lot of money. Brewster, who had been a butler and general factotum, knew more about that than she did. Brewster had come to New York as a matter of course, he was a man faithful to the Van Ordens, and that family was now extinct. He had liked her from the first, she realized, because she did not care about the money, because she was unaffected and because, unlike the British, she had no class consciousness.

And with the disappearance of Maureen it was fortunate that she had the solid Brewster to bolster her. It had been a tremendous shock when she received the news. The dull ache, the sense of guilt had never left her from that moment to this. The long boat trip had been well-nigh unendurable, it had altered her, she realized, it had changed her entire outlook upon life. She could never be carefree until she found the girl. She could never be herself until she had repaired, somehow, the damage.

Even Ben Hancock, she thought, had remarked that the child needed more attention. It was in Central Park and they had been rowing on the lake amidst the swans and Maureen had been radiant, and then they had gone to the house on 20th Street and the nurse had taken the child for the evening.

"It don't seem right," he had said. "Seems like we oughta tuck her in, or somethin'."

But they had gone dancing, then to her performance, then dancing again until late and she had not even kissed the sleeping child good night. Not even a good-night kiss, she repeated. How often had Maureen lain awake, waiting for her mother?

It had to be made up, she told herself. Somehow, by some means, it had to be made right. The past, she well knew, could not be mended, but the future could be managed. No matter what the child wanted — she must have it. There was money enough, and as for the rest, it was up to her, Laurie, to provide.

She heard a noise in the hall, there was a stealthy tap on the door. She walked across the room and hung up the towel and put on a robe. The gunslinger, she thought, Cole Strand.

She waited, unafraid, not even thinking about the man. She heard Brewster's voice.

"Madam does not wish to be disturbed."

"Who says so?" Strand's voice was soft and even, with a southern inflection.

"Your pardon, sir, she has left instructions."

She found a bottle of French brandy in one of the cases, also two small glasses of exquisite workmanship wrapped in chamois. She put them on the night table, smiling to herself, and sat upon the edge of the bed. There was a derringer in her other bag, but she did not attempt to reach it.

"I merely wanted to pay my respects to a lady, sir. If you'll take her a message? My name is Cole Strand," the purring voice went on.

"Madam is weary," said Brewster.

"I see. Tomorrow, then?"

"Tomorrow we proceed to Cobre," said Brewster, not friendly, not unfriendly. "Madam has no desire for social affairs."

"My compliments to the lady," said Strand. "She has a superb watchdog at her command."

"Thank you, sir," said Brewster. "But — 'dog'? Did you say dog?"

"Figure of speech, I assure you. 'Watchman' would have been more salubrious. Your pardon?"

"Certainly, Mr. Strand."

"Good night — I didn't get your name."

"Brewster, sir."

"Ah, Brewster. Good night, Brewster."

There was only an instant's hesitation, then the British voice came, "Good night, Strand."

Soft footsteps sounded, going away. Laurie Pomfret Van Orden opened her door. Brewster, wrapped in a

41

voluminous burnoose, purchased long ago in the Near East, came into the room with flushed countenance.

She said, "That was beautiful, my friend. Just the right tone. You are learning."

Reciting a lesson, dubious but obedient, he said, "They only understand strength. Politeness is good, but stubbornness is better. He is a dangerous man, ma'am."

She poured the brandy, handed him a glass. "To your courage and kindliness."

"To your wisdom and beauty, ma'am."

They sipped. She looked like a young girl, perched upon the bed in her robe, her hair piled atop her head shining in the lamplight. He sat upon a straight chair, without stiffness, a poised, burly man in his forties, his round face showing a faint touch of worriment.

She said, "You know I could have gone on to Cobre."

"Yes, madam."

"I'm scared, Brewster. Scared."

"You should not be frightened."

"But I am."

"You've had the courage to come this far. You have been many other places, searching. You have not faltered."

"But this could be it. The Pinkerton was very sure."

"Then, madam, you should be happy."

"Oh, I am — I am. But scared. Does she hate me?"

"How could she hate you? She is your daughter."

"My flesh and blood. But I deserted her. In my heedlessness, in my selfishness. When she needed me."

"You can only learn by finding her."

"Are you anything, ever, but slow and sure and kind?" she demanded, her voice rising. "I need advice but I don't need that British stolidity. I need someone who is also afraid, to share with me."

"I am sorry, madam." He finished his brandy, put down the glass with care. "It is my part to stand by."

"Yes — yes," she murmured. "You're a rock. You're Gibraltar. There is no one like you. I know that I'm lucky. Just stand by, friend. Just stand by."

"I have ordered food," he said. "The girl will bring a tray. With coffee. They have no tea."

"Yes, Brewster." She was flaccid, her mind would not hold to her determination, the fear had undermined it. She leaned back against pillows. "You will take care of it."

"Of course, madam."

She closed her eyes. The taste of the brandy was rancid. She should not have taken it before supper. She should not have stopped here. She should have gone ahead to Cobre and learned whether the detectives had been wrong again or if her child was there. She felt old, not for the first time. Laurie Pomfret, as she always thought of herself, growing old — it was a hideous thought, like a weird dream. She opened her eyes and reached for the brandy and finished it.

Tomorrow, she thought, it would be better. Tomorrow, with daylight, she would regain strength and confidence. Daylight always helped. She had been a night person too long, now she needed the sun.

The rain sloshed against the windows, beat upon the roof. The woman coming with the food. She braced herself, sitting up straight.

"Charge!" she said. "Charge straight ahead. Thank you, Brewster."

CHAPTER
THREE

The red lamp gleamed defiantly in the window of Mrs. Jay's house. A heavy, quick storm had passed over as Ben Hancock went past the livery and down the alleyway. Buck Buchanan's body lay in the establishment of Con Boyd, the stage had been delayed by a flash flood, the moon had come coyly from behind black clouds. Luke Post would be coming in late this Friday night. As predicted, the Cobre Annual Ball would be held on the morrow, with Buck's funeral postponed until Sunday or Monday, no one seemed to care much which, Ben ruminated, mounting the steps and turning the knob of the door which was never locked.

The parlor was small because Mrs. Jay did not approve of lingering on the premises. She had an arrangement with Jim Madison just across the way to refrain from selling liquor, to restrict her business to providing the girls for those who wanted them. In return, the girls were allowed to work Madison's saloon and gaming room, for which Mrs. Jay received some unstated portion of their extra earnings. Ben Hancock took no part in this transaction; he had always been skittish when it came to taking money from madames.

He would accept free services from the girls, but the money, somehow, seemed tainted. Many people had thought him squeamish in this quixoticism, but few had spoken to him about it.

Mrs. Jay came into the room followed by Chompy, but the pimp took one look at Hancock and went out into the alley and smoked a cigar. The madame was a middle-aged woman with an aging countenance illuminated by huge, shadowed brown eyes. She wore her hair piled high atop her head and affected ballroom gowns during work hours, probably because she had young, rounded shoulders and chest. Her voice was husky, masculine and badly placed.

"You didn't have to turn that stud Neddy loose on my girls," she said. "He's like to wear out Cora. She don't want to work tonight."

"Never mind the boy. What about the little parade the gals put on? Didn't I warn you about that?"

"It's that goddam weed," she protested. "They grow that stuff right over in Centro now. The Mexicanos. How am I goin' to stop them from smokin' the damn stuff?"

"If it's not the weed it's laudanum," Hancock agreed. "If they'd only stick to suds or whiskey. Reckon you can't control 'em too good. But what's the matter with Chompy, letting 'em walk the streets?"

"Chompy! If I could find a good pimp you think I'd have him around? He's a nothin', in spades. He's a yella hound, the dogs should forgive me."

"There's no good pimps," Hancock told her. "You have to be responsible your own self."

"Shoot, the country's gone to hell in a basket. The railroad, keep it down, the railroad people are watching. Sickening. Might as well move to Texas."

"You wouldn't do that, now, Mrs. Jay."

She grinned. "Well, not Texas. I been in Texas. I been in Colorado. I been to Kansas and Montana. This is the best place I have been."

"You run a clean house, we know that. Just keep the gals off the street is all I ask."

"It's that Daisy. She no more than got here than she had them all thinking they were somebody. Like they were real citizens and all. Damn little rebel."

"She wasn't on the weed today."

"She don't need it. She's the best gal I ever had exceptin' for her ways of cuttin' up. But she has been dippin' the laudanum. You know what that leads to."

"I warned her often enough."

"You and me, Marshal." She sighed. "They all either marry quick or they die quick."

"Or if they got brains they turn madame."

"Thanks. Maybe you better talk to Daisy some more."

"It won't do any good."

She winked lewdly. "It's on the house."

"And thank *you*." His voice grew hard.

"No offense, Marshal." For an instant she lost her aplomb. She dwelt upon the edge of his approval or disapproval and she well knew there was a line she dare not cross. She arose and went up the stairs.

Hancock sat in a plush chair and gloomed at the painting of a nude woman on the wall. He felt helpless and when Daisy came in he did not arise.

"Talk, talk, talk," she said. "You're beautiful but please talk to me — and not at me."

She sat opposite him, attired in a fresh, loose robe caught tight at the waist. Her hair was brushed back and tied with a ribbon. The lost innocence of her expression caught him again and confused him and angered him.

"I don't know what I'm going to do about you."

"How about you? Sending that boy Neddy in there. Was that nice?"

"Never mind that."

"I had to bite him. Then he just about wore out poor Cora."

"You kicked him, too."

"Didn't I, ever?"

"And you tore up the cot."

"I was pretty mad about everything." She grinned. "Why keep this going? You know I don't give a damn."

"You've got to either give a damn or get out of town."

She jumped up and drifted across the room like a small puff of smoke and perched on his knee, letting the gown fall open so that one breast pressed against his shirt front. "You wouldn't run me out of town. You can say it but you wouldn't do it. No use, Marshal, I know."

He put an arm around her incredibly tiny waist. "Daisy, I'm the only law in the county right now. There

48

are things happening real fast. The town is changin' every day. If you'll just calm down and stay off the streets, it'll help."

She got up from his knee and ran to the foot of the stairs, changing again, always altering mood and demeanor. "Oh, la. The marshal wants help from the whore!"

"Why not?"

"Nobody gets help from me. Not even you." There were tears in her eyes but not of sorrow. "Why should I have consideration for anybody? The hell with that. Just leave me alone, that's all. Leave me alone!"

She was gone up the stairs. He could have followed her. He sat still, thinking that she was right, there was no reason for a kid her age driven to whoredom to do a damn thing for anyone, any time. He got up and went heavily into the night. The moon was high over Cobre. He started for Madison's place for a drink. He felt low in spirits; the day had been a long one and a bad one. He heard the sound of horses and the creak of harness as the mud-covered stagecoach rattled into town. He changed direction and went toward the Wells Fargo office where Speedy Jackson, working late, came to attend the strongbox and the mail.

Luke Post descended, a thin cheroot in his fingers. He wore a hard hat and clothing made especially for him by a Denver tailor, well-fitted, sober. His boots were black and narrow and shiny. His face was quiet, closed-in, a gambler's face, but he was a handsome small man with bright, inquiring eyes. He held out his hand as Hancock approached.

"Howdy, *amigo?*"

"Damn glad to see you, Luke boy." It elevated him to shake hands with this old friend. He had, Hancock realized, been walking on the verge of events, unsure since the problem of the railroad had encroached upon Cobre and his own future. "Sorry about the flood."

"It was right interestin'," said Luke, indicating the descending passengers. "People gab a lot durin' a storm. A fella can learn what's goin' on."

"Then you got a load of the local gossip?"

"Railroad, railroad — and more railroad."

"Yeah." Hancock spoke to Speedy. "You see that Luke's gear gets over to the hotel, will you, please?"

"Luke? Luke Post?" The telegrapher-agent peered. "Proud to meetcha, Luke. Heard plenty about you. Give a lot to see you behind a faro layout."

"You sure would," Hancock assured him. "Bein' you're the prime sucker."

Jackson winced and laughed and the two friends turned toward the office-dwelling-jail down Buxton Street. There were few people about. They talked of the immediate past and the hopeful future, easily, as men who had been together often over many years.

They went inside the office and Hancock took one of the flat pint bottles out of a drawer and reached for a pitcher of chunked ice melting on a shelf.

"All the comforts of home," Luke observed. "Got an ice plant, I see."

Hancock poured into tumblers. "Spoiled rotten, we are. Let's set outside where you can look over the burg."

They tilted rawhide chairs against the wall. The moon had achieved such brilliance that the mountains were visible amidst clouds of all descriptions. The rain had made the air electric; reflected lights illuminated the long street.

"Looks like Cobre's plumb growed up," Luke said. "Like most every other town with action. We gettin' to be oldtimers."

"Beats all," Hancock said, pouring into the glasses. "Up the trail at fifteen, scared to death of the whores in Abilene. Drunk on rotgut, tossin' away the thirty per month. Back down the trail and start over again. It's a pure wonder we made it up to now."

"Just tough, that's all. Too mean to cash in." Luke tasted the drink. "This here is plumb good. Shows how things do get better. Local stuff?"

"Chinese. You hungry or anything?"

"We ate up the road. Mexicano, real good. Makes the whiskey taste cool and nice. How's it with you, *amigo?*"

"Had one of them days. Whores smokin' that Mex weed. Apaches killed the sheriff. Had to kill the Apaches."

"They can be mean as snakes."

"Town's quiet but this railway business has got everybody stirred around."

"The sheriff, huh?" Luke sipped the whiskey. "Could be you'll run for the job?"

"Looks like. And it looks good for the railroad comin' in. That's why I sent for you."

"Then we'll actually make money on that land you touted to me?"

"You don't rightly need it. But I do," said Hancock. "Wearin' a badge don't help at the bank much."

"That's why I never put one on."

"I don't know myself why I ever started," Hancock confessed. "I know why I stuck at it, but how come I started?"

"It was a job without work. You always was kinda pure-minded. I see you don't wear your gun."

"Gets to be a nuisance, hangin' on your hip. Sign of progress. Civilized, we are."

"Here's to it, whatever it is." Luke lifted his glass, found it empty, held it out for more. "There's money in it and you know what makes the mare go."

"Yeah." Hancock looked down Buxton Street. The town was sleek, well-lit by coal lamps, of which the city council was very proud. "I'm ready. I had it up and down and here and there."

"Like I always said, lawin' makes a man old before his time. Dealin' faro is easier."

"You may be right." Hancock finished his drink, reached for the bottle, stopped when the night was split by the sound of horses and the yelling of men.

Luke reached instinctively for the short-barreled .38 he carried in an especially tailored pocket of his correct trousers, but Hancock shrugged and picked up the whiskey and made himself a drink.

"Matt Buxton's little brother and his bunch. They're the only ones still hoorahin' the town. They had to plant my Apaches this morning. Made 'em edgy, I reckon."

52

Five men rode by, waving mock salutes to the men on the porch. They tied up at Madison's saloon. Jed Buxton threw back his head and let go with a wolf howl. Then they were gone from view.

"That pup," sighed Hancock. "Another bad part of a no-good day."

"You want to go down there?"

"No use. Jim can handle them up to a point. Young Buxton's no damn good but his brother takes care of damage."

"I heard about his brother on the stage."

"Yeah. He aims to make me sheriff."

"You don't say." Luke drank again.

"It's the new way. Or maybe the old way in new times. You keep your nose wiped and you do all right."

"It's better than robbin' banks." Luke laughed. "You mind the time we was broke in New York and had notions about holdin' up that tin bank?"

Hancock grinned, feeling easy again. "I remember what did happen. You found that wolf den where they tried to run one on us and cleaned it. I remember them toughs from the Bowery didn't like it none."

"We only shot one of 'em. That gal of yours hid us out from the police," Luke said. "You remember her? Laurie?"

"Laurie Pomfret." He remembered her in the pit of his stomach, he couldn't forget her.

"Singin' gal. She sure loved you a heap."

"She was a something. I wonder whatever became of her?" He looked across the street at the shop of Linda Darr but he was seeing a lovely, wild, laughing girl in a party gown, drinking champagne and kicking off silver slippers.

Luke was observing, "She is a female I wouldn't worry my head about. If she can't take care of herself, flowers don't bloom in the springtime."

"She was pretty great to us."

"To you, she was great. Very great."

"She wouldn't leave New York."

"You didn't own doodley squat to take her anyplace."

Hancock shook off the memories. "Hell, that's all past. We were young bucks. Scares me to think about us like we were then, tryin' New York."

"We didn't scare, them days. Just another wide place in the road to us, it was." Luke waved his glass. "Big, but what of it? Loco, we was."

From Madison's place came a raunchy, raucous yell. It was young Buxton. A girl laughed on a husky note.

"Tough on women, that Buxton punk," Hancock said.

"That's progress? One thing we was taught, never be mean to women."

"You mind the time Laurie took us to the show? The gaslights? Them trains runnin' overhead? The elevator, first time we was in it?"

"Damn little room going up, up. She sure laughed at us. We must've looked simple."

They chuckled softly together. Hancock went into the office for another pint. The moon had gone soft behind fat and fleecy clouds. Across the street, curtains moved and Linda Darr peered out, saw them together, was satisfied, going to her sewing . . .

Linda Darr was a woman with purpose. She held up the gown on which she was working, went to the wall mirror and looked at herself by lamplight. Her brow was wide, her face tapered to a sharp little chin. Her mouth was small but the lips tucked up at the corners when matters went well, giving her a youthful aspect, warmth with a touch of hidden force. Her only wrinkles were at the corners of her hazel eyes.

Yet she was getting along for that country, she admitted to her reflection in the only pier glass in Cobre. She was twenty-six, a fact she kept well hidden. Of her past she said nothing and the custom of the country accepted this without question. She parted her flannel wrapper and admired herself. She had a fine, long body, shapely legs, a small waist. Men looked at her on the streets.

She looked only at Ben Hancock.

She flushed, closing the robe against her nudeness, remembering the night she had almost given in to him. It had been a close call, atop a sunny hill, on an afternoon when they had driven out for a picnic. She had wanted him. She had wanted a man for a long time now, since her husband had been killed up North.

She did not speak of her husband, either. No one knew that she had been married. If Ben had known that afternoon he might not have listened to her pleas as she put him on his honor. In this country widows were fair game.

She had been, then, strong enough and clever enough to resist him when she had not wanted to. She could now keep him at arm's length, allowing him just enough familiarity to keep him anxious. They went to social gatherings as a pair, the town accepted them as a couple. It looked well for the future, she thought. He had not yet proposed, he would be slow to do so, she knew, but she had the patience to wait, to refrain from pushing him.

Meantime there was Daisy. She had learned through the whores, who secretly came to her for dresses they could never find occasion to wear, about the fascination Daisy held for the marshal. Sometimes on lonely nights she hated the girl. Other times her intelligence told her that she should be grateful for the banking of the fire in Hancock through dalliance in the house of Mrs. Jay. She was a practical woman through experience of living with Tammy Green, who had been sweet but hopelessly inept, who with great diligence and optimism tried everything and failed, until a winter in Butte had killed him.

Calm again, she piled her hair high. It was auburn and thick and she thought tomorrow night she would wear it in the Lily Langtry Coil which she had learned from a periodical well hidden from the prying eyes of town women.

She took down her terra cotta rhadanos skirt of electric-blue jersey and held it against her nakedness. The effect was startling. She put it back on the rack and held a modified Spanish blouse, low-cut, against her chest and thought vividly of the hip-high lisle stockings and the slippers with pointy toes and high heels which would show off her ankles. Ben Hancock would not be able to resist her, she truly believed.

She wanted him, she believed in him. Now he might well become sheriff. His property across the coming railroad would provide for them both. She did not ask for the wealth of the Buxtons or Jerry Kay and the mine magnates, she had no lust for power. She had known privation, now she longed for security.

And love, she added; she needed the love of a man, more than anything she needed that. Poor Tammy had loved her in his fashion. She missed his physical being, the warmth and safety of nights in his arms. Women did not admit to this openly, but naked before her mirror she gladly proclaimed it to herself.

It was love, she repeated as though to convince herself. If it were purely avarice, there was Jed Buxton. He had made a nuisance of himself until she had appealed to Matt to keep him away. That had not been easy because Matt had wanted her to marry his brother and attempt his reformation. She had known better than that, after Tammy.

But Tammy had been honest. Jed had forged bank drafts on his brother, he had beaten a sheepherder almost to death over a rifle, he had raped a Mexican girl and been caught at it, he had committed a hundred breaches of the peace in and around Cobre. Only Matt had saved him from the penitentiary.

Money was not enough. She knew her place, it was middle-class comfortable, with children to bear and attend and a decent man to provide. A sheriff would be nice in a land still raw and only slightly tamed.

She put her finery away with careful, deft hands. Tomorrow night she would make Ben eager and then when he made love to her she would force him to ask her. She was certain the time was ripe.

Down the street came the sound of revelry from Madison's place and she thought she recognized the wild laugh of Daisy. She knew Jed was on the prod and for an instant she hoped it was Daisy and that the little whore was catching it from the brutal scion of Candlestick. Then she was ashamed, feeling herself unchristian.

Jim Madison's place was long and narrow and the bar stretched its length to the door of his private office. There were mirrors and chandeliers and real oil paintings and a faro layout and several poker tables and other tables where customers could sit and drink and play with Mrs. Jay's girls preparatory to using the rooms upstairs. It was an opulent establishment, designed to fit the new image of a railway town.

Jim Madison wore gambler's black although he was no hand with cards. He was an entrepreneur whose specialty was buying at a low price, refurbishing, then selling as times improved. His judgment had not always been correct, therefore he was not wealthy and suffered from gastric problems and enervating headaches. His long thin nose, small tight mouth and watery eyes proclaimed that he dwelt always on the verge of fancied disaster.

The Candlestick crowd led by Jed Buxton were a problem to him. He was not a thorough coward but he feared the power of wealth. Now he played solitaire in a corner near the table across which Daisy and Jed faced one another. He knew Daisy had been dipping laudanum and that she was not a proper whore but kind of weird. He wondered why she stuck around Jed, who was equally unsound.

The other Candlestick men were distributed around the room, playing faro for bit pieces where Jack Dover dealt, or leaning against the bar with schooners of beer. They were peaceable when Jed did not stir them to action. Still, it was unhealthy to have them in the place at any time.

When the rails came, Madison thought, he would take his profit and move on. Cobre would soon have more law than it needed, with Hancock as sheriff and a new marshal, and the women and preachers would make trouble for any saloonkeeper. There would be more and more commerce, which would bring more businessmen, the kind who drank at home with their families and never gambled over green baize. The mine people would join in and Cobre would be dead.

He could hear the talk between Daisy and Jed, although he kept his head down and pretended he did not. His stomach kept getting worse and now the headache started.

Jed Buxton was wearing his fancy duds, bright silk shirt and matching rebosa, fawn-colored tight pants, shiny patent leather boots, flat-brimmed hat strung down behind his neck by a rawhide cord. His hair was too long. He had a weakly handsome face, marred by overconfidence and an underlying sullenness. He stared at Daisy.

"I been thinkin' about you."

"Ha!" She laughed on the wild note. Her bare feet were in *huarachos*, her fair hair drawn severely back. Her eyes were wrong, as they had been all day.

"I been thinkin' about takin' you outa here," Jed went on, swelling out his chest. He was feeling his liquor.

"Ho!" The laugh was louder.

Cora, the cowlike girl from Mrs. Jay's, came in and sat dumbly at another table. Larson, the foreman of Candlestick, wandered over and ordered a beer for her. Monty Dipple, tough, casehardened, scarfaced, came to serve it, glanced at Madison, shrugged, went back to his place behind the bar.

"I truly mean it. When Jed Buxton says somethin', he means it, gal."

"Keep meaning it," Daisy told him. "Nobody cares."

"Matt keeps telling' me, get married, get married. We could get a nice li'l old spread from Matt." He drank whiskey straight from a bottle.

"Very funny," Daisy said. Her speech was slurred but the eastern accent was plain. "Very cruel."

"Whadda you mean, cruel?" he demanded.

"Some of the girls might believe you."

"You callin' me a liar?"

"Ho!" Again the soaring laughter.

Now that, Jim Madison thought, was damn bad. She was giving it to him, hard. The way she stared, the way she laughed at him, that was bad.

60

Jed took another swig. "I tell you, it's an idea from Matt. Whores have made good wives before now. Gettin' hitched would take ol' Matt off my back, too."

"And close his pocketbook. You think you could make it on your own? Ha!"

Madison felt the gas forming in a big bubble, so that his stomach hurt. She was asking for it, big trouble. He wished he could interfere, but he had no standing in this dialogue.

"A place of my own." Jed seemed to be talking from inside, not hearing Daisy at the moment. "Me and the boys. Horses. Matt can have his dumb cows, I'd raise horses. Me, I'm the best with a horse. I can top any bronch I ever seen."

Madison frowned, risked a look. The damn fool was half serious, maybe more than half. Whiskey talk was recognizable, there was a lilt to it that all bar owners knew. Jed was actually talking out of a half dream, maybe a true dream released by alcohol. It didn't seem possible.

Daisy yawned. "Why don't you try Cora? She's really stupid. She might believe you."

"I tell you it's a notion I got, for real." He leaned forward, glaring at her.

"Just get rid of that notion," she said.

Now Jed was hearing her. He popped his eyes, clutching the whiskey bottle. "What? What'd you say?"

"Who wants you to take her out of here?" Her laugh rang again.

There was now a burning sensation in the region of Madison's heart. Cora was openmouthed, Larson was frowning. The faro dealer quietly departed through the side door. Customers departed.

"You loco or somethin'?" demanded Buxton.

"Not me. Maybe you, not me." Her voice tinkled like broken glass.

"You don't wanta leave the whorehouse?"

"Certainly not."

Jed sat back in the chair. This was something out of his recognizance, this was something for his whiskey mind to reckon with. Madison wished he had not eaten *chile rellano* with his *enchiladas* that evening. He looked toward the bar, suffering. Monty Dipple lifted one shoulder, shook his head and served a beer to Muley Ward. Beneath the bar was a sawed-off shotgun. Dipple edged closer to it, but the Candlestick men would know about that, too.

Madison misplayed a card, spread the deck, pulled it together, shuffled without much skill. Only Cora, Monty, the Candlestick crowd, himself and Daisy were now in the saloon. It was a spot he would have left if he dared.

Jed was staring at the girl. She was high as a kite and twice as independent. Her eyes were vague and she seemed to be looking inwardly at something she did not like. The silence was scarifying.

It was time to sell out and Madison wished a buyer would walk in this very minute. The hell with the railroad, he thought, the hell with anything, he would take a loss and get out and start again anywhere so long as it wasn't Cobre.

★　★　★

The Cobre Hotel lobby was neat and of ample size, with one big chair and several smaller ones and a bench under the windows. Behind the desk Mel Hunter watched over the scene, a nervous man with an uncertain smile. His wife, May, was a thin woman, always hovering, resembling her husband so closely that they were often taken for brother and sister. Their son Johnny was precocious, a fine student, a spindly boy always in evidence in the background.

Wide stairs curved upward to the rooms, all of which were high-ceilinged, comfortable. The decor was Spanish-Mexican, there were tile insets along the edge of the floor where the rugs did not reach.

There was a small bar off to the right in the rear of the building. Pedro Gomez wore a white Mexican jacket and poured the best available whiskey. This was a semiprivate room in which cowboys and miners were unwelcome. Hamilton Grey, judge of the circuit court, stood with Matt Buxton, holding a glass in his hand.

"To law and order," Matt said, lifting his glass.

Judge Grey frowned, did not drink. "Surely you jest with me, Matt. You choose to make your own law."

"Now, Jedge, that was long ago. It was different. Held court mebbe once a year. Hadda fight 'Paches, greasers, drought, weather from the mountains. Hadda hold grass and water for the cows. Hadda hang rustlers. Different times, Jedge, bad times."

"And you took what you wanted."

"Lots of 'em took. I held. Hired good men. Buried 'em, one by one. New boys, they ain't a patch on the deaders we buried."

"And now you would use law and order to maintain your position and indulge your brother."

"Not me." Matt wagged his head, jowls quivering but good nature emanating from him. "Storekeepers, bankers, mineowners, they need the law. Buyin' and sellin' bits of land, goods over a counter. My brother, he's a problem, sure, but I pay him out."

"This town has churches, schools, lights in the street at night. Its peaceable citizens want to build for a future. Your brother is a menace to them, to the town."

"I know about Jed. But lemme tell you, I'm for law and order. I got mine, I can hold onto it, law or no law. They need it, them people. Let 'em have it."

"They are going to get it." The judge sipped at his drink. "Nothing can stop progress."

"Sure. Progress. When I come there wasn't nothin' but Injuns and no-good land. I progressed it."

"Before you were the mountain men," remarked the judge. "They took very little. They showed you the way."

"Knew several. Dirty dumbheads. Trapped, screwed the squaws, drank up the bust-head rotgut, died in the gutters of Taos, a bunch of 'em. Not my kind."

"There is still your brother."

Matt sighed. "Hate to talk about him. More complaints?"

"Several."

"You take 'em up with Ben?"

"I intend to."

"Good man, Hancock. Make a good sheriff." Matt reached for the bottle. "Jedge, you know I ain't got any kids, don't you?"

"I am aware of that." Deep lines showed suddenly in the distinguished features of the older man. "I sympathize with you."

"Just Jed. Raised him from a pup. His bein' so much younger, you see. Didn't have enough time to spend with him. Maybe laughed at the wrong things, like Virgie says. Spoiled him rotten."

"Understandable, Matt. But he's a grown man. It is time to put a curb upon him — even if it means a jail sentence."

"I know — I know."

"Your money keeps him from trouble — serious trouble for himself."

"Shouldn't do it, mebbe," muttered Matt. "But there it is. My fault, I got to pay."

"I'll tell you frankly, the next time he is arrested I am going to see that he is punished. No fine. Punishment."

There was a moment of silence. The jurist was not many years older than Matt. A bearded, somber man of intelligence, he was several years from the East, he knew men like the Buxtons, he was grimly opposed to their disregard of others. This was the breed which had opened the country, cultivated it, made it go, but every stratum of society has its day, the judge knew, each had to give way to the new. Matt drained his glass.

"You reckon, Jedge? You really mean it?"

"I'm serious."

Matt's round face smiled, the eyes twinkling. "If it comes to that, we'll see. We'll larn, won't we?"

"In court."

"Mebbe in court. One way or the other, I 'spect. Nice talkin' to you, Jedge. Always is."

He went out of the bar and up the stairs. He knew Jed was across the street in Madison's. He thought for a moment of going over there and watching things, but that would be no good. Jed had to have his little fling. Brag as he might, the boy hated the sight of blood, the burying of the Apaches had been avoided by him, but he had seen the remains and now he was blowing off steam.

Virgie opened the door of the room before he got to it, half dressed, always concerned, now definitely upset.

"Matt, this bouffant dress ain't right for me atall. I should've listened to Linda Darr. I'm too damn skinny for this kinda rig."

The dress was moire silk, the skirt stiff and wide so that it stuck out in 'A' fashion from her narrow middle. Thin ankles and bony, long feet showed beneath the flurry of petticoats she had donned in order to try on the outfit.

Matt's eyes softened. "Honey, you look good to me in just anything. And better in nothin'."

"So! You been drinkin' again!" But her large eyes gleamed, her smile was warm and soft and ready.

He dug into a sagging pocket and brought out a slim pint. From his vest he produced a small glass. "Brought you a smidgen from the Chink. Bastard tried to claim he was all out but he found one for you."

"You!" She took the whiskey and opened it. "What did Judge Grey have to say?"

"Like always. Oratin' as if he was Dan'l Webster."

"On Jed again, I s'pose?"

"Oh, sure. And everything else. He's a real scold, the jedge."

"He's a good man and a big man."

"Big with the railroad. Scares folks."

"He plays fair, Matt."

"Well, yeah, it's mainly Jed. Like Jed stands for all the bad things."

She threw down the whiskey, came to him, put one arm across his heavy shoulders. "Matt dear."

He gently pulled her close. "I know, honey."

"Jed's a big boy now."

"I know." But the little spike was driven between them for an instant and she adroitly abandoned the subject, moving away, scowling at the mirror on the wall. "This dress just won't do."

He followed her, as he always did, abandoning any other thoughts. He looked her up and down. "Hey. Leave off half a dozen of them petticoats. See how that looks."

She brightened. "I swan, Matt."

She began hauling off the underskirts, of which there were several. In a moment she spun around and around. The dress magically fell into folds, making her slender, almost pretty. "I always did say you was the smartest man in the world. But my lands, a dress! You jest know everything."

He held out his arms and she came into them. He said, "Smartest thing I ever did was dab my loop over you."

"Never! You coulda had a pretty lady." She chuckled, kissing his ear, confident.

"All the way from nothin' to here. You did the work around the house and the barn. You took the bad times. You gimme the only good advice I ever had."

"I loved you then," she whispered in his ear. "I love you now."

"I ain't deservin'. I know it and I want you to know it." He laughed softly. "Don't say things real good. Never could."

"You say right things to me." She tugged at him, urging him toward the bed.

He said, "Might's well take them new duds off altogether now, mightn't you?"

"Turn out the lights, you fool jackass," she said, deep in her throat. She picked up the flat bottle and took a pull straight from its mouth.

He blew out the lamp.

Judge Grey came to where Hancock and Luke Post were finishing the second pint of the Chinese whiskey, lifted a hand, sat on a third chair beside them.

"Judge, you're acquainted with Luke here."

"I am indeed. Mr. Post, how do you fare?"

"Just dandy, thank ye, Judge."

"Just had a talk with Matt Buxton."

"Good man, Matt."

"Is he?"

"We rate him high," said Hancock.

"Anything I should know?"

"Reckon not." Hancock was puzzled. "You got somethin' on your mind, Judge?"

"Nothing particular perhaps. I take it Mr. Post is your partner in the property of which we spoke?"

"Couldn't have swung it without him."

"The railroad, gentlemen, is the future of this part of New Mexico. Cobre must have it."

"I mind when end of rail meant booze and whores," Luke observed. "Times have sure changed."

"Now it means transportation and advancement of business," said Judge Grey. "It means peace. Which brings up the question of Candlestick."

"I don't see the problem," Hancock said.

"Mr. Reynolds fears the power of Matt Buxton as expressed in the behavior of Jed. Remember, the right of way also crosses part of Candlestick."

"Matt won't stand in the way."

"He figures to gain," Luke pointed out. "If he don't have to drive his cattle to rail they weigh out fatter."

"You remember the case of Jed Buxton and the Latin girl?" asked the jurist.

"Matt paid off. The family took the money and moved North," said Hancock.

"And our Latin friends are becoming a factor in politics up there. A lawyer has spoken with the family. Moves are being made to reopen the matter."

Hancock said, "Only it won't do. Matt can handle it."

"Reynolds doesn't like it." The judge lit a cigar. Luke reached for the bottle. "No, thanks. The real problem is, of course, fear that Cobre is a one-man town. They do not appreciate the thought."

"Ask Jerry Kay at the bank. Ask anybody. Matt has plenty of power. But not like you say," Hancock said.

"But Cobre can lose the railroad if it isn't proven."

"You aiming that at me, Judge?"

"In a way. You'll be the new sheriff."

"It's not right. Matt will support me."

"There's Jed."

"So far he's paid Jed out fair and square. I'm not close to Matt, nobody is but Virgie. But he's been square."

"Reynolds doesn't like him."

"The hell with Reynolds, then. Does the railroad expect to run Cobre? Is that it?"

"They expect equal representation. They could get it in Centro."

Luke said, "I checked out Centro. Full of Mexicans and dirt. No good."

"The railway could make it good. Rails bring law and order as well as business. You know that."

"Law and order. I kind of feel I brought it here, at least a good part of what we got," said Hancock.

"True. And you will profit thereby, thanks to the information I gave you on that acreage. You deserve that. I could have purchased it myself, Ben."

"I know that." But he could not argue. He felt cornered, that the judge was laying too much responsibility upon him. "I know you wouldn't do it.

70

Nobody would blame you, but that's the way you are. Well, the way I am, I'm grateful to you. And I'll do what my job calls for. I don't figure to do any more."

"Just remember about Matt." The judge smiled in the half light. "You're a good man. Do I hear the strains of the Cowboy Band?"

"Practicin' for tomorrow night. The Annual Ball." Hancock was depressed. Things had been going along so smooth, now the surface was ruffled.

"I am weary from today's drive," said Judge Grey. "'Sleep that knits up the raveled sleeve of care,' as the bard said. Just think of what law and order really means, Ben. It is the same for all, each and every one of us. Good night, gentlemen."

"Good evenin', Judge."

They watched him walk toward the hotel. Hancock went inside and got out another bottle.

"Hadn't meant to start this soldier. But that man sometimes gets me reelin'."

"Makes you feel like you're back in that little red schoolhouse we never did attend much," Luke agreed.

"He put it right on me."

"Could be."

"He figures me to buck Matt if need be."

"If need be." Luke poured with a steady hand. "Well?"

"Well — what?"

"Don't tell me you wouldn't — if need be."

"Matt's always sided me." Hancock was unhappy.

"Gimme a reason he shouldn't."

"Why should there be a reason? Hell, a man gets along with people — that don't mean he's owned by 'em."

"There's a storm brewin', Ben. The old judge was tellin' us plain enough. The railroad and Buxton."

"Matt's got a lawyer here, Tim Finnegan. Smart as a weasel. I put Jed in jail, Finnegan's right there. Matt pays him, the banker hires him, the mines hire him. Now the judge is here and he don't like Finnegan's ways."

"Cobre's gettin' mighty big."

"On account of the railroad. The mines want it too, you know. Real bad they want it."

"Big ranches like Candlestick always ran things. For Matt Buxton, that's the way it is. He won't give up."

"There hasn't been any problem until now. And all on account of that no-good dumbhead, that Jed." Hancock drank again.

"You seem to cotton to Matt, kind of."

"He's got points. Tender as a suckin' dove to his wife. Virgie's a fine woman. Matt deals square, like I keep sayin'." He thought of Linda, watching from across the street, and wondered if he could ever feel toward her as Matt felt toward Virgie Buxton.

Luke said, "The judge is square too."

"Straight as a string. You know about him? His wife checked in and it broke him up. He quit politics back East and come out here, federal appointment. Lives alone, just for law and order. I'm beginnin' to hate those words. Law and order, law and order, law and order. Bulls' balls!"

Luke smiled. "You put that badge on years ago, *amigo*. Didn't nobody make you do it."

Hancock subsided. "Oh, sure. I know. Judge is right. What I can't get down is politics."

"Politics is part of it. You mind the rangdoodle in Dodge when the mayor tried to run us out?"

"I remember. Yeah, that was politics — but there was a heap of Sam Colt in it, too."

Luke said, "You got the jimjams tonight. Lemme go over to the hotel and catch up on some of that knittin' the judge was quotin' at us. See you in the mornin'?"

"Sure, Luke. Guess I really got stirred up a bit. Layin' everything on me, the way judge did. I'll take a lady out to supper, make me feel more salubrious."

"Lady?"

"Gal over yonder. Tell you about her tomorrow."

"Me, I'm more interested in the ones you already told me about. At Miz Jay's. So long for now." Luke ambled across the street and toward the hotel.

Hancock put away the booze bottles for future refilling. He locked up the office, letting the steam within him die down. He walked slowly across the street and tapped on Linda's door. The liquor was rolling in him a bit, but he felt steady enough. When she opened the door she was wearing the robe and his cheeks grew warm, but she carefully turned up the lamp and opened the curtains so that they could be seen from the street.

He said, "How about some chile at Romero's?"

"A nice notion. Come in."

He stepped inside, removing his hat. "Why don't you close them curtains, gal? You don't like me any more?"

"Just as much," she replied, winking at him. "You've been drinking just enough, haven't you?"

"I wouldn't say that. A few more and I'd turn out the light myself."

"Oh-ho! Brave marshal. Now you sit there while I change. That's my ball gown on the rack. Do you like it?"

"How can I tell? Try it on and we'll see."

"No, thanks." She slipped into the living quarters. He dared not follow her there so long as people could watch from outside. She put on a skirt and shirtwaist over hastily donned underwear. She brushed at her hair, threw a long cloak about her shoulders, giving him no chance for maneuvers of any sort, coming back into the shop, passing him to the door, saying, "Now you can turn down my lamp."

"Clever," he grunted. "Real cute." But he did as she asked, mocking himself, knowing that the liquor had inflamed him and that she was quite right in her actions, thinking how good-looking she was and how she would make a fine wife, circumspect, dependable.

Then, when the lamp was low, she lifted her face and kissed him on the cheek. "You're always good to me, Ben. I do appreciate it. I appreciate you."

"Well, thankee, ma'am." He tried to make it sound comic, but there was more to it than that. He understood what she meant and he knew he could have her. He had only to mention a ring and name the date.

74

A very long time ago he had asked Laurie Pomfret to come West with him, but he had never proposed marriage. The prospect of such a violent change in his habits appalled him, the proper words stuck in his throat. He took her arm and they walked down Buxton Street in perfect amity but with the situation unchanged. Romero's was at the far end of the town; it was a nice walk in the early night of moonlit Cobre. She leaned close to him so that everyone who saw them would know how it was, how close it was to coalition.

They were abreast of Jim Madison's place when Daisy screamed. It was a high, weird, scary sound, that of stark fear and this from a girl who seemed not to know fear. It was recognizably Daisy, both to Hancock and to Linda.

He said, "Go back to the shop, Linda. Lock your door and wait for me."

But she could not move. She stood rooted to the spot as he went up the steps and headlong through the swinging doors of the saloon. She could see his legs, the rest of him cut off by the door, when the shot sounded above the echo of the screaming. She heard him thunder in a voice she had never known, "Drop it, you bastard!"

She knelt to see what was happening. She saw the body of someone on the floor and she saw Jed Buxton. Hancock was slapping Jed. A gun dropped to the floor. Ben kicked it away. His hand went back and forth as Jed sat on a chair, slap, slap, slap, slap. Jed's face was crimson.

Linda crept closer as Luke Post went past her with a revolver in his hand. People's voices were raised in questions, lights appeared at all the windows along the street.

Monty Dipple's nasal, tough voice said, "Easy, now."

Then Luke snapped, "Nobody move. Just hold it."

She moved closer, could then see the blood oozing into a pool, and without volition pushed her way through the batwing doors and went past the tableau of men, the Candlestick riders held under the guns of Post and Dipple, Jed half conscious, Ben holding him by the shirt front. She knelt beside the girl, noting her youth even now. She stared at Cora, a pallid hunk of quivering, scared flesh; at Madison with his long nose, his eyes furious, his mouth twisting. Then she put a finger on the place in Daisy's neck where she knew there should be a pulse.

She said, "I believe she is dead. Shouldn't someone get Dr. Farrar?"

Post motioned to one of the Candlestick men — it was Muley Ward. People were standing on the porch of the place now, but no one came in, not with the guns out and leveled. Dipple had the shotgun on the top of the bar, Post stood spread-legged, his gambler's eyes darting here and there. Ben slammed Jed hard into the chair.

"You don't have to kill him, Marshal," said Larson in a monotone. "Things is bad enough."

"He shot her in the back." Hancock wheeled on Madison. "You people let him do it."

"It was too quick," protested Madison.

"Like he says, too damn quick," agreed Larson.

Madison seemed unable to dam the flood of speech. "They was havin' it back and forth. Jawin', jawin'. By God, I half believe he meant it."

"Meant what?"

"The marryin' talk. Tryin' to convince her. She was high all day, you know. Beer made her higher. It went on and on. There was nothin' to be done about it. On and on. Then he was quiet awhile and she laughed. Then he said somethin' I didn't hear and she said somethin' back which I didn't hear neither. Then he hit her hard in the face and said somethin' else and reached for his gun. Then she screamed. Then she ran, hollerin'. Then he cuts down on her. In the back. Right in the back."

Matt Buxton heaved through the door, shirt stuffed untidily into his pants, a bull, charging. "What the hell's goin' on here? Jed?"

"Keep away," Hancock told him. "Stay away from him, Matt. He's under arrest."

"Don't tell me what to do." Matt almost ran into the gun in Luke's hand, stopped dead. "What the hell is it?"

"Murder," Luke told him.

"Who the hell are you, holdin' a gun on me? Damn it, do I have to keep askin' what the hell?"

Hancock said, "Your brother just shot Daisy."

"Daisy? The loco whore? What did she do to him?"

"Not anything to get shot in the back about." A muscle quivered in Hancock's neck. He spoke to Linda in a voice she had never heard. "Go home, Linda. You don't belong here."

She arose, dazed, looking once more at the girl, then at Jed Buxton muttering curses beneath his breath. She went out the side door and knew that her world had turned upside down. She bent her head, hurrying homeward.

Inside the saloon Matt Buxton seemed to be leaning against a strong wind. He asked, "That the truth, Jed?"

"The hell with you. Goddam 'em all. Damn the world. Goddam the stinkin' marshal. He hit me. Goddam everybody. Goddam God!" His voice rose to a shriek.

"Don't talk like that, boy!" Matt said.

"No use, Matt," said Hancock. "He'll need God on his side, this time."

"Yeah," Matt said heavily. "Can I come in now? Can everybody put down them guns?"

"Just so your people keep quiet."

Matt glanced around at the Candlestick men. "You heard him." He walked to where the girl lay, looked down upon her. "Dead, all right. Larson?"

The foreman's voice was uncertain. "Yes, boss."

"You seen it?"

"I was settin' with Cora there. Jed was boozin' from the bottle. She was drinkin' beer . . ."

"Who cares what in hell they was guzzlin'? What happened?"

"They was havin' it back and forth and somethin' was said . . ."

"What was said?" Matt pounced, looking for a loophole, a way out. "Jed?"

"Goddam all of you." The voice maundered. Jed's long hair had fallen in lank strands about his reddened face.

"First he hit her. Then he shot her," said Hancock. "I was a minute too late."

"Hancock slapped Jed some and knocked his gun away and hit him some more," Larson said with a touch of spite. "He slapped him pretty good."

"Hancock ain't wearin' a gun, neither," Luke interposed. "Sure is a mean thing, a marshal without a gun hittin' a poor, armed killer."

"Never mind that," Matt said. "I want to know the story from everybody. I want Lawyer Finnegan here. I want this to be told straight while it's fresh."

Dr. Farrar entered by the side door, followed by Muley Ward. He went directly to the body of the girl, a small, sharp-faced man with the authority of an experienced medico.

"The body is still fresh, Matt," Hancock said. "See the blood runnin'? Bled a lot, didn't she, for such a little girl?"

Matt stared at Ben, at the body, at his brother, his lips moving without sound. Then he walked to Jed's table and picked up the bottle, pouring a drink, draining it. "Poor Virgie," he muttered. "Poor Virgie."

Hancock took out keys, tossed them to Luke Post. "You mind stickin' this thing in a cell? I want to know a few things around here, too."

"I don't mind, but you better go over him first."
Luke had not put away his pistol. "Fancy boys hide out
fancy weapons sometimes."

Hancock jerked Jed to his feet. Matt put out a hand,
then drew it back. Jed cursed steadily, his voice rising.
Ben jammed him against the bar, bent him face down,
began searching him. He found a knife between the
shoulder blades and a derringer concealed in an ornate
belt buckle. He spun the prisoner around and shoved
him toward Luke.

"Nice tools to wear into town for fun," he snapped.

Larson said, "You see, boss? Marshal's bein' awful
high and mighty, ain't he?"

Hancock whirled. "You, Larson. You take your men
and ride. And I don't want you back in town until I
give the word. Understand?"

"I only take orders from the boss," Larson replied.

Matt Buxton's tone was weary. "You heard him.
Ride."

Larson didn't like it, but he knew he had to take it.
He gestured to the others. He marched past the bar,
pausing to remark to Dipple, "Be seein' you later,
Monty. Better keep that shotgun handy."

"Any time," said the bartender tonelessly. His tough
face was impassive.

The boot heels of the Candlestick riders clicked out
through the doors. In another moment they had
mounted and were gone. Luke motioned to Jed,
directing him to the door.

"Damn you too. Damn everybody. Damn everything."

Luke stuck the pistol deep into flesh. "I ain't so experienced at this. Better go. This trigger's real light."

Matt said, "You go with him, Jed."

"Damn you, big brother. You better get me outa this. I didn't do nothin'." Now there was a small light of reason in the bloodshot eyes. "I don't remember nothin'."

"You go."

Jed went, Luke staying close to him, through the assembled crowd, across to the jail. He was, Hancock thought, already looking for a way out. There was nothing in him that regretted his act, he was merely seeking means to get free to cause more trouble. He was like an animal, a canny beast of prey, cutting down his victim, then beating a safe retreat. If ever there was an evil person, Jed filled the bill.

Dr. Farrar had finished his examination. "One shot through the back. She never knew what hit her."

"She knew it was going to hit her. She screamed loud enough," said Hancock. "Somebody get Con Boyd."

Outside, a boy scurried toward the carpenter shop-undertaker across from the jail. People were asking questions but it was comparatively quiet. There was fear in the town. The butcher, the baker, the candlestick-maker were all involved if the Buxtons and the marshal were involved. Many of them were staring at Hancock; they had never seen him as he was now. They had never realized his innate toughness and his involvement with his job, his responsibility toward the law. It was evident in the set of his jaw, in the way he carried himself, in his anger and his aggressiveness.

Lawyer Tim Finnegan came in and stopped a moment, surveying the scene, his red hair disarranged.

Cora, forgotten, stood against the wall, one hand to her vacuous face. Neddy Truman came in and handed a horse blanket to Dr. Farrar, who covered the body. The other whores hovered at the side door and windows, peering in, chattering among themselves. Mrs. Jay stood like a grenadier behind them.

Hancock spoke to Neddy. "You want to go over and stand guard with Luke?"

"I sure do."

Jeb Truman came forward and moved into the saloon. "I can spare him, for you, Ben. Poor li'l gal." He spoke to Matt. "I don't hold with hoors. But this is a pukin' shame."

"Mind your own business," Matt said without heat. He had espied the confused Cora. He motioned to Finnegan. "Talk to that one. Lean on her hard."

Finnegan asked, "Did Jed do it?"

"He don't remember," said Matt flatly.

"Ah," said the lawyer. "Yes." He went to Cora, but Hancock was before him.

Hancock said, "Cora, you don't have to talk to anybody now. There'll be a hearing."

"I don't know. I don't know what's goin' on."

Hancock shoved her out the door. "Mrs. Jay, take care of her."

"Now just a minute," Finnegan began.

Hancock cut him off. "You do your job. I'll do mine. All right?"

Finnegan looked at Matt, shrugged. "Plenty of time."

"Not too much time. Judge is in town," Matt told him, then said to Hancock, "Ben, Larson had somethin' there. You actin' mighty high."

"Any objections?" Red anger was in him. He had been involved with Daisy, the strange little whore. "There'll be no bail this time, Matt. No payoff."

Matt said to Finnegan, "He sent my men outa town."

"You have no legal right to do so," said the lawyer. "You know that, Marshal."

"I know when to prevent a riot, too," Hancock said. "You all had better clear out of here. Tell your troubles to the judge when you see him. I want this place closed."

"You have no legal . . ."

Matt Buxton shook himself like a bull coming out of a river. He took Finnegan's arm. His voice changed, became conciliatory. "Ben's doin' what he thinks is right. Come on, we'll palaver."

Rancher and legal representative went through the doors and down the street to the hotel. Hancock inhaled, exhaled, went to the bar. Monty Dipple poured him a drink.

Madison said shakily, "He murdered her. I never seen a man murder a woman like that."

"I want to know all about it," Hancock said. "I want a piece of paper. I want to measure where they were when it started, where she fell."

"What? Why?"

"Because of Lawyer Finnegan," said Hancock. "Because Matt Buxton will never stop tryin' to prevent his brother from hanging."

"Hangin'?" Madison hadn't thought of that. "Why, nobody could hang a Buxton in Cobre."

Hancock drank, swallowed hard. "Maybe not. But if the judge says it's to be done, here's one will try damn hard to see it done."

Linda Darr sat in darkness. She knew fear, for Ben Hancock, for herself. She knew Candlestick and its power, as she had known the power of other entities in other places. And she knew Ben would never back down a step. She had learned that tonight when she saw him in action, a man generally mild, slightly corrupt, suddenly becoming another person altogether, tackling an armed drunk, unthinking of peril, taking command, bending people to his will, which was the will of the law. This was not the Ben Hancock whom she had planned to gently corral and marry.

Nor would he ever seem the same to her, she realized. It had been like the tearing away of a veil. All the safe, sane little dreams she had entertained were shattered by this vision. The straight path she had thought to travel had developed turns and twists and sudden blockage. Her world would not be the same again in this place. The moon came in her window and she shuddered, drawing the shade against it. Sleep would not be easy.

Book Two

JUSTICE ON TRIAL

CHAPTER
ONE

A bright sun mocked Cobre's morning, splashing over the town as Ben Hancock came out onto the porch of the jail-office-dwelling quarters which had become the focus of attention for so many of the citizens of the county. The mountains, looming in every direction, were still the colors of the rainbow, with violet and pink and russet undertones, thrusting toward a sky decorated by white clouds. It was quite early but the town was never more awake.

Dan Melvin, who had not slept at all, came with a copy of the *Bulletin*, banner headline shrieking of murder. "You must take complete charge, Ben. There'll be violence. The law must take its course. Violence must be checked."

"Until they hang him?" Hancock accepted his paper. He watched Melvin hustle along with copies for the town leaders, the people who counted and therefore might buy advertising for special editions.

Breakfast sat uneasily on his stomach. People walked by, looking covertly at him, scrutinizing him even as they bade him good morning. It was insulting. It was also alarming. Few truly understood his position.

Neddy Truman came hustling along, wearing his deputy's badge, his square young face lowering. His anger seemed to be permanent.

"Mornin', Marshal. They try to break him out yet?"

"Take it easy," Hancock warned him.

"You ain't heard him cuss me. All night he yowled. He's lowdown, rotten. Maybe crazy, I dunno. He's spoiled, like carrion meat."

"We're going to keep him on ice. Understand that. If they try to get him loose, we'll shoot. But don't let him get too far under your skin, Neddy."

"I'd hang him myself." Neddy looked troubled. "Why, if anyone said yesterday I would feel like that, I'd of called him a liar. I ain't the same as yesterday. It's his fault, the dirty bastard."

Hancock said, "It's a lousy job, guarding him. Luke may help, give us shorter spells at it. Maybe I shouldn't have asked you to do it."

"No, it's my job. You always used me before." Neddy was earnest. "Poppa give me a book to read, see?"

It was one of the Little Blue Books so familiar to Hancock. He examined it and said, "Shakespeare, huh? *The Tragedy of Macbeth.*"

"You read it?"

"I read it and a hundred more of 'em," Hancock told him. "Smoked Bull Durham for years just to get the books. It reads right, Neddy."

"Never did have much chance to look into a book," Neddy confessed. "It'll take my mind off him — the bastard."

They went into the office and Hancock took from the rack a shotgun which he loaded with buck. He handed Neddy an extra pocketful of shells. The youth handled the weapon with the skill of an outdoors background.

Neddy said, "There's hell to pay all over town. Speedy told me Finnegan and the judge both been sendin' telegrams. Matt's still in town."

"I know." His own sleep had been sketchy but he had not felt the urge to communicate with anyone. "Luke'll be over directly. Just stick with it for a couple of hours."

He unlocked the big door and they went into the cells. In the smallest, tightest cubicle Jed Buxton slept, his mouth open, snoring. Neddy lifted a shoulder in disgust, then moved a barrel-shaped chair to a position from where he could maintain a strict watch. He cradled the shotgun at his knee, took out the little blue book.

Hancock said, "Luke'll bring him some food. Remember that you're the law, Neddy."

"It ain't easy. But I'll remember."

Hancock went out through the big door, locked it. He put the key around his neck and it felt heavy at his chest. He saw Luke entering and went to the office.

Luke was wearing a loose coat of light wool and striped trousers. Today the revolver was under his arm in a spring holster.

"Can't say it's a good mornin'," the gambler observed. "Pretty, all right, sunshiny. But not good."

"You see the judge?"

"He seen me. He was very strong. The hearing'll be Monday. The trial the following week."

"That gives Matt plenty of time."

"Sure. And Finnegan. And some citizens."

"We been through that before."

"Every lawman's been through it before." Luke shook his head. "That's when you fellas have the real trouble, when the good people begin to weaken."

"I been thinking on it."

Luke said, "Now, if Jed busted out and got clear away it would sure cool things."

"What about the judge?"

"All right, what about him?"

"He'd break me. Oh, the railroad wouldn't care. Matt would sell them his land. They'd be rid of Jed."

"And we take our profit from our acreage. And we vamoose," said Luke. "Simple, ain't it?"

"Real simple."

"You don't like it."

"Oh, I like the part where we take our profits," said Hancock. "I like that fine. I got that coming to me and all the rest. I could even take Linda with me and make out. Lots of places I could make out."

"You and me, we could open a big saloon. There's a spot in Montana I already own."

"I know."

"But you're a lawman. Damned if I understand but I know the way you always been."

"I ain't so proud. It's just that — I don't know. Maybe I'm plain dumb." He broke off.

Linda Darr was coming across the street. She was sober of countenance, subdued. There were circles under her eyes.

"Miss Darr — Luke Post," said Hancock.

"I saw him — last night."

"Pleased to meet you," Luke said. "Last night was no introduction, now, was it?"

She said, "People are talking. The town is divided. I'm worried."

"Nothing to worry about."

"They're betting Matt will take him out of jail."

"Take the bets," Luke suggested.

"They're saying he'll send for men. Gunmen."

"Don't fret," Hancock said. "We're awake."

People were gathering at the city hall at the far northern end of the street. The day was different from all days before, Linda thought. "They say if Jed hangs, the town hangs with him."

"You think that?"

"Matt will rip up anything to save his brother."

"And he won't sell right of way to the railroad," Luke interjected. "I heard that already this mornin'."

She looked at them, saw that they were as one. They were hard men in their own right. She saw Hancock with new perception. They would reserve their opinions, listen to her and others but act from their own thoughts. "I just wanted to tell you what I heard."

"Thanks, Linda," Hancock said. "I appreciate it."

It was, by his tone, a dismissal. She retreated from that which she recognized as a man's world and returned to the shop. She watched Hancock take leave of Luke and go down the street. She saw Judge Grey come from the hotel to intercept him. She retreated to her back room and put on the pot for coffee. She felt resentment against the man's world from which she had been barred. She also felt that she must do something — but she had no idea what.

She could still see the little girl on the floor with the blood seeping from her, feel the stillness of the young neck which she had touched. She could see Hancock's face, flinthard as he slapped Jed Buxton and altered, she knew, the history of Cobre. Something had gone that could never be regained.

Judge Grey was saying, "It happened, Ben. I had not thought it would be so soon."

"It happened."

"Counselor Finnegan has been importuning me since breakfast. Habeas corpus, any amount of bail. He is shrewd. Not a great legal mind, but clever enough. There will be much noise and confusion."

"Jed says he don't remember anything."

"He had unquestionably been forewarned by counsel, in case anything ever occurred. It will not stand up in my court."

"Who'll prosecute, would you know?"

"I have wired for Mr. Edward Evans."

"Whew!"

"There is a time when the public needs the best."

"Matt will holler about that. Evans is top dog."

"Matt will do much hollering. They have already just suborned one witness. Cora — Jones?"

"A poor witless whore. They've got the Candlestick men, of course. I don't know about Jim Madison. Monty Dipple will stand up, I think. But hell, Judge, Jed shot her in the back. No jury will turn him loose."

"I cannot comment on that, Marshal. However, I must caution you to consider the ramifications."

"I been considerin' them. A whole heap."

"Bring him to trial." There was a light in the eyes of the jurist for a fleeting moment, a flash of zeal. "Let the law run its course. But see that he comes to court."

"I aim to do that."

He saluted the older man and went on down the street toward the city hall. The council was gathering. They would be sounding out each other, talking in circles, wishing they were some place else. They would be thinking in terms of dollars. They would not know, not yet, which way to jump. They would be waiting to hear more from Matt. And they would be wondering what Ben Hancock would do, because Sheriff Buchanan was dead and there was no one else they could turn to.

They were not of his West, most of them. They had come here when it was safe and they had invested money, time, labor, in mining, in merchandising, in banking. They had imposed their ways on the town and he had adjusted to their ways, thinking it best. Now it was different, now it came down to him and his job and the judge and the court and they would be scared.

Like Neddy, he thought, who had been an easygoing boy yesterday, taking the drunk whores in the cell, laughing and scratching. Neddy was not the same boy today, nor was Ben Hancock the same man, he began to realize.

He had been forced to kill three Indians and see a sheriff dead. He had been forced to see a little girl whore dead and to arrest her murderer. It had all happened in one day in the new, peaceful time, under the rules made by the newcomers in a town where he did not even wear his gun, where he had been a constable patrolling a quiet little town.

Now he was all the law enforcement the entire county had and he was different, he felt changed inside, and by Linda's attitude he knew that it showed upon him, that people could see it. Overnight, he thought, everything had changed. The judge was right but the judge didn't know as much about the people as he should. Cobre would twist and turn and Matt would make moves and the people would look to the marshal to see how he would act and then they would make up their minds — and probably change their minds more than once.

It was a problem of law and people but it was also a personal problem. He wore the badge. If it had not meant lately the same as it had meant in Dodge and other towns, it was still a bright and shining sign of office. Furthermore, he had always known down deep that Jed Buxton would push him too far one day. He had tried not to think of it, but it was there, especially in the wakeful night. And he knew that Jed Buxton was wrong, as wrong as any man could be.

Jed had escaped punishment for crimes including murder. He had broken all the laws. He had his

94

Candlestick riders and he had a rich brother — did that make him any more than an outlaw riding the trail with his gang? If there was law, then it must be enforced and here the judge was altogether right. There was no separating murders into separate bags. He would act, Hancock thought, as his training had taught him, as his instincts directed. He had been wearing the badge long enough to have confidence in himself.

Yet it was — different now, he felt, uneasy as he came to the end of the street. The city hall was a low, wide building of frame and adobe, quite new. It was filling up with people. There had been no official notice but a town meeting was certainly about to take place. The council and all other important folks would be on hand.

Mayor Lou Taggart's office had a window on the street. He beckoned and Hancock went inside and through the door which Taggart closed tight. The mayor was a burly man, but soft. He wore burnside whiskers and sweated in a dark suit and a high collar which made him appear neckless.

"Wanted to talk to you, Ben. This is a difficult time for us all." Taggart was an eastern man with a twang to his voice.

"It'll be worse." Hancock knew this man well. The mayor had come West from upper New York State with some money, not a lot but enough to invest in several enterprises. He was not a worker, but he was canny and he could turn his hand to selling things or arguing for small points. He had a few dollars in every small business in town. He had a fairly slick lingo and a beaming personality and an eye on Santa Fe and politics. He was as honest as he need be, no more, and somehow he was vulnerable.

"Matt talked to me this morning early. He wanted me to go over the head of Judge Grey and turn Jed loose. He offered — all sorts of things."

"That's plain dumb."

"Certainly. You wouldn't turn Jed loose without a court order. Matt said — well, he said you could be handled." Taggart peered anxiously, awaiting a reply.

"Just how did he mean to handle me?"

"I don't know. I swear I don't, Ben."

"With guns?"

"Lord in heaven! I hope not!"

"Jed used a gun. On a gal."

"I know — I know." If Taggart had been a woman he would have wrung his hands. "What I'm worried about is the railroad. It means so much to all of us."

"It sure does, don't it?"

"Well — Matt suggested Jed could escape. You know, get away in the night."

"Yeah. I've thought of that one, too."

"There are always ways and means — you know? More ways than one of skinnin' a cat, we used to say."

Hancock regarded him with jaundiced eye. "I'd rather not think of even one way. Kinda like pussycats."

Taggart walked to the window. "This could ruin us, all of us, the town. We have to think of the majority, Ben."

"You meanin' I should let Jed go?"

96

"Not exactly. I — oh, if Matt sent him away and we were well rid of such trash and — I don't know."

Hancock said, "Taggart, nobody appointed me to this job. I ran and got elected. Since Buck's gone, I'm all the law we got in the streets. We got Judge Grey in the court — I'm the rest of it. I aim to do my part right. Savvy?"

"Yes. I understand." Taggart wiped away sweat. "I guess you're right. Still — the town . . ."

"The money?"

"Money is essential. It makes the mare go."

"You sure got a lotta cute sayin's," Hancock told him, weary of the conversation. "Shouldn't we get in there and hear from the others?"

The council was already on a dais at the back of the building: Abe Getz, Con Boyd, Gus Mueller and Del Hunter. The varnished benches held various other citizens, not including Mrs. Jay or Jim Madison. Cobre had been polishing itself for the coming of rails for some time now, so that surfaces were spick and span. The joints down on Maine Street, the Mexican quarters, the miners' shacks were supposed to be invisible, Hancock thought — as he would not have ruminated yesterday.

He found himself scrutinizing his fellow townsmen, ticking them off, estimating them. Dr. Farrar was a staunch, fearless individual, drunk or sober, and mainly he was sober enough to attend to his practice. Abe Getz was also a solid man, unassuming, quiet. Mueller was a stout German who looked like a butcher and kept the

General Store. Hunter looked lost without his wife, nervous, scared.

Father Donner of St. Mary's sat beside his friend Reverend Doerr of the Methodist Church, each sober in black, equally neutral, ineffective men of the cloth, without much influence — or force either, Hancock knew. Church was still a woman's business on the frontier, men attended only when persuaded by their wives.

Then there was, amazingly, Jeb Truman. The smith wore his apron and there were coal smudges on his folded, massive arms. Lawyer Tomas Rosario, representing his fellow Latin Americans, stroked his dragoon mustache next to Hod Simms and Asa Boyd. Mr. Jerry Kay, banker, a lean old veteran who eschewed politics but whose bank was a profound factor in the county, wore his string tie and rested his congress gaiters in the aisle, blue eyes hard and sharp.

As they ascended the platform, Con Boyd intercepted Taggart and Hancock, whispering, "Got her all laid out, nice and pretty. Crowded, though. The sheriff and the whore . . ."

"Shut up, Con," Hancock told him. He sat down at the end of the row of chairs. Taggart went to the lectern.

"Of course this is not a regular meeting. It's that we have this — er — situation. Everyone's worried and we thought we might — er — talk it over." His voice wavered between anxiety and unction.

Jeb Truman said blunt and clear, "You talkin' about murder, Lou."

"Uh, be that as it may. I mean, the court has not decided."

"Coroner's jury decided an hour ago," Truman said.

"Yes. Well, we will follow the law. That is the only way. We must maintain peace."

"For the railroad," Truman said. "Y'all follow it like sheep. If they say this ain't no playpen for Jed Buxton, that's the way it is. If they decide Candlestick's more important, that'll be all right with you."

"Now, Jeb, let's not be persnickety."

"Ain't got time to mess around," Truman told him, rising. "Got work to do. Thing is, can this here town hang Jed Buxton? Now, I'm agin them hoors, keepin' up the racket all night, all that. But I'm worst against murder. If the court says hang him — I'm for it. Now I got to go to work."

He walked out with steady gait, a massive man steady as a burro on a mountain trail. The door closed behind him amidst a sudden silence.

Jerry Kay climbed to full height. Everyone turned to him, paying strict attention. He had been early in the West and his position was solid. He was as authentic as the mountains which surrounded the town.

He said, "Jeb done told you. I don't see it no other way. Matt's a friend of mine. Don't make any difference. Ben Hancock is doin' his job; I expect we better let him hire as many men as he needs. It's the only way there is. Reckon that's the reason I'm here, to see Ben gets help and the town pays for it."

Taggart looked haggard. "Yes, Mr. Kay is correct. If anyone on the council is opposed, let him speak up."

Gus Mueller asked, "How much we pay? For how long? How many deputies yet?"

Ben said, "I can get along with Neddy at four dollars a day. Luke Post will work for ten as chief deputy."

"Fourteen a day? For how long?" insisted Mueller.

"Two weeks. Maybe more."

"That's now fourteen a day for fourteen days, maybe more." Mueller was suffering. "That's now . . ."

Jerry Kay said, "One hundred and ninety-six dollars plus found. Cheap at ten times the price."

"All over a leetle whore gal," muttered Mueller. "*Gott im Himmel.*"

Dr. Farrar drawled, "Helen of Troy was an adultress."

Hancock rose and stepped to the edge of the dais. "Matt Buxton has promised Jed will never hang. We all know that. It's got everyone scared. It's been put on my back. You want me to do it? Or you want me to quit?"

"No!" Taggart spoke quickly. "No, don't quit. You do what you must, we'll put up the money. Only . . ."

"Only nothin'," Hancock told them. "It's my show."

Kay said, "He's all the way right."

"Of course he consults with the council."

"No," said Hancock.

"Police business for police." Kay lifted a lean hand. "You better agree, gentlemen. Or turn Cobre over to Buxton."

"We agree — we agree," Taggart said. The others sat tight a moment, then nodded. It was over with fewer words than Hancock had expected. He left while the iron was hot and Jerry came out of the building behind him.

"They'll be meeting and jawing and trying every which way to figure angles," Kay said. "It's a chicken-shit town, but what town ain't?"

"But without towns you got no county and without counties you got no Territory nor a State and then where are you?" asked Hancock.

"Better off, maybe. This Territory is kinda loose," said Kay. "Even for a Territory, way they change governors back there in Washington. But we got Judge Grey and he's a man I put in with. You go ahead, Ben. I'm with you."

Dr. Farrar came up behind them and added, "Me too, Ben. When Matt's bunch gets you I'll patch you up for free. Best I can, that is."

"Thanks, Doc," Hancock said. "Decent of you people to stand behind me — even that far behind."

They grinned at one another and parted. Hancock swung straight down Pass Avenue to the corner of Maine Street. The shades of the house were tight drawn but Mrs. Jay was awaiting his visit. She was attired in plain black and her expression was severe, with a tremor of fear just below the surface. Hancock sat on the velvet-covered chair as before.

Cora was slumped in a corner, patently drunk. She resembled nothing so much as a scared cow. Carrie, a frail, pretty consumptive, held a handkerchief to her lips and arched her brows at Hancock. The former farm girl known as Sadie, with her heavy legs and thick ankles, perched upon the staircase. Mrs. Jay waved a hand to include them all.

"They all want to say they're sorry. Except Cora. Matt and Finnegan got her so she don't know who she is or where she is."

Hancock said, "We're all sorry."

"I want to say we demand justice," Mrs. Jay stated in flat, somewhat hopeless accents. "We got rights. Nobody should be able to slaughter us like cattle."

"You'll get what the courts say."

"You mean Jed Buxton'll hang? Huh!"

The whores cackled. Hancock looked at them, suggested, "Like to talk to you alone, Mrs. Jay."

She waved her hand and they all skittered a moment, then went up the stairs. Carrie came close to Hancock and said, "Now Daisy's gone, Marshal — any time — any time."

"Upstairs!" Mrs. Jay commanded. When the girl had vanished she went on, "She's next best to Daisy, at that. A tart in her heart but she has qualities."

"Uh — sure," said Hancock. "Now, about Daisy."

"She was trouble, but I liked her. And I meant what I said, she had rights."

"Did you know anything about her, where she came from, her full name?"

"Nothing. Not a damn thing." She went to a table and picked up a japanned box no more than six inches wide and a foot long, decorated with cherubs and a benevolent angel. "This is all she had. She came here in a raggedy dress and asked for those ginghams. I had

102

'em made for her. She'd had experience, young as she was."

"How old was she?"

"I don't know. But you could tell she was a child. They start that way sometimes."

"What about the dress she wore here? Maybe there's a label in it."

"She burned it. When I got her the gingham she made a bonfire in the back yard and burned several things."

"She didn't have a real name?"

"Everybody's got a real name. I asked her. She said she came out of the nowhere into here. Then she laughed. She said she was Daisy because daisies don't tell. Then she laughed again — you know the way she did."

"Yes. I know." He had heard that laughter in the night, upstairs behind locked doors, and at moments it seemed as though she were crazy and at other times it was low and warm and hugely exciting. He knew all about Daisy's laughter. He shivered.

Mrs. Jay said, "I've seen plenty of 'em come and go. They don't last long, poor geese. Daisy was a leader. They were jealous of her, but she led 'em. When trouble came she laughed and teased and pretty soon nobody cared."

"I suppose she never got a letter or a card."

"Nothing. She was just — here. She wasn't crazy or anything, you know. She could make good sense. She had some grief. Somethin' deep inside. She took to the laudanum, then she found the Mex weed to smoke and that sailed her. But she wasn't crazy."

"No, I never thought so."

"That Jed busted up this place a couple times. You know that. Matt paid, sure. But nobody mended the bruises on my gals. And he never did hit Daisy."

"He hit her last night. Then he shot her."

"He should hang higher than Haman."

"That may be, too." He stood up, the box under his arm. "I'm real sorry, Mrs. Jay."

"I'll tell you something," she said tightly. "If they don't hang him, I'll move out of town. I couldn't hold up my head if somebody killed one of my gals and didn't pay for it. Like we're nothin'."

"I know how you feel," Hancock said.

Mrs. Jay's face softened. "She sure was a nice piece, wasn't she, Marshal?"

"The best," he told her and went out with the box, thinking of madames and whores and how they had their pride — honor?

Did everyone have his code? he wondered. Did Jed Buxton have one, twisted, criminal, yet preventing him from abusing Daisy until the final, ultimate act of violence? He could not decide in his mind. He only knew he felt a sense of loss, a pity which had not been in him yesterday.

Cobre seemed on the surface to be doing business as usual. Wagons came and went, people walked back and forth and in and out of the stores. There did seem to be a few more people in evidence than usual. They drifted into small knots here and there, talking together in low tones. They spoke to him soberly, then whispered as he went by. At the hotel hitching rack he saw four familiar horses bearing the Candlestick brand. He veered from the walk and into the lobby, his jaw set.

Larson, Pitts, Ward and Farr sat about a chair in which Matt Buxton had planted himself. Finnegan stood behind the fat rancher like a courtier at the throne of a king. The Hunters, nervous as land crabs, fluttered behind the desk, and young Johnny was poised to run errands and eavesdrop on the proceedings.

Before Hancock could speak, Finnegan said in his lawyer's voice, "I have a paper here that says you cannot bar these men from town. It is signed by Judge Grey."

Hancock read the paper carefully. The riders stirred but were silent. Matt seemed to be deep in thought.

"And they are not to carry arms," the marshal said.

"We checked 'em with your man down yonder," Larson said. "You satisfied with that?"

"No. There's always the hardware store where your boss can buy guns," Hancock said. "I'm not satisfied but what the judge says goes."

"You push too hard," Larson began, but Matt glanced at him and the hard-faced, tough foreman was silent.

"Want to talk to you, Ben," the rancher said.

"We already talked." Hancock started for the door. Matt got up and followed him, barring his way.

"You really want to hang my little brother," Matt said.

"If I have to."

"I thought we was friends."

"That's up to you. I'm not mad at anybody."

Matt lowered his voice. "You could let him get away. The boys'll make it look good. I'll cover it for you like a blanket."

"No bet, Matt."

"You can still be sheriff. The railroad won't complain if we get Jed away. I'll send him to Mexico."

"Can't possibly." He felt the temptation. The way Matt made it sound, the escape hatch was wide open not only for Jed but for Hancock.

"I'll deed that acreage to the railroad as a gift. You'll come out smellin' sweet as apple cider."

Hancock struggled with what had built within him, trying to find words to make himself clear. "Matt, supposin' I agreed. That's the minute you'd lose respect for me, forever. I got to live, with me — and with you."

"No, Ben. I'm your friend. We always been friends." Matt was utterly sincere, he was pleading as he had never pleaded before.

"Not quite. You always been Candlestick. I've been town marshal. We got along, sure. But friends? You think so?"

Matt seemed to consider this. "Well, you're as good a friend as anybody around here. I never had time. Look, Ben, why have all this trouble over a li'l old whore who accordin' to everybody was no good nohow?"

"She was alive. She's dead. She was human."

"Just what I say, she's dead. Can't bring her back. Why wreck the town?"

Hancock's anger had begun to boil at Matt's categorization of Daisy. He could see her bleeding on the floor of the saloon, hear Jed's raucous profanity. He had to make an effort to keep his temper in check. "Matt, you're tryin' to buy and I got nothin' to sell."

Matt licked his lips, his eyes went to Finnegan, then back to Hancock. "Ben, you're gonna look real bad in court. Finnegan's gonna put you on the stand. The way you slapped Jed around, like you hated him. And that Daisy — she was your favorite whore."

He felt himself turning cold all over at the threat. He said, "The hell with you, Matt."

"Cora, the dumb one, she'll testify."

"And who'll believe her?"

"You laid the little whore regular. You deny it?"

"That's nobody's business."

"You think testimony like that'll help you to be sheriff?"

"Yesterday it was you that wanted me for the job," Hancock told him. "That was before your brother turned murderer."

Matt flushed, his neck swelled like a frog on a lily pad. "You're pushin', like Larson says. You're polishin' that star."

"You helped me to get to wear it." He felt easier as the rancher grew angrier.

"My brother ain't goin' to hang!" Matt threw the words from the middle of his immense girth.

"That's for the court to decide."

"Nobody hangs Jed for killin' a whore. I'm tellin' you and the judge and the world."

"Keep telling it," Hancock said. "You can't make me believe it."

"Jed was stone drunk."

"He could shoot good enough. In the back."

Matt seemed about to burst. Then he gained control and exhaled. The sound of the town came through, the jingle of a cowboy's spur, the tinkle of a woman's laugh, the squeak of a wagon wheel.

"Most people ain't got brains. Muscle but no brains. I thought you was different."

"Not me. I'm a tin star, like you said."

"I raised my brother. Maybe — no, not maybe, for sure — I raised him wrong. I'm responsible for him."

"Sorry."

"He'll never stretch hemp, Ben."

"Could be, but I'm holding him. Anybody tries to take him could be cut off at the hips. That's for Larson and anyone else you bring in. It's for you too."

Matt stepped aside, leaving the way to the exit clear. "Hear you plain, Ben. Finnegan said to give it a try. Might have knowed. You're an old-timer. Like me. Maybe a damn fool as who ain't once in awhile. I'll be stickin' around."

"You do that, Matt. Me, I'll be around too."

Hancock went out into the hot sun. There was no wasted venom between them, he knew. An iron bar, but no doubts as to where each would stand. Each was aware of the strength and weakness of the other. The struggle would go on until Jed's fate was decided. Matt respected Hancock and the marshal sure as hell respected Matt.

He let a farm wagon pass, then cut across the street kicking dust. Luke was on the porch, chair tilted, hat over his nose, a shotgun tilted at his side. Jim Madison occupied another chair. Hancock spoke to them, went inside, stared a moment at the black box, then put it in a wall cabinet for later reference. He went out and joined the others.

Luke said, "Madison here, he's talkin' some."

"I ain't runnin' out, Ben," Madison said quickly. He took white powder from a twist of paper and drowned it in a gulp of whiskey.

"Some kind of drugs?" asked Ben, grinning.

"Somethin' new Doc gimme. Aspirin."

"I thought you took bismuth for your stomach."

"This here is for my headache."

"You know what? I could have a headache my own self today," Hancock said, sighing. "It's a time for it."

Madison tapped a slight bulge beneath his arm. "You ever see me carry a gun? You're seein' it now."

"Candlestick men checked theirs," Luke said.

"Better take it off. You don't wear it, you don't have to use it," Ben added.

"That an order?"

"Just good advice. Candlestick won't come at you."

"They came here yellin'," Luke said. "They went around and yelled some to Jed. Neddy had the shotgun on 'em all the time. I had this one ready. But then they come to me all mealymouth handin' over their guns. Me, I'm lookin' for a pinwheel or somethin' smart. But they just laughed and put down the hoglegs. Like they knew somethin' I didn't know."

"Judge Grey gave Finnegan an order. They like that. They come in alone?"

"They was ridin' behind a lady in a light rig. A thin lady with big eyes."

"Virgie Buxton," Hancock said. "She must have gone out for 'em. She'll do anything for Matt, anything. She don't hold with Jed worth a damn but she purely loves Matt. Damn if the world ain't complicated sometimes."

"It ain't simple," said Madison. "I want out of this town, I decided. Things is too tetchy."

"The judge'll want you to testify," Hancock told him. "You want to tell about last night?"

"If I had my gun on me." Then he shook his head. "No. It was too quick and I'm not gun-fast. Dipple had the shotgun right at his hand and couldn't get it up in time."

"They were arguin'?"

"It was funny. You know? Jed was tellin' her he wanted to take her outa Miz Jay's place."

"That's an old one," Luke said.

"No, it was funny. Jed's got a nasty way with the gals, we all know that. But last night, I dunno."

"You sayin' he was serious?"

"I ain't sayin' he wasn't. A saloonkeeper, he hears a lot of guff. Jed, he was drunk. I just don't know."

"And Daisy, what'd she say?"

"Laughed. Like she did. Said she liked it at Miz Jay's. He couldn't get over it. Kept hammerin' at her, sayin' nobody liked bein' a whore. Daisy laughed and laughed."

"What did she say before he hit her?"

110

"I didn't hear. I moved away. Larson was settin' with Cora. He hit her quick. She hollered and started to run."

"That don't figure, Daisy running."

"You didn't see his face. The look. Like he was ready to kill. You see that look and you fight or run. She didn't have anything to fight with."

"No. She didn't," said Hancock. "You tell that story to the jury, they'll hang Jed all right."

"And then Matt will come at me. He's already asked me not to go to court. Made a few threats. Hell, whores are a dime a dozen and all that. But Daisy was different and I seen her killed."

"You said you wouldn't run out," Hancock reminded him.

"Matt just ain't used to not havin' his own way. Matt could be real bad if he had a mind."

"You tell the truth and I'll mind Matt. Let the court make the decision."

"Well, you're right. I dunno." Madison spoke vaguely, his mind turning over, his inner thoughts perturbing him. "You come by, I'll buy the drinks."

"Just stick around and tell what you know," urged Hancock. "We'll see you later."

They watched him walk across the street, stoop-shouldered, plodding. He was a man disturbed, his eyes went toward the hotel as if he expected to be attacked by the Candlestick crowd at any moment.

"Not a man to tie to," Luke observed. "He means good, but he wouldn't stand up."

"That reminds me," said Hancock. He took a badge from his pocket. "Ten dollars a day and found. You ready?"

"Not me." Luke recoiled. "A star? On me?"

"I know how you feel." Hancock chose his words with great care. "I need somebody to side me. I need a man's been around some. You can see that."

"You got me. I don't need the money, I'll just stick and see it through."

"*Amigo*, you can't do that. If we're with the law, we need to be sworn in. Maybe it's kinda foolishment to you. But that's the way it's got to be."

"Neddy wears his like it's a medal." Luke shook his head. "I'd feel like a damn fool."

"You going to quit me?"

Luke shifted uneasily, muttering, "That punk in the cell. He yammers all day. Settin' around, that don't wear good for me."

"You going to quit?"

Luke said, "Ah, the hell. I wish I could. Lawin' is dumb. I could be over breakin' Madison's bank. I could be doin' well at Miz Jay's. I could be sittin' on my royal in the hotel, watchin' Matt Buxton stew."

Hancock smiled for the first time that day. He pinned the badge delicately to Luke's lapel. He said, "Raise your right hand."

"Cow dung," said Luke, but he obeyed.

"You're a deputy," said Hancock, wisely omitting further ceremony. "Pay starts as of yesterday."

"Whiskey, too?"

"I'll see Ching Hoo later. We're runnin' low. He always pretends he's fresh out of the stuff but I happen to know he's got a barrel stashed."

"He's a great man," said Luke. "Always did cotton to Chinks. Decent people."

Hancock went inside, opened the big door. Neddy was seated in the chair, the little blue book in his fist. He grinned, removed two wads of cotton from his ears.

"Big mouth's runnin' down. I think he's gettin' hoarse. This here cotton sure helped."

"Smart bastard," snarled Jed Buxton from his cell. He sat on the bunk, his hair combed back, his eyes bloodshot, a stubble of light beard on his face. "Where's that fat damn brother of mine?"

"Busy," Hancock told him. "Take some air, Neddy. I'll set a spell, then send Luke in; he hired on."

"Thought he would," said Neddy. "He swore he never would, but I thought different." He held up the book. "Some goin's on in them days, huh? Bloody goin's on."

"Bad folks, them Macbeths, thought they could solve everything by killin' people," Hancock said.

"That Shakespeare had some fine words."

"They tell me he was the best."

"Books," Jed Buxton said with great scorn. "Some damn lawmen. Readin' books."

"He never did read one," Neddy observed. "Some rich punk, never read a book." He departed as Jed screamed curses at him.

Hancock sat down in the chair. It was an act of strength to remain calm beholding the prisoner, hearing his caterwauling.

"Smart bastard, him and his book," Jed said. Now he was suddenly calm. He peered at Hancock. "No bail, huh?"

"Your hearing is Monday."

"I killed her, huh? You know that?"

"You know it."

"Lawman, I don't know nothin' about it. We was talkin' and drinkin' just goofin' around. Then I drew a blank." He paused, his face fox-pointed, his eyes narrowed like an animal at bay. "Then you was knockin' me around and I seen her layin' there on the floor. It's all mixed up in my head."

"Finnegan will be proud of that yarn." It was difficult not to open the cell and drag him out and beat the truth from him.

"It's the truth. I don't remember nothin'!"

"Trouble is, there are some who do remember. Like me. I was there."

"You didn't see it —" He broke off, realizing he had blundered. "I mean, you — I mean, I . . ."

"You mean you do remember. I saw enough. You were holding the gun, it was smoking. She was dead."

"My brother will get me outa here." The foxy look was gone, he was scared again, blustering against the wind of realization of his true position. "I want my brother."

"You can have him any time he's ready to see you."

"Nobody can send me to jail for killin' a two-bit wide-mouthed whore!"

"They're not planning on sendin' you to jail, bub."

The rubbery face changed again. "You sonofabitch. You cheap lawman. My brother put you where you are. Now you're talkin' about a lynchin'."

"No lynching," Hancock assured him.

"You think a jury would hang me? ME?"

"I wouldn't know. It's what we call first-degree murder. Usually that calls for neck-stretching." He suddenly realized he was enjoying the changing expressions on the face of his prisoner. He was wishing for the hanging, he wanted to see the weakling walk up thirteen steps, to watch the last remnants of manhood wiped out of him. This was wrong, he knew. He got up and went to the door and unlocked it.

Luke appeared. Jed was yelling again, one obscenity atop the other. Luke took out a small roll of cotton. He made a big show of putting it in his ears, saying loudly to Hancock, "That Neddy's smart. I got me a book out of your desk. This here'll be the most eddicated jailhouse in New Mexico."

He had a paperback called *The Pinkerton Ferret*, a wild piece of a writer's imagination. Hancock laughed, made gestures, went outside and refastened the door.

Neddy was on the porch, watching the traffic. He looked up seriously and said, "Ben, I been thinkin'."

"You'll strain yourself."

"Luke told me a story about Dodge. A lady named Dora Hand."

"She was shot and killed by accident. Fella was lookin' to get Dog Kelley."

"Fella named Kennedy? Father was a big Texas rancher?"

"That's right."

"Dora Hand was a nice lady, Luke said."

"Some said from Philadelphia. Played piano like I never heard it played."

"But she was a hoor?"

"Hard word, but she was — well, careless sometimes."

"Bat Masterson was sheriff. A posse rode out after Kennedy."

"Sure. Chased hell out of him."

"Somebody shot Kennedy. He lost his arm, didn't he?"

"I wouldn't know. Somebody shot him when he wouldn't stop for arrest. He got off."

"That's it. He got off."

"I begin to salivate what you're drivin' at," said Hancock, drawling deliberately in the patois. "It won't do, Neddy."

"Seems to me, 'course I'm just a dumb kid, it would save a lot of trouble. Jed gets away. I'd be plumb happy to be waitin' on the road to Mexico."

"You'd shoot him?"

"Not in the elbow. In the ass at least. You ain't sat in there with him, Ben. He stinks. He stinks outside and he stinks inside. I've had to kill a mad dog. He's worse'n a poor mad dog."

"Murder."

116

"I don't see it that way."

Hancock said, "Neddy, you're a good boy. Don't start thinkin' about murder. There's no excuse for it. Sometimes you got to kill — I had to shoot some Indians yesterday. I didn't want to. I had to. They would've killed me. That's self-defense."

"I'll give that bastard first shot."

"But you'd have it in mind to get him."

"Well, hell, yes!"

"No good, Neddy. Stay with the law. Stay with that badge you like to wear. Think what your poppa would say."

Neddy considered. He looked down at the little blue book in his pocket. "Macbeth was wrong."

"This is a rough country. I been through it. I was with that posse out of Dodge. Fact is, nobody knows who shot Kennedy, they tell it different. I may have done. But he was escapin'. We didn't turn him loose. He got away and we chased him, a legal posse."

"And he got off."

"Because a smart lawyer made it accidental shootin' and his father had money."

"Matt's got money."

"That was years ago. Cobre ain't Dodge City. You just do your job, improve your readin' and let us take care of Jed."

Neddy nodded. "All right. But Ben — you better take care of him good."

Hancock sighed. There was no use talking any more. Not so long ago he had been identical with this boy in his thinking. Now he knew better. Nobody wanted

117

vengeance on Jed Buxton more than he, but he had changed with the times. He walked down the steps and up the street again. The sun was high now and the color had gone from the everlasting mountains. Every midday this happened and it was a time he did not like. Cobre and all around it on the high plain flattened out, lost shape. It seemed cold, but that was in the mind, for the sun was hot. The distant towering piles of rock seemed stark and forbidding. The peaks stretched toward the sky as though in prayer. At other times they seemed to glower, threatening to march down in the town, but today it was supplication, as if they knew Cobre had enough trouble.

He waved to Abe Getz in the store and realized the proprietor wanted to talk. He paused and stout, red-cheeked Becky Getz came and stood beside her husband. The interior of the shop was always orderly and clean with glass cases of jewelry and bolts of cloth and spools of thread and what was loosely called "notions." It had a fresh, wholesome odor.

"This is a circumstance, Marshal, no?"

"You could call it more'n that."

"A boy we seen raised right here."

"Right here didn't do a good enough job."

Mrs. Getz said, "A nogoodnick, Jed Buxton. But also the girl? A nogoodnick?"

"A live human being," Hancock told her.

Getz said, "Yes, a human. Never mind how good or bad a girl, she was alive. There is talk, talk, talk, Marshal. Finnegan slips here, he slips there. Talk."

"A lawyer's mouth," said Mrs. Getz. "A lying and a thieving. Nogoodnick, that Finnegan."

Her husband made a gesture, spreading his hands. "I am no fighter, Marshal. But this boy, he shot this girl. I have seen worse things. In the old country, much worse. But here, it cannot be, nu?"

"It hadn't ought to be."

"I just want to tell you, Marshal, I am with you and with Judge Grey. Some say nothing should be done, on account of Candlestick, on account of the railroad. Mixed-up talk. I say do. Whatever, we should do."

"Thanks, Abe. Makes a man feel good to know people are with him."

"A nice town it is," sighed Mrs. Getz. "A shame already. Altogether a shame."

Across the street, Linda was at her window. Hancock said, "We do what we can," and went over to the dress shop. A running boy and a dog almost upset him. He went into the shop. It was cool and Linda was perturbed.

"Anything new, Ben?"

"Nothing."

"They called off the Annual Ball."

"Reckoned they would, it's too tight around here."

"Two funerals tomorrow."

"Yes. Two. Nice Sunday in Cobre."

"Finnegan was here." She spoke nervously. "He asked me not to testify."

"Sure. He's got Cora talkin' double."

"Cora?"

"The other — gal — who was there."

"Oh. Yes, I remember. Finnegan talked about her, and about Madison and about how Matt feels, all broken up."

"Matt? Broken up?"

"He said that."

"He'll be broken up real bad if Jed goes to trial," Hancock told her.

"It's a bad thing." She looked drawn today, subdued. "Everything is wrong today."

He could not reach out to her. His voice was flat. "I know, Linda. We just follow the law from now on. There's nothing you can do about it."

She turned away and he touched his hatbrim and went back out on Buxton Street. Finnegan was smart, he was spreading the gospel and mixing it up with threats of Candlestick's muscle. If anyone could swing popular opinion it was the sleek lawyer with Matt behind him.

The stage came in, turning to brake in front of the Wells Fargo office. It was a brave picture, Mitch Mitchell on the box, Reb Johnson riding shotgun. The six good horses ambled down the street, shaking their heads, snuffling from the climb up the southern trail. The brakes squawled, the whiffletrees swung, Mitch flourished the ribbons, clucking to a stop, talking to his steeds. The stagecoach, too, would soon be a part of Cobre's past and the past of all the towns on the rails, relegated to the tules and the byways of the West.

Speedy Jackson appeared, out of breath as usual, confidential. "The wires have been hotter than hell's foundation. Matt's been at the governor for hours.

Governor refers him to Judge Grey. Finnegan runs racin' around with his tongue lollin' out and waggin' at both ends. You think you can keep Jed in the hoosegow?"

"We try, Speedy, we try."

"You got two good men. That Luke, everybody knows him. Neddy's all right." He broke off, said in awe, "Hey, looky yonder! What is this come to Cobre?"

Hancock was looking. He saw a burly man in clothing too warm for the day, wearing a derby hat. The man was extending an arm and a gloved hand was grasping it. A dainty booted foot extended itself with some recklessness of display, a dust-covered traveling dress of high style fitted up and down the form of the most shapely woman Hancock had ever beheld. He stared, rubbed his eyes, stared again.

It was Laurie Pomfret. There could be no doubt. No one in the world resembled Laurie. The blood ran to his face, congealed there. His hands were damp. Disbelief flooded him, then receded as a gladness ran through him. He started forward.

The woman smiled, as always. Looking around the commonplace of another western town she saw Speedy's open-mouthed admiration, saw other men pause to watch. Then she saw Ben Hancock. She shook loose from Brewster and ran.

Brewster followed her glance, automatically reached for the luggage Mitch was handing down. People now stopped to stare at the meeting of the marshal and the lady.

"Ben!" she shouted so that all could hear. "Oh, Ben Hancock, praise the good Lord."

He said, "Laurie, what in heaven's damn name — Laurie!"

They stumbled together. It was as though each had come to the end of a long, exhausting search. To Hancock it was a trip he had not known he was making, a complete emotional culmination of something of which he had been utterly unaware. To the woman it was relief, joy and perhaps more, much more than she knew in that instant of recognition.

She was babbling in his ear, "Oh, Ben — Ben — I had no idea you were here. It's so good, so good to have you here, waiting. It's Maureen, I've been looking for her all over the country. The detectives traced her here — oh, Ben!"

He had not the slightest notion of what her words meant. He was held in the moment, only conscious of the tremendous sensation of seeing her again, of the feel of her in his arms. It had been over a dozen years yet she was as familiar to him as though it had been yesterday.

He managed, "I'm plumb flabbergasted, Laurie. It's crazy. I've been thinkin' about you. Come on, let's get out of this sun to where I can really look at you."

She was weeping a little and laughing a little. Brewster, imperturbable, had the luggage. There was so much of it that Mitch climbed down, beaming, to help. People moved heads on shoulders and down the street Linda Darr looked from behind her curtains, her face pinched and drawn.

122

Laurie said, "Brewster — Brewster! This is Ben Hancock. Remember, I spoke of him only last evening?"

Brewster inclined his head, "Indeed, madam. How are you, sir?"

"Take the things up, wherever — I asked for a suite, Ben — I never know what I'll get for accommodations. It's been such a hard, long trip."

He had never seen her like this. She had always been gay, laughing, in control of any situation. Now she was ready to come apart at the seams, he thought. He was confused, but he took her arm while all Cobre observed the handsome pair as they made their way to the hotel, close as Siamese twins. It was an odd sight to those who knew the marshal, it was a matter for sly glances at Linda Darr's place and for whispers behind closed doors.

Brewster, erect as a Grenadier, stalked through traffic and by his very bearing made a path across Buxton Street. Hancock followed in his wake, scarcely listening to Laurie, bemused still. They paraded into the lobby, Mitch following with hands full of bags. Matt was sitting in the chair he had adopted as his own and the four riders provided a background. The Hunters stared from behind the desk and little Johnny came scuttling to ascertain whether there was a gratuity in it for him.

Matt said, "Ben, want to talk to you."

"We've been through that." Then Hancock said vaguely, "Later, Matt. Later."

Hunter said, "Mrs. Van Orden?"

That registered with the marshal. She was married.

She signed the register and asked, "May I go right up to my rooms? You do have a suite for me?"

Hunter said nervously, "I'm terrible sorry, Mrs. Van Orden. The only suite — well, Mr. Buxton had to stay over and — there's been an upsetment in town. I'm sorry."

"But I sent you a telegram. You corroborated my reservation."

"I know, ma'am. I can give you two rooms together, real nice."

"Three rooms. I require a bedroom for myself, one for Brewster and a sitting room between."

"It can be arranged, ma'am," said Hunter eagerly. "Three rooms, yes, ma'am."

Hancock said, "Get at it. You want to go up and sit down for a spell? Or you want to wait till they're ready?"

"Brewster will handle it," she said. "Is there a private place?"

She smiled in her fashion, bestowing a glance upon the riders and Matt and the Hunters as Johnny scrambled. The Candlestick men fumbled with their hats, impressed, but cold-eyed. Matt just stared, his enmity apparent to her, confusing her for the moment.

Ben said, "In here," leading her to the small bar. There was one table in the corner and they sat down, regarding one another, their eyes wide and eager.

She began, "What a trip. But all stage drivers are gallant, they are great men. People have been kind."

She broke off, catching sight of his badge. "You're an officer?"

"Around here right now I'm the only one."

"But that's wonderful. You can help." She waved a hand. "Let's start at the beginning. Let's tell each other everything, every single little thing. Oh, Ben."

He took the hand she reached out to him, remembering it, remembering caresses and the times that had been in New York. "You're married?"

"I was, I was. An Englishman, a nice man, Donald Van Orden. He passed away. He left me a million pounds and he left me something better. Brewster."

"You — you're aimin' to marry him, Brewster?"

She was startled. "Brewster? Why, he's not a man. Oh no, I mean, he is of course a man. But in England he was a servant. Over there, servants aren't men."

"They don't marry, have kids?"

"I said it wrong. He's wonderful, my Brewster. I'm teaching him to be our kind of man. I want him to be — like you."

"Heaven forbid." He could be light and easy now that he knew she was unattached, unpromised. "You look great, Laurie."

She gripped his hand. "And you look greater. We had times together when we were young."

"Good times. The best." It was true. He had forgotten everything, all the troubles, sitting across from her.

"We were too young. Stupid. No real knowledge of what life was all about. Just fun. And I let you get away."

"My fault. I was stubborn as a mule."

"No one's fault. Just the way things were." Her voice changed, she shook her head. "Then there was Maureen."

The name meant nothing to him. "Maureen?"

"You called her Baby. You were very good to her. My little girl, remember?"

"Oh, the baby, sure. Bless her little heart. How is she now?" He recalled the tiny curled fingers in his palm and how they had strolled the shady streets while Mummy slept until he had to carry her because she was so little and easily became weary and how she would fall asleep on his shoulder. "Sweetest kid I ever saw. Couldn't talk any but laughed a whole lot."

"And I neglected her. She loved you because you spent time with her. I never found the time. I was having fun."

"She said things like 'mamma' and 'dog' and like that. There was trouble with the diapers. You had a maid for 'em, you never did like the diaper business."

"Yes. I had a maid. I never had time." Her face twisted in sudden pain. "Of all the foolish, evil things I ever did, neglecting Maureen was the worst. She made Donald nervous — oh, he was all right, just older and not used to babies — girls. He was uncomfortable in New York, too, and I had never seen Europe. It seemed so simple. We had a governess then. I promised to come home to her. I stayed away too long."

"Why, Laurie, time gets away on all of us."

She said agonizedly, "She ran away."

"She did what?"

"Maureen ran away. She got hold of some money, not much. She disappeared. Donald had died, we were settling his estate, very complicated. I hired the Pinkerton agency, took ship and came home."

"The Pinkertons, yeah." He did not think much of the agency. "They never found her?"

"I paid them a lot of money. They traced her to Chicago. They lost her, they said she was heading West. I thought of you then, but she could not possibly have remembered you, she was too young when we were together. I began to follow westward. She kept going that way."

"That seems strange, in a way. The West is no place for a young girl."

She said, "Ben, they said she had come here. To Cobre."

"Here? Why, that's impossible." He blinked. "She'd be, lemme see — how old?"

"Fifteen, almost sixteen." She fixed him with her lovely, tormented eyes. "You might know, Ben. Is there anyone that age new in town? Working in a household, perhaps? She knew nothing more useful than housework. Unless she learned to cook, something like that?"

"Nobody in town could be your baby. Cleaning women, they're Mex or colored." He broke off short. Horror gripped him in his bowels.

Laurie was reaching for a large reticule. "There is, luckily, a picture. The governess had it taken to send me before Maureen ran away. Here — here it is."

If he had ever needed a poker face it was now. He tried hard for it, but he had never had any skill in disguising his feelings. He accepted the pasteboard gingerly, turned it to the faint light in the little room. It was a posed, slightly unnatural likeness from a fashionable New York studio.

Laurie exclaimed, "You do recognize it! You've seen her."

His mind was reeling, words stuck in him. He choked and she leaned forward, whitening, hands clenched.

"Ben, please. Tell me."

When he found his voice it was strange, dull. "You better come take a walk with me."

"You do know where she is. Oh, Ben I don't care — anything, just so I find her. There's so much to make up for. Just take me to her."

"Yes. I can do that." He could not tell her right out, he had to spar for time. The past and the present pinched him in. The whole of it was too much for him, he needed time, even a short time. His mind worked disjointedly, seeking answers where there were none. He followed her from the little bar, into the lobby. Brewster was coming down the stairs. He beckoned to the servant to join them; if she ever needed support in this world it was now.

Matt repeated, "I'll want that talk, Ben."

One thought did escape, come menacing to the fore. Hancock's voice was brutal, savage, threatening. "You'll get it, Matt. You'll get it."

128

He led the way across the street, stumbling once in the dust, narrowly escaping being run down by a carriage, nearly tripping over the ubiquitous boy and dog. Laurie was silent, the fear of impending disaster upon her, afraid to question Hancock. Linda Darr saw them from her window and ducked swiftly lest someone accuse her of spying. Luke was inside the cell area, guarding the prisoner. Neddy was taking a nap in Hancock's bedroom. The office was empty.

Laurie's gaze darted around, rested on the oaken door. "Is that the jail? Is she in jail?"

"No, she's not in jail." Hancock went to the wall cabinet and removed the japanned box, his hands shaking.

"She's in trouble. She's in bad trouble."

"No, Laurie. She's not in trouble."

He wiped dust from the box. There was a small, decorative latch to keep the lid shut. He was clumsy picking it open. He sat down and put the box before Laurie.

"Yes. It's hers. I gave it to her. Yes."

She removed a pair of long evening gloves, once white, now soiled. There was a dried blossom, unidentifiable, crumbling. There were two separate letters in a round, firm, child's handwriting, neither finished. There were other small objects and at the very bottom another cabinet photograph.

"Dear God in heaven," whispered Laurie. The picture was of her, long ago, in stage costume. Beneath it was another, from the same negative which Laurie had shown to Hancock.

129

He said dully, "Sometimes the string don't run right."

"Ben, what is it? Tell me!"

He pulled it all together, trying to find a way to tell it without hurting, knowing he could not. "She — she called herself Daisy. She was in Mrs. Jay's house."

"House? Did you say 'house'?"

"That's the way it was."

Laurie shook her head. "That's nothing. I'm prepared for that. Her father — my own weakness — the life I led her. The Pinkertons — they hinted — Ben!"

"Yes?"

"You said 'was,' didn't you?"

"Yes."

"She isn't here any more?"

"That's right, Laurie. She's gone."

"Gone." She folded her hands on the desk. "You mean that she is dead."

"Yes."

She was fighting herself hard. "Buried?"

"Not yet." He found a way to go on, somehow. "It only happened last night."

"Last night? God help me! Did she die — in the house?"

"No. In a saloon next door to the house. What can I say?" He got up and saw Brewster, whom he had forgotten, iron-faced in the background. He walked toward the man, touched his arm, saying, "I'm sorry. Damn sorry."

"Yes, sir. I, too, am sorry."

"How did she die?" Laurie asked. "Was it painful? Was it awful?"

"It was awful but not painful. A man — a punk boy — shot her."

"Shot her? Oh, no!" Laurie wailed now, "I could have been here. I didn't have the courage to come on through. Right to the end, I failed her."

Brewster spoke. "Please, madam. You could have done nothing."

"He's right. It was done too quick. Nobody could do anything."

Laurie demanded, "The man who did it, what of him?"

Hancock nodded toward the big door. "In there."

"You arrested him?"

"I was a mite too late. I got him, but I been kickin' myself — just a few seconds sooner." He shook his head.

"And you didn't kill him." Her features broke apart, she put up one hand. "No. I didn't mean that. You're an officer, there's the law. It was my fault, all of it. Always and ever, my fault."

"I don't hold with blamin' people for what other people do," Hancock said carefully. "She was wild, Laurie. I mean, real wild. You didn't do that."

"I didn't help. I wasn't there."

She was about to break, he thought. He found the flat bottle and Brewster took it from him and poured two drinks, but Hancock produced a third glass and the servant accepted it, bowing, and they all drank down the whiskey.

"I'll be all right," said the woman. "I want to know more. I want to know all about it."

"Daisy," said Hancock, "Daisy was the way she was. Her own gal. They take laudanum and they smoke this Mexican weed and they mix it with beer and — wildness. She was real crazy at times."

"You knew her well, Ben?"

"I knew her." He gagged on the words.

"Of course. You're the law, you'd know them all. Was it that bad?"

"It was pretty bad."

"But no pain? I mean — the shooting."

"She never knew what hit her." He did not choose to speak of the child's moment of terror, the last scream.

"The man. He must be insane?"

"No. Just a rotten punk kid. We'll take care of him."

"Oh, yes," she said. "That must be. The law."

"We have law, Laurie. He'll be tried."

"And hanged," she said. "Oh, yes, if it costs me my last English pound, he'll be hanged."

"I believe he will." He felt as though he were encased in a sheath, unable to express himself, to get to her and comfort her.

"Who is he, this killer?"

"Jed Buxton. His brother is the fat man you saw in the hotel lobby. Matt Buxton, a rancher."

"The one who wished to talk with you?"

"That's him." She was, he realized, concentrating on details in order not to crack.

"Was he — the one — her lover?"

"She didn't have a lover. She wasn't like that."

"Then he was drunk or crazy."

"Maybe a little of both."

"Matt Buxton. Is he an evil man?"

"No. He's a lot older'n Jed. He feels responsible for his brother."

"Why was she killed? Why?"

"They had words, her and Jed. People heard them talk. Back and forth. She laughed at him," he finished lamely.

"She laughed a lot, not always nicely," Laurie said.

"Yes. Then something was said between them that nobody heard. And he shot her."

"Just like that." Laurie paused, went on. "Laudanum. I used to give her that for a toothache."

"Everybody did. You can buy it in the general store."

"Yes, anywheres, I remember. And the other — the weed —

"Madam!" Brewster pleaded.

"It's a plant. They dry the leaves and roll them into cigarettes. It came up from Mexico years ago. The — gals — they use it. Seems to ease their way."

Laurie said, "And the house, the men. God! She didn't deserve all of that, did she?"

"No. Nobody deserves all that."

"I did it to her. I'm guilty as sin. I did it."

Brewster cleared his throat and said, "Please, madam."

She turned to him, her eyes swimming. "Poor friend. Halfway across the world and this is what I give you."

"Think of yourself, madam."

"Myself, mother of a whore."

133

"Now wait. No use thinking of it that way. What's the good? It don't help none."

"Is there any other way to think? Tell me, Ben, tell me."

"I know you. I won't have you bring yourself down like that."

Her voice grew hoarse and coarse in her throat. "If I had spent less time in bed with men and more time with my child it would not have happened."

"Madam!" Brewster pleaded."

She put her head down for a moment. The two men looked at one another, then their glances went sideways because it was too bitter to know how it was with her, it was a thing which each would have preferred to be private. Yet there was an understanding between them, Hancock knew, the Britisher was staunch, a man to take along.

Laurie reached down for something, pulled herself erect. In an entirely different tone she asked, "May I have another whiskey, please?"

Brewster gave it to her, three ounces straight. She threw it down, held tight to it, then managed a faint if forlorn smile. "I have said it. For the first time I managed to say it. Now it is in the past."

"Leave it there," Hancock begged her.

"I think I can look at her now, if it's all right."

"Just across the way, Con Boyd's place." Hancock started automatically for the big door to check with Luke. He stopped but she nodded to him.

"No, go ahead. I want to see him, also." Her shoulders were a bit too high, her chin too hard, but her eyes were clear and steady.

Hinges groaned as the heavy portal swung open. Luke cranked around in his chair, squinted, pulled the cotton from his ears and came to his feet, trailing the shotgun.

"Laurie? Laurie Pomfret?"

"Luke," she said, taking his hand. "I didn't know you were here. I'm so glad."

"Why, sure." He was baffled. "It's real good to see you."

Hancock said, "Luke, Daisy was the baby. Laurie's baby. You remember."

"The baby?" Luke's face filled with sudden emotion. "Oh, no! That ain't right."

Laurie said, "Thank you, Luke." She looked past him to the cell where Jed Buxton hung onto the bars, his initial smirk vanishing, jaw dropping as the words permeated his understanding. "So this is the hero who shot my daughter?"

"He cries a lot," Luke told her. "He's pure punk."

Jed found his voice, wailing. "What am I, a critter in a cage for people to stare at? You got no right showin' me off like this. Whereat's my brother?"

"Now he's crying for his big brother," Hancock said. He addressed the prisoner. "You think Daisy's mother hasn't got a right to take a look at you?"

"What the hell do I care for the mother of a whore?" bellowed Jed. "What's she expect?"

135

"She expected her daughter to be alive," Hancock retorted. "She had a right."

"The hell with her. Mother of a damn whore."

Laurie said coldly, turning from him, "He will hang, won't he?"

"We sort of plan on it."

"He is sleazy, isn't he? Cheap. Not worth saving. It's written all over him."

"He don't grade much to the ounce," Hancock agreed.

Brewster was standing in the doorway. He said quietly, "Madam, please?"

"Yes." She looked at Hancock and her face was white but calm. "I won't leave here until he hangs."

She turned and walked out, Brewster at her elbow. Luke wiped his brow, whistling under his breath. Jed Buxton flung himself onto his cot, his mouth all awry and moist.

"Mother of a whore. You bastards, I'll never hang. You better get my brother in here, damn your eyes."

The fear had come up in his throat, Hancock knew. It was growing. There were sweat stains at the armpits, beads of it on his forehead, his hair hung lank and lifeless. He looked subhuman at this moment, even as he ranted.

At the big door, Luke drew close and whispered, "What the hell, *amigo?*"

"She came lookin' for Maureen — the baby. Daisy."

"Jeezus, what a bad mess-up."

"It'll get worse, now she's here and rich and ready to stay here." Hancock sighed. "But it's awful good to see her."

"Whoa, now. Slow down, boy. What about the gal across the street?"

"Linda?" There was Linda Darr, he remembered. He had not thought of her in any important way since the moment he laid eyes upon Laurie. It was not a time to try and examine that part of it, he thought. One thing at a time — and what Laurie's presence meant to him needed no thought, it was a feeling, a lifting of the spirit. If he was different today, then this was something to help, he knew instinctively, this was a page from the past come fresh and plain and good.

Luke whispered, "You don't reckon Daisy knew you?"

He started and a dark shadow fell. "Why, she was just a wee baby when I was with her."

"Still and all."

Hancock said heavily, "Yeah. Still and all."

"It'll come out at the trial."

"I know, Matt threatened me."

"That'll be bad."

"Bad enough. But just so Baby — Daisy — didn't know."

"I don't think so," Luke said thoughtfully. "She couldn't even talk, I mind."

"Long as she never knew." Now he was sweating.

"We'll never find out." Luke hesitated, then said, "Just go slow, *amigo*."

"Yeah. I'll do that." He went out and locked the big door. Laurie and Brewster stood together, looking across the street. He went to them and took her arm as Brewster ranged on her left, so that she was between them crossing the street to the undertaking establishment.

Con Boyd was in his carpenter shop. He put down his maul and peered at them. The clean odor of shavings and sawdust permeated their nostrils.

Hancock said, "This is Daisy's mother — Con Boyd."

The little man's eyebrows shot up to his hairline. "Her ma?"

"Yes. She wants to see Daisy."

Boyd, who had seen so much of life and death, recovered quickly. He dusted his work clothes and said, "Why, ma'am, I'm plumb sorry about this. I fixed her up good. I ain't fancy like, but I done the best I could, she was so purty."

It was Brewster who interposed in his British manner, coldly impersonal, "If we might view her, Mr. Boyd?"

An offset wing of the building housed the mortuary section of Boyd's business. There was no showroom, merely a long, rather narrow hall with high windows to bar the curious young of Cobre. The light was dim and the smell of formaldehyde was too strong. The sheriff lay on a plank supported by wooden carpenter horses and Laurie started at the sight of his sunken, bearded features above a white shroud. The two men steadied her, although at this moment Hancock rather felt the need of something solid upon his own part.

Daisy was already in a coffin, a pine box, unpainted, resting upon a trestle. Hancock could not think of her as "Maureen" — it would have been better for him if he could. Now he could think only of the girl in the dark night of a room upstairs at Mrs. Jay's, tormenting himself with guilt.

Laurie released herself, standing firm and alone, her eyes heavy-lidded, staring. The dead girl seemed asleep, excepting that Boyd had not been able to alter that last expression of fright, as though in sleeping she was suffering a nightmare. Pennies on her eyes could not conceal that terror.

Laurie said in a strange voice, "I think I'd like to be alone for awhile."

The three men went wordlessly from her. Hancock stood in the sunlight. Cobre was parched and stark, new clouds threatened, the mountaintops were ugly, bare. Now all was changed, he thought, himself and everything. Nothing would ever be the same.

CHAPTER
TWO

Supper was over in Cobre on the evening of the day after the death of Daisy-Maureen. Matt Buxton sat in his chair in the lobby of the hotel and drank his fifth or sixth glass of whiskey. The Candlestick riders, unused to inaction and confinement, were restless and uneasy.

Virgie came down the stairs and went to her husband, leaned close and whispered in his ear, "Matt, why don't we go home?"

"Can't. Not yet." His voice was guttural but kindly.

"What about the ranch?"

"Arizona can take care."

"We ought to be home."

"I know — I know. I'm astudyin'."

Judge Grey came into the lobby and Virgie stepped back but remained behind the chair. The riders moved. Del Hunter and his wife and the boy slid together behind the desk, huddling like chickens in a rainstorm. Matt arose and the judge paused, regarding him without expression.

"I want Jed out of there. It ain't safe for him, Neddy with a shotgun, that Luke Post a known shooter."

"Impossible."

"Someone raises a ruckus around the jail and Jed might get killed without a trial."

"That would be unfortunate." Judge Grey glanced at the Candlestick riders. "It would be better to keep the peace, wouldn't it?"

"I want the right to see Jed, visit private."

"You have that right. You may also be accompanied by counsel."

"You been wirin' the governor. You been doin' everything to keep Jed in a cell."

"Quite right. That's where he belongs for this time. Monday he will be heard. A week from Monday he will be tried," the judge said.

"If it's second degree at the hearing we get bail. Right?"

"If it's second-degree murder I would grant bail."

"You know it won't be. You'll see to it."

"That, Matt, is insulting." Judge Grey walked past Virgie and went up the steps to his room.

Virgie said, "You see? It ain't any use."

Matt said, "Larson."

The foreman jumped. "Yeah, boss."

"Make a pasear around town. Check on the jail. I'm goin' over, you cover me."

"Without guns?"

"I'll get guns when we need 'em. Just keep a watch. If we can find a way without gettin' him killed, we'll spring him outa there."

"No," said Virgie. "You're wrong, Matt."

Larson said, "We get the kid out of the cells, we can handle Post and Hancock."

"You reckon?" Matt was doubtful.

"What I mean is, we can try. Hancock don't wear his gun. Dave, he's as quick as Post."

"Mebbe," said Dave Pitts. "I'll try him. I'll try anybody you say, boss."

"That's good." Matt got up and went to where Virgie had removed herself. "Darlin', I got to see Jed. I got to try somethin'. Nobody else is goin' to."

"Jed's a growed man. This is wrong. You start anything, someone else is gonna get killed on account of him."

"He's my brother and they can't hang him." He was cold and as far from her as he had ever been. "Why'n't you go upstairs and rest? When I get back we'll have a good dinner and talk some."

"You'll talk. I've said all I can. If you won't go home, if you won't let the law alone, there'll be trouble."

"They might lynch him."

"You know better. There's some thinks he should hang, sure. But nobody's lynchin' him. You're just tryin' to make bad look good. It ain't like you, Matt."

"They won't hang him."

"I'm more'n sorry. I know how it is with you. Me, I can't blame myself for Jed's ways. He's bad, all bad. He's gutless and rotten. It's a sad thing you think you got to protect a bum like Jed."

He watched her go up the stairs, moving slowly, as though she had aged overnight. His heart beat faster, he thought how good she was and how she had always stood by him and how lucky he was to have her. But he was driven. He could pursue no other course than to show the town that Candlestick was paramount. He had been there before Cobre and he would be there forever, he told himself, and he would get Jed out of town and out of the country and that would solve everything . . .

He turned to leave but his way was blocked by the imposing bulk of Brewster. The lady, Mrs. Van Orden, was staring at him in an odd fashion. He bowed and waited.

"You are Mr. Matt Buxton?" she asked.

"Yes, ma'am."

"I am the mother of the girl known as Daisy."

His eyes grew round as saucers. "You are what?"

"I am Mrs. Van Orden. Daisy was my baby."

"Why, ma'am, that's hard to swallow. A lady like you — I mean, I am plumb took back."

"And sorry. Everyone is sorry."

"Well, ma'am, I'm more'n sorry."

She regarded him closely. "Are you? Yes, I believe you are."

"Yes. My brother, you see, I don't hold with his ways. I can't explain mebbe, but I never did. What happened, it's mortal cruel."

"I see. But you feel responsible for him, for that dreadful, evil young man."

"That's somethin' I can't help." He put up a hand. "You feel responsible for the girl?"

"Deeply."

"Would you, no matter what, want them to hang her?"

"I didn't want her to be shot. In the back, I have learned. In the back, sir."

"Yes'm." He faced her, head up.

"So you will make trouble."

"Not to be known, yet."

"You're a rich man."

"They say."

"Mr. Buxton, I have over a million dollars. Your brother will pay for his deed. You understand?"

"It's plain."

"Good evening, Mr. Buxton."

"Evenin', ma'am." It was hard to control his emotion, watching her go up the stairs with the big Britisher. His heart was heavy. She must suffer, he thought, she must suffer terrible. Me, I remember Jed when he was a button and I hurt and blame myself, figure how she must hurt.

He had, however, no choice. He went out into the town, the riders following, covering him. The streets were nearly empty at this hour while suppers digested in the bellies of Cobre. He felt naked and alone, going down to the jail. His mind was getting back to work, going back and forth and up and down and around the situation.

The advent of a rich and angry mother complicated matters, he knew. There was no use to be mad at anybody, things had to be faced. Hancock had done his job, was doing it. Madison had told his story as he saw it. Monty Dipple would stick to what he saw. Cora, the dumb whore, they could handle her. Finnegan would take care of that part of it.

144

Truth was, Jed had torn it this time. The affair of the little Mex gal had been bad enough. This was it.

Finnegan came trotting out of his office and fell into step but Matt did not speak to him and the lawyer always knew when it was wise to keep silence around the master of Candlestick. The riders clanked their spurs and people came to stare and wonder and worry.

At Getz's store the riders swung out and vanished into shadows, Larson ducking across the street behind a late-coming lumber wagon. Matt went onto the porch with Finnegan and Hancock rose from his chair. There was light from within and from the oil lamps in the street, and from the moon above.

Matt said, "Ben — want to see the boy. Alone."

"Sure, Matt." They went indoors and Luke Post put down his paperback. "You know Luke. So you want to see Jed alone? You and Finnegan?"

"That's it."

"There's only one way."

"I got a right. Judge says so."

"Sure. But we have to search you."

"What?" Matt was astounded, then furious. "Never try that."

Hancock shrugged. "You made your brags he wouldn't hang. You're not going to slip him a gun, not in my jail."

Finnegan said, "This is outrageous. Matt wouldn't do such a thing."

"You, too, Lawyer," Hancock told him. "You want to see him alone, we search you."

Matt said, "I'll see about this. I'll see the judge."

"You do that." Hancock turned away. "See you later."

Matt swallowed hard. "Okay, Ben, okay. But I ain't forgettin' this." He put a small, nickel-plated revolver on the desk. "I carry that in town case of robbery is all."

Hancock said, "Perfectly all right." He stepped close to Matt and ran expert hands over him as the fat man squirmed.

Luke was going over the outraged Finnegan. He found a derringer and a heavy clasp knife.

Hancock said, "All right, here you go," as he opened the heavy door.

Neddy was on the job. He stood, the shotgun at ready. In the cell Jed snarled and snapped and cursed his brother, Finnegan and the world.

Hancock said, "I'll just leave the door open. Neddy, you come here and watch 'em. They can talk but if they pass anything through the bars, nail 'em. Luke?"

"Right here," said Luke, picking up his shotgun.

"Okay, gentlemen, be our guests." Hancock went into the office, then out and onto the porch, looking up and down. He said to Luke, "The Candlestick boys are around. I'll be checking."

He did not take his gun belt. He did not really expect an attack on the jail and he had no wish to instigate trouble by wearing his gun. He walked down toward Getz's store. He was still a bit shaken, bemused by the experience of the afternoon. He had managed an hour's disturbed sleep but he could not orientate himself, he felt suspended in space. He crossed the street and saw that Linda's light was on and knew he had to face her sooner or later. Since her place was a good observation point he braced himself and doubled back, tapping on her door.

She admitted him. There was in her something which she could not conceal and in that moment some part of him cracked and splintered and she was a stranger.

"It's been a hard day," he offered, ill at ease.

"Daisy's mother, they tell me," she said, her voice level and cool. "Several people took the trouble."

"Yes, Daisy's mother. From New York."

"New York. You and Luke, the gay old days."

"That's right." He did not, he found, care what she said.

"She was your woman."

"She was a singer." He felt he was being evasive but again it did not really matter. "She's a widow now."

"And rich. She told it that she was rich."

"Probably real rich." He moved to the window and inched the shade so that he could see Pitts, Ward and Farr strategically placed about the jail. Luke was ready with one shotgun and Neddy with the other. Matt and Finnegan were inside, unarmed. There was no sign of Larson and this was a worriment. "Can I use your back door, please?"

"You always have." She led the way and at the exit said, "It will be strange when the lady finds out about you and Daisy, won't it?"

He was utterly shocked. He stared at her in the lamplight. "Why, Linda, you hate me all of a sudden, don't you?"

"It will be embarrassing, won't it?"

"Like you say."

"I only had to see you together, you and the lady. I only had to hear a few words from kind friends." Her face was stony. "Don't come back, Ben. I'm shamed enough."

"Good evenin', Linda," he replied.

He went into the alley between Linda's place and the bank. He felt slightly nauseated. The venom in the woman's tone, in her stare, was like a blow in the belly. In an instant all that had been between them was vanished; his increasing thought of marrying her, of raising children by her, all was wiped out in that one small exchange. He walked slowly to the mouth of the alley, scarcely knowing why, his sense of danger allayed, dormant.

He stood a moment in the semidarkness, gathering his wits. The Candlestick men were approximately where he had seen them last. They were most likely merely standing guard on their boss, he thought. Yet it was a tetchy time; Matt was dangerous because he thought through every move and he never stopped thinking about his objective.

Behind him Larson's voice said harshly, suddenly, "Skulkin' around, huh, lawman?"

Hancock reacted like lightning, swinging about, coming in low, grabbing the foreman, slamming him against the wall of the bank, seeking the gun holster to see if he was armed. When his fingers did not find a gun butt he whirled again and pushed Larson out onto Buxton Street.

"You ought to know better than to come on a man in the dark, you damn fool," Hancock said.

The Candlestick men came running, someone down near the hotel sensed action and called to a friend. Lights went on. Larson came hard and fast, swinging a fist.

"You sneakin' polecat," the foreman bellowed. "I'm sick of your ways."

People came running. Little Johnny at the hotel yelled, "Fight! Fight!"

It was the worst thing that could happen, but Hancock's blood sang, he felt released. The foreman was big and saddle-tough and strong. It was an uneven match, but it was a release to the marshal. He evaded the rush, moving more easily in town boots than the cowboy in high heels. He had been in a hundred street encounters, he knew the tricks, he had no fear. He could see Luke with the shotgun ready, he saw Matt and Finnegan come running, saw Neddy slam the big door and retreat within the cells. All the time he was making the moves.

Larson had long arms, heavy wrists. He swung low, at the crotch, and Hancock turned a knee, pivoting. The blow had power enough to drive him against the bank. He rolled to the right, letting Larson chase him.

The Candlestick riders were jumping up and down like kids in a schoolyard, cheering for their man, giving him loud advice. They would not get into the action unless Larson was being beaten, Hancock thought; at least not with half the town looking on — and with

Luke at their backs. As long as they were enjoying the fight they were not attacking the jail.

Larson was proving agile as well as strong. Once the first heat died in him he was canny and clever, striking out from the shoulder, shrewd, telling blows. Hancock caught several punches on his forearms and one slipped through to the ribs before he could get into the open.

Linda Darr was at her window, watching from behind the curtains. Speedy Jackson came on the run and immediately began making bets that Hancock would win. There were plenty of takers as the marshal beat a retreat in the face of Larson's charge.

Hancock felt his wind going. He was soft from town life and Larson never ceased his attack. A fist grazed Hancock's ear, turning it scarlet, deafening him. Another dug into his breastbone and further depleted his breath. He had to make a stand, he knew, or be knocked down and kicked unconscious.

He crouched, altering the level of the engagement, letting Larson close in as Candlestick shouts rent the night air. He hit for the middle, above the belt, chary of bruising his gun hand on the buckle. He struck quickly, once, twice, three times, practiced, thudding blows. Larson came up tall, grunting.

Hancock straightened, jabbed. His left fist caught Larson's nose. He kept on that target, snapping his punches. Blood spouted.

Larson roared and tried to grapple, his eyes streaming tears. Hancock avoided the maneuver by sidestepping, but ran into a roundhouse swing which

150

sent him across the boardwalk and almost through the window of the bank.

Larson charged, knees high, stomping at Hancock's toes, his spread fingers seeking the eyes. Hancock managed to tincan left, then right, gasping. He was on the verge of defeat, he knew. He choked, then magically gained second wind and found his feet under him as he danced away.

He had a target now. He stabbed at the nose. Larson yelled in rage and pain. Hancock stuck him with another left and the blood ran down over the collar of Larson's shirt. The foreman made a dive, choking on the gore. Hancock kicked his knee from the side, rolling him in the dust.

"Stomp him, Ben!" Speedy shouted in glee.

Hancock grabbed for the collar, his hand slipped in the blood, Larson kicked him in the shin. Everyone was whooping now, so that the town shook with the noise.

Larson got to his hands and knees. Hancock kicked him in the ribs and rolled him. Every time the foreman started to get up, Hancock kicked him again. He drove him to where Luke looked directly down from the porch, kicking him with methodical purpose. Larson's efforts became weak, he fell across the steps. Hancock picked him up, spun him, punched the nose once more, feeling the bone splinter. Larson fell onto the porch.

Hancock said to Luke, "All right, lock him up. Make sure he hasn't got a gun. Disturbing the peace'll do it."

Matt Buxton stepped aside as Luke half carried Larson inside the building to the big door. Finnegan was at the far end of the porch, keeping himself well out of it, knowing the rule of the country, winner take all.

Matt said, "Reckon he'll need Doc Farrar for that nose."

Hancock picked up his hat, dusted it. "That'll be all right. The town pays."

"Disturbin' the peace, that's ten dollars?"

"You paid it often enough for Jed."

Matt pulled out a bill. "You goin' to keep him tonight, I suppose."

"Under shotgun guard."

"This'll pay him out for the funeral tomorrow."

Hancock accepted the bill. "I'll give you a receipt."

From the street Muley Ward called, "You goin' to let him get away with it, boss?"

Matt paused on the way inside. "He already did."

"I'll take him next," Ward said. He was the biggest of the riders, a notorious ear-biter.

"You simmer down," Matt told him.

Speedy Jackson, collecting his bets, called, "You can whup 'em all, Ben. Hoohee! Drinks are on me."

The crowd dispersed, talking among themselves about the marshal's prowess, reliving the excitement. The Candlestick men hesitated, then went reluctantly toward Madison's place. Linda Darr's light went out. Hancock wrote a receipt for Matt. His left hand hurt but he had saved the right hand. Finnegan came in and waited, watching.

Matt said, "Thought it was a play, didn't you?"

"No. You wouldn't do it that way."

"Why not? It could've worked."

"With the town gawkin' at you?"

"The hell with the town."

"No, Matt. You and Finnegan and all the mine people and the other ranchers are no bigger than Cobre. People live here, a lot of people. You can't tromple on people."

The fat man took the receipt, folded it, put it away. "Towns. The hell with 'em. You treat Jed right, you hear me, Ben? Any expense, extras, I'll pay."

"No extras," Hancock told him.

"Give him what he wants."

"He's gettin' what he deserves," Luke Post said. "How come a man like you to raise such a pulin', whinin' muley calf?"

Matt turned and looked the gambler up and down. "You too, Post. I hear you puttin' anything on him, you'll be took care of."

Hancock interrupted, leaning on his good hand, the knuckles of the left swollen and bleeding slightly. "Matt, just stop that. I told you a hundred times the day would come when Jed would get it. Now don't come here and ride us. Luke's my deputy. So is Neddy. Way it is, we're all the lawmen Cobre's got. We don't have to take any guff from you, understand?"

"You ridin' high again?"

"I'm hangin' on. Larson tried me. You can try me. I'm sick and tired of mealymouth."

"You'll never hang my brother!"

Finnegan plucked at Matt's sleeve. "Better go back to the hotel. Talk won't help."

153

"And think on this, Matt: If Jed's convicted and there's no one else to do the job, I'll manage the rope around his damn neck." Hancock's voice was thick.

"I hear you, Ben." Matt had regained control. "I hear you plain. You said we was never friends. From now on, as I stand here, we never will be."

He waddled out of the office. Finnegan followed. The law officers watched them go, then Luke exhaled noisily and took Hancock's left hand, peering at it.

"I'll put on some water. That fat man, he means to make us trouble. I was you, I'd start wearin' a gun. Saves wear and tear."

Hancock sat down, aware of aches and pains. "Man like that Larson, he'll sure wear you down. Doc'll be here to attend his nose, I'll let him look at the hand."

Luke said, "It ain't broke. You know, it's right good we got Judge Grey around. Wasn't for him I don't mind admittin' I'd be a might put out."

"I don't mind tellin' you, *amigo*," Hancock sighed. "I don't mind at all. I am put out."

Matt Buxton paused on the verandah of the hotel. He looked across the street and said to Finnegan, "You got law books over there. What about it?"

"Nothing until Monday." Finnegan was weary in the head. He was walking on ice he cared not to risk but he was a hired man, he well knew, he had no alternative.

"Check the boys in Madison's. Tell 'em I want them in church and then at Buck's funeral tomorrow."

"Church?"

"Shined up and prayin' for Jed — for all of us."

154

Finnegan said, "Good idea. If they'll do it."

"They do what I say. Church'll keep 'em in line."

"I wouldn't try to break Jed out," Finnegan ventured. "Let me see what I can do with Judge Grey."

"You can't do a damn thing with him. I'll do what I think will work. Good night, Finnegan."

He went into the hotel and through the small bar and into the restaurant. Virgie sat at a table, her shoulders hunched. He kissed her cheek and lowered himself gingerly into a chair opposite her. Ramos, one of the many sons of the lawyer Tomas Rosario, brought a cup of steaming black java and Virgie poured whiskey into it. When the boy had gone she regarded her husband.

"Ben beat up Larson, didn't he?"

"Ben's a tough hombre. Tougher than I thought."

"Did you put Larson up to it?"

"Hell, no. A dumb play. Finnegan talked to the mayor. There's a great man, Taggart. Got him to call a caucus of the council tonight."

"What good is that?"

"Want to feel 'em out."

She shook her head and asked, "Did you see Daisy's mother?"

He nodded. "She braced me. Rough tongue."

"People will be sorry for her."

"People will be sorry for a lot. I want Jed out of there. One way or the other."

"You're wrong. I keep sayin' it, you don't listen."

He put a wide, dry hand over hers. "Virgie — Virgie. I put it on you."

155

"I ain't going to say it again, Matt." Her large eyes softened, moistened. "What you got to do — you got to do."

He said, "Would you drive out to the ranch?"

"Alone?"

"Marshal's got my gun. Didn't want to ask for it back. He's got all our guns. I buy some more, everybody in town knows it."

"Guns." But she had given up. She loved him enough to do anything he asked and he knew it.

He said, "Tell Arizona. Drive back in the mornin', we done that before, it ain't all that far. There'll be the funerals. Stack the guns in our room. We won't use 'em until we positively have to."

"Matt, of course I'll do it. But more blood."

"Just in case, Virgie. A show of guns can do it without shootin', sometimes. And tell Arizona to bring every hand in for the funeral. Just leave a couple boys to handle the herds — he'll know who to bring."

She did not say anything further to deter him. She knew his determination, she knew his implacability.

He said, "If Jed gets out I promise to send him away."

"Ha!"

"I mean it, this time. I come to that. I'll give him cash and a horse and tell him to git."

"You do mean it."

"I do. He's torn the blanket."

"He'll come back."

"If he does I'll let them hang him."

"You wouldn't."

"I would. He's ravin' and bawlin' and makin' a fool of hisself. He's no damn good. If it's my fault, so be it, but he's through here."

She said, "All right, Matt. I believe you. I better get the horses hitched. I can be back before sunup."

"Come around back. I'll have the boys tote the guns, and remember about Arizona."

"I wish I could forget."

"It'll be all right, Virgie. I'll go over to Madison's and show myself. Want them to know we ain't hidin' our faces."

"Yes, darlin'," she said. "Don't drink too much, now."

She went out of the dining room and upstairs to get a wrap. He thought about her some more, he spent a good deal of his thoughts upon her. She had worked so hard in the fields and around the house on the ranch that she had been unable to bear children. It had ground her down, he knew. Jed had never got to her heart; she had wanted one of her own and Jed had always been a problem. It was a crime and a shame and Matt wished he could do something about it. He drank off the coffee and whiskey and got up to lumber down the street to Madison's place.

Mayor Taggart stood upon the lawn of his house on School Street, parallel to and above Buxton Street, and stared at the white moon over Cobre. His wife, a small woman with a prominent nose and wispy brown hair, placed a hand upon his arm.

"It's not to worry. Worriment breaks the spirit."

157

"Someone must worry," he told her.

The house was imposing, of red brick, a cupola atop its third story, bay windows in front and on one side. Within was an entrance hall, with rooms right and left and a stairway leading up to four bedrooms including the attic chamber. Fireplaces were on first- and second-floor front rooms. The furniture was from the East, horsehair and plush. The bank held a mortgage on it all, also imposing.

Tinkling notes from the only piano in town came through an open window. Gary and Timmy, twin small boys, who took lessons from Sister Joseph Cupertino down the street, were practicing. It was a discordant sound.

Taggart said, "Better put the boys to bed. They get underfoot among their elders."

"Please not to worry," she repeated. "It is not your part to carry them all upon your shoulders."

"A man makes plans. He tries to be sure that life is safe and good for his family. Then something like this happens."

"Judge Grey is here. He is a fine, godly man. Have faith, Lou dear. Have faith." She was very constant at mass, a pillar of Father Donner's flock. She went into the house and he heard her admonishing the boys in her colorless, patient voice.

He leaned against one of the rare cottonball trees. Buxton Street lay below him, with all its lights and life. Behind him were the Burro Mountains, to the north the Mogollons, to east and south the Coopers and the San Andres. They towered to the clouded skies, stars twinkled at their peaks. They were too much, he thought, too many, too enormous. He longed for the rolling hills of upper New York State.

There had been disappointments there, also. Always there had been some kind of frustration not of his making. It had been the mills which shut down, causing him a serious loss of capital. Now they were prospering again, he knew, but for him they had proven worthless. That was why he had come West with what money he had left — and what money his wife inherited from her barkeeper father, the late Harry Moriarty. Now he was threatened in Cobre by the clash of law and Candlestick. At least there had been no violence back in New York, no shooting of people. The very thought of shooting made him nervous. He had paid his way out of the war in '65 to avoid guns. Had he known the West was not tamed he would never have removed here.

Gus Mueller came lumbering up Alamo Street from below. He was not the kind of man Taggart would have chosen as a friend, but he did have a sense of values, the mayor thought. Mueller would be neither rich nor poor, he was hard-working and thrifty and his family worked with him in the store, early and late. Mueller had no dreams of power or glory, he was a safe, solid citizen.

From the other direction Abe Getz and Con Boyd were approaching, two small, serious men, very different from one another. Boyd was trustworthy but Getz was a maverick, as they said in the West, he should never have been elected to the council, although

159

Taggart had not dared oppose him for fear of being faulted for prejudice. Not that he had anything against Jews really, it was just that Getz was — different. Del Hunter agreed on this. He saw Hunter now, hustling after Mueller, afraid of being late, nervous as always. Hunter could be handled better than the others, he was not a forceful man. This completed the city council, and Taggart steeled himself for the discussion to come.

Mueller, slightly out of breath, was first to arrive, puffing, "They got to build the town on the hill already. Such a crazy."

Taggart shepherded them all into the high-ceilinged, imposing parlor. The council arranged itself as comfortably as possible on furniture not designed for easy reception of the human body. There were neither cuspidors nor ashtrays since Mrs. Taggart was unable to endure tobacco in any form. Con Boyd looked around, then went back out to dispose of his chaw.

Taggart said, "Well, here we are. Actually the men who run Cobre, duly elected to office."

"That's a joke," said Boyd.

"The city charter says it is true."

"Jerry Kay, Matt Buxton and Ben Hancock run Cobre," Boyd said bluntly.

"The sheriff was one of them," contributed Mueller. "Ja, Boyd is right already. Figureheads, we are."

Taggart cleared his throat. "The men you mention are of the old breed. They are from another day. When the railroad comes, they will be archaic — forgotten. They are the old. Look at us, we are new. We came here to make this country a fit place to live. Boyd is from

New England, Mueller from Chicago, Getz from New York City."

Abe Getz said mildly, "Everybody is from some place, no? The Indians, they are from here."

Taggart chose to ignore this. "The Apaches have been subdued by the government troops. Business is prospering. The mineowners, the railroad people, the banks will be the powers of tomorrow. We belong to that group."

"Not me," said Boyd. "I'm just a carpenter and an undertaker."

"You are a councilman of Cobre," Taggart assured him. "In a year or two you will be a wealthy man. So will we all — if the rails come here."

"Are you saying the railroad may not come?" asked Hunter, chewing at his mustache. "Have you bad news?"

"I have heard that our Latin American friends in Santa Fe are making overtures, putting up cash, trying every means to divert it to Centro," Taggart stated flatly. "This tragedy which has struck us, this nasty murder, has them worried. A friend sent me a lengthy telegram urging that we act in some way to dispose of the matter at once."

"The matter, *nu?* The killing of a girl?" Getz shook his beard to and fro. "And how, may I ask, we should do this? Maybe turn young Buxton free to kill again?"

"That is impossible. Judge Grey would turn the railroad against us," said Taggart seriously, without flinching at the notion of freeing Jed Buxton.

"Then what?" demanded Boyd. "Looks like we're over a barrel for certain."

"Matt will start a war if Jed don't get off," Del Hunter said. "Then who gets hurt? Property owners. And whose children are in danger? Not theirs, none of them have children."

"If there is a war, we must be separated from it," Taggart declared.

"How can we do that? We own property. We can't move out," Con Boyd said. "We're here, that's the trouble."

"I say we remain neutral," Taggart said. "I say we send telegrams to the governor and to the railway people. We tell them that the mayor and council have no part of the hostilities, we are against violence. I say we ask that if Matt Buxton starts shooting, the governor sends in the militia."

"Militia, is it?" cried Getz. "That proves we are good, reliable people? That we ask for militia?"

"It proves we don't approve of either Matt Buxton or Hancock's militant attitude," Taggart told him.

"Neutrals, we are? In the midst of a fight? Me, I am no gun-shooter. But violence you have never seen. Cossacks riding, slashing, raping. Just because we were Jews and helpless. You don't know from this." Getz arose, a small, neat man, his beard quivering with indignation. "You want to turn your backs on Ben Hancock, who made our town a good one? On Judge Grey? On Matt Buxton? Just make a game, like they are not ours? We disown them?"

162

"We can protect ourselves in that way," Taggart said. "When this all blows over, they will know we are responsible people."

"*Ja*, we save money in the end," Mueller said. "Dot is a goot notion you got there, Lou."

"I think so too," said Hunter. "We can wash our hands of the whole thing."

"I'll go along," said Boyd. "It might work with Reynolds and the railroad people. If they know we're just plain citizens here, caught in a trap like, they might think better of us."

Getz said, "I see. I see too much. It is no use to argue. You will vote. Therefore, may I respectfully, gentlemen, offer my resignation from the council?"

Taggart said coldly, "As you please, Getz."

"No hard feelings, no?" Getz smiled at them now. "You see, I am newer to America than most. From different eyes I see it. If a man murders, there is law, strong law. In Russia the law was only for the rich, nu? So me, I must be for the law, for Marshal Hancock, yet I must feel pity for Matt Buxton. But for Jed, nothing. If there is a fight, I know my part, I know my side."

"*Mit* a stickpin? You will fight? Ho, ho," said Mueller.

"Only to hope not," Getz said. When he was emotionally upset his English grew ragged. Rather than display his anger, he took his hat and went to the door. "Send your telegram, but leave off my name."

He left the house. He heard Mueller say as he went out the door, "A Jew. Always a Jew. Leave him go already. Him we don't need."

His name, Abe thought, walking down to Pass Avenue, pausing to look at the moon, at the peacefulness of the town at this hour, his name was something these people could not even pronounce. They did not know about the Russian way of life under the Czar. No use to try and tell them. They did not even comprehend that there was a bigger country than the United States with millions of inhabitants. They saw only their own country, thought only of their own dollars, their property.

He knew the value of dollars better than they who had not starved in a strange city. He had struggled to get started, to save enough to leave the ghetto. Becky had helped. And then their only son had died of a plague which swept New York's slums and they had come West, a lonely, unhappy couple seeking a new life.

And it proved to be a new life and a better one. What his friends did not know, Becky was again with child. Into the new land they would bring an infant to become a natural born citizen.

And they wanted him to be a neuter, for that is what they were, not neutrals but neuters. They had waited for the West to open up, then they had come with their eastern ways, yes, the Getzes among them. But the Getzes had already come to a new land and this was their second experience and if one couldn't learn by experience, Abe thought, one could not learn any time from anything.

He went down the hill to his waiting wife.

★ ★ ★

It was the quietest Saturday night he had ever seen in a western town, Hancock thought, walking along Buxton Street. People knew that there was a crisis at hand. He saw Abe Getz walking from Pass Avenue toward his own place and they both paused as if to pass the time of night.

Getz said, "I have just resigned from the council."

"Like that, is it?"

"They want no part of trouble. There will be trouble, nu? Truly, they are mice."

"New people," Hancock said, "either learn about the country or turn into mice."

"Thank you," said Getz. "I will be waiting. Worse than this I have known in the old country."

"Lock your doors and keep plenty of sand and water handy," Hancock advised him. "A fire would be the worst."

"Matt Buxton would burn down the town to save his brother. Tomorrow it is two funerals. Next week?"

"Can't even guess," Hancock said.

They parted. Speedy Jackson had closed up the Wells Fargo office for the night. The general store was being handled by Mrs. Mueller, just in case a late shopper needed a loaf of bread, but only one lamp was burning. The fire house was deserted and Ching Hoo was in the yard tending his still. There was a light in Finnegan's office but Tomas was over in the Mexican quarter, where people respected him above all law and government. Mrs. Jay's was closed tight.

Madison's was busy, but without the boisterousness of the normal Saturday night. Miners and cowhands

165

and farmers and plain citizens talked in low tones over their drinks. Matt Buxton and the Candlestick men, excepting Larson, of course, were around a table playing poker.

Hancock came down on the east side of the street, walking slow. His gun felt strange on his thigh. He was dogweary, he realized. There had been little sleep and he had been involved with too many stupendous subjects in the past two days. At the hotel he paused, thinking of Laurie and how she must be mourning for Maureen — and for herself. He did not believe in self-blame, yet he too was mourning, not only Daisy, but his own derelictions. If he had only tried harder to learn who she was, to dig a little, to help her in some way!

"In what way?" he muttered, going past the hotel, knowing he was unable to relate to Laurie while guilt rode him with bloody spurs. Daisy didn't want to help, he argued. She was past that in some cockeyed world of her own, with the booze and the dope and the weed.

He would have to convince himself of that. He would have to shuck that burden before he could come to terms with Laurie. And he knew that between Laurie and himself there was a bond, it had been proven by the electricity of their meeting. She had been there, deep inside him, all these years and he had scarcely known it. She had been a pleasant dream of the past. Perhaps he had been unfair to Linda, he thought, coming to his office, noting that her lights were out. Perhaps he had been comparing her unconsciously with

166

the woman from the East whom he had made love to so long ago.

He could not feel guilty about Linda. True, a small-town woman has few chances to marry and he had taken her time and possibly given her encouragement, but he had never really popped the question. She had played the woman's game of holding him at arm's length; he was wise enough in their artifices to be aware of that. It was even Steven, the way he saw it.

He went up the steps to the porch. In the darkness Luke sat smoking a cheroot.

"Quiet," Hancock said. "Too quiet."

"You better get some shut-eye."

"Is it showin' on me?"

"You look beat. Take a few hours."

"All right with you?"

"I'm thinkin' a bit. About this town and all. You know somethin'? I always did like towns best. Everybody talks about the trail, the great outdoors, the scenery, the huntin' and fishin'. Never did give a damn about it. Sleepin' on hard ground, bugs, snakes, rain, snow, what the hell's so good about it?"

Hancock grinned. "Never thought of it that way, but since we were tadpoles we never cottoned to that life."

"No. People want to live, they build towns. Get to see each other for company or fightin' or whatever. No Injuns, not anything you can't duck behind your own door. Me, I'm thinkin' this place might be nice if the rails come. Lively."

"Profitable."

"And safe," said Luke. "If we pull through this rangdoodle, a nice, safe place."

"We'll give it a hassle," Hancock said. "I'll take that nap now."

His room was in order. Both Neddy and Luke were men of good habits, he thought comfortably. He took off his belt and his boots and loosened his collar. Other than that, he could not undress with Candlestick men in town. He stretched out and tried to think of Laurie Pomfret Van Orden but his eyes fell shut and exhaustion claimed him.

CHAPTER
THREE

The Sunday morning stage came in and Cole Strand debarked with two carpetbags, clad in fresh gray as always. Cobre people in their Sunday best were scattered about town talking in hushed accents, solemn of mien. Speedy Jackson, his ebullience diminished, came from his office, recognized Strand, blinked recognition.

"Well, Cole, howdy."

"In time for the funeral, I take it."

"Funerals. Two funerals. They prayed over Buck in the church. Takin' him out now. The preachers didn't want Daisy. Goddamn them."

"Daisy was the whore?"

"A hell of a nice kid, any old way. You heard about it down Lordsburg?"

"Bad news travels with the stages."

"Yeah, well. There's a lot more to it. You need me? I got to get the bill of ladin' and receipt for the box and then go to Daisy's buryin'."

"Don't let me take up your time, Speedy." Cole Strand walked across the street to the hotel. Johnny Hunter was behind the desk, otherwise the lobby was deserted. Strand signed the register and accepted a key.

169

He went upstairs and opened his bags and carefully hung up his clothing. He removed a gun belt from its receptacle. It was of soft gray leather which he had caused to be fashioned in El Paso. He found a cloth and rubbed the smooth butt and the barrel of the Colt .45, not because there was need but because he liked the feel of the revolver. He hung it in the belt. It was not a day to wear it in Cobre, the smaller weapon in the spring arrangement beneath his shoulderpit would do.

He wondered which room housed the woman. He had not been so excited about a female in a long time, and on just one sight of her in Lordsburg. He knew what was in her, the big thing, and he knew it was only a matter of persuasion, she was that kind. Women were his only real preoccupation besides — the other thing.

He washed dust from his hands and went out of the door and locked it and walked downstairs into the lobby. Johnny asked if he wanted anything and he bought a *Bulletin* and refused the change from two bits and put himself against a wall, from whence he could keep watch on the surroundings without moving his head, a constant precaution.

He was running a bit low of ready cash and this seemed the town and the time to make some form of profit. The elements of war were here in Cobre, he thought, and war was his business. A safe war, of course, in which he had the advantage, he added to himself, and where his luck would carry him through. He firmly believed in his luck.

He held the paper before his face but his mind went fondly to the good fortune which had blessed him since the time he had been a drover going up the trails, like Luke Post and Ben Hancock, whom he had known well in the past. He had behaved no different than they, gambling, whoring, brawling in the cowtowns.

Then there had been the scrape in Fort Worth when he had pulled his gun on Wes Thompson in a saloon. Both had been drinking or they would not have quarreled over the girl, Beebee, a notorious whore. On such trifling happenings hang many a career, Strand ruminated. Wes was a known fast gun, a killer, and when he went down a new reputation was born. It was enough to start him as a dealer and lookout man in gambling joints. He had never worked a day since Thompson's gun caught in the holster.

On the other hand, it was necessary to have further good luck, and along came Asa P. Colligan before some faster gun could down the youthful Cole Strand.

Colligan was a brainy one from a southern college, a consumptive with reckless courage. He had forced Strand to practice with the guns, either hand, from all angles, he had established the style of the gray clothing. He was a man of great imagination, as in '76 when the James gang was broken up in Northfield.

Colligan took Strand and picked up a couple of Missouri ruffians named Halsted who were familiar with the terrain and the status of county banks. In quick succession, wearing the notorious dusters and carrying the famed wheat sacks of the Border outlaws, they held up three institutions of savings to the tune of over $75,000, the blame for which accrued to the James boys.

And Colligan was smart enough to do away with the Halsted brothers, who might some day have talked to the Pinkertons, being loud drunks. After the first killing, Strand had found, no others meant a thing, it was just the way life had to be. The strong survived, Colligan pointed out, the weak deserved their rest.

Colligan had known a lot, all right. Too much, in fact, Strand thought, and then the newspaper rattled a little. There had been the thing about women as the illness debilitated the older man, and then there had been the other thing, which Strand never did believe.

Colligan had accused him of wanting to die. Said that luck, as Strand called it, was a myth. That some day Strand would work himself into a corner where he had to be killed, that secretly this was what he wanted, that he went against superior force with too much happiness. It was true that something caused him to laugh a bit in battle, but Strand had noticed others in his trade who did the same; in fact it was a sort of badge or something for them to smile as they killed. All this had wound up in a big fight while they were hiding out for awhile in the mountains above El Paso and now Colligan was buried there, or at least he was a skeleton at the bottom of a deep, worked-out mine shaft.

It had not been as easy to kill Colligan as it had been with the others. How many were there on the record? Not the legend, which had him down for twenty-two, that was for sure. They had all the famous ones down for more than they ever had shot, Masterson, Thompson, Hardin, all of them. The truth was he had downed six notorious fast men in front of witnesses and

172

in fair gun fights. That was enough to establish him as the number one man.

He never did count the cashier in the Missouri bank and the Halsteds, nor, of course, Colligan. Nor the Mexicans they had robbed and slain. He had been lucky enough to be challenged by the big ones and fast enough to get out with his life and that was enough.

He had also been lucky with women, especially after getting rid of the puritanical Colligan. He had developed a sharp sense of discrimination, he knew which of them to pursue and how to attain them. He knew how to treat each, he had a sixth sense which enabled him to judge whether to beat them or entreat them. He seldom failed.

Over the top of the newspaper now, in Cobre, he saw Laurie Pomfret Van Orden as she descended the stairway. The familiar, desired, warm sensation crept upward from his toes, tingling, anticipatory. He lowered the paper just a trifle to allow recognition, no more, not yet.

She did not look his way. She was wearing mourning black, her face was veiled, she stared straight ahead. Beside her was the large Britisher, his hand on her elbow, equally inattentive to the surroundings. They went out onto the verandah and stood at the top of the steps.

Cole Strand arose and followed them. He saw Ben Hancock waiting with a buggy from the livery stable. He started to go out and claim an introduction, then noted the solemnity of Hancock, the lack of animation among the three, the gentle manner in which Hancock handed the lady impersonally into the rig. His predatory instinct roused with the view of the dress tightly stretched over the long, graceful legs and delicate ankles of Laurie, but he held back, his instinct sound, waiting to watch them pull away.

Then he saw that there was a small procession. Past the carriage came Con Boyd's funeral wagon, heading for the burial grounds on the flats east of town. He turned and almost fell over Johnny Hunter.

"What's Mrs. Van Orden got to do with this here funeral, son?"

"Name's Johnny," said the Hunter boy.

Strand produced a two-bit piece. "All right. Tell me." Johnny smirked. "She's her mom."

"Whose mom?"

"The hoor. Daisy. That got killed by Jed Buxton."

"You tellin' me that lady's the mother of a whore?"

"She told it herself. I heard her. Right here. In this very spot. She told it to Matt Buxton."

"You heard her?"

"Ask anybody. Whole town knows it."

"Seems impossible," muttered Strand. He gave the boy another coin. "Is Matt stayin' here?"

"Oh, sure. He keeps sayin' he won't see Jed hung. But my notion is, Judge Grey and Marshal Hancock, they're too tough. Jed killed her. He'll hang, all right. They won't let me watch, though. My folks already told me."

"Tchk, tchk," Strand said, shaking his head. "Some folks are plain inconsiderate."

174

"My old man is nervous. He won't even go to the hangin' himself."

"You don't say. What else you know about the lady?"

"Miz Van Orden? She's real rich. She spends money like it was nothin'. Got three rooms. She and Ben Hancock, they're old friends."

"Old friends, eh?"

"Yep. Known each other for years. Mom says they musta known each other too good, whatever that means."

"I see." Strand provided still another coin. "You do keep your eyes and ears open. I may ask some more questions later on."

"Dan Melvin from the paper, he always comes to me," said Johnny with pride. "I may be a reporter some day."

"You'll be a dandy." Outside the hotel a carriage drawn by a spanking team of bays pulled up. Matt Buxton grunted his way to earth and held up a fat hand for Virgie. Larson, his nose in splints, held the reins. Muley Ward, Sandy Farr and Dave Pitts rode rear guard. Matt was disgruntled, Mrs. Buxton looked bone-weary and sleepy.

Strand went out onto the verandah. The feeling of good luck was strong now. He waited for the Buxtons as they came slowly up the steps. Virgie went past him and directly upstairs. Matt stopped, scowled and sat down in one of the outdoor chairs. The riders tied up and came and made a group in the background, staring at Strand.

"Howdy, Mr. Buxton," Strand said.

"Strand," said Matt acknowledging him but not welcoming him. "Bad news brings you quick, don't it?"

"Not exactly. I was headin' this way anyhow. Heard about your trouble. Everybody has by now."

"I bet."

"Thought we might have a private powwow."

"Not from you."

Strand asked, "You don't need help?"

"Not with you."

The flat, dead tone brought color to Strand's cheek, but he smiled easily enough. "Nothing personal, I take it?"

"Take it any damn way you want," Matt said rudely.

"You wouldn't want to hire me?"

"Soon hire a snake."

"That's pretty rough, Buxton." The tone cooled, grew crisply arrogant. "You don't own Cobre."

"Wouldn't want to own it. Wouldn't make any difference. Just not interested."

Strand shrugged. "Fair enough. Maybe Hancock'll need another deputy."

"At ten per day? You?" Matt chuckled grimly. "Better leave it alone, Strand."

"You suggesting I leave town?"

"Good notion. But suit yourself." Matt got to his feet, motioned to his men. He went into the lobby. The Candlestick men came onto the porch. Dave Pitts shifted his gun holster, the others fanned out.

Strand said, "Pitts, you're supposed to be pretty good."

"I'm good enough."

Strand managed a wide grin. "That remains to be seen. Larson there, he got his nose fixed. I wonder which one of you will get it next and what it'll be?"

Pitts said, "We mind our business. What about you tryin' the same deal?"

"Sure, glad to. Just tell your boss I'll be around. For the hangin'."

He went past them down the street toward the jail. He was boiling, inhaling deeply, fighting a red demon which writhed in his guts. His hands clenched, fingernails dug into palms. No man talked to him in the accents used by Matt Buxton without paying one way or another. Profit was important but there was that other thing, that will to kill which had for a brief instant almost sent him against the guns of Candlestick despite the certainty of suicide. Was it, he wondered, the warning of Colligan that prevented him? Or was it the knowledge that the situation in Cobre was, one way or another, made to order for his talents? Both, he decided, and his heart ran slower and the blood faded from his face. Both of those reasons and the hunch that his luck was running strong.

He came to where Luke sat on the porch with the shotgun at hand, and was able to smile in his flat-faced fashion. "Luke Post, as I live and breathe. Howdy?"

"Tol'able, just tol'able. How's it with you, Cole?" Luke gestured to a chair. "Set awhile?"

"Thankee." He deposited himself, tilted the legs, leaned against the wall. "Wooo-eee, you got somethin' going around here, they do tell me."

Luke said, "You heard good."

177

"And you wearin' a badge."

"You like it?" Luke touched the star with mock pride.

"Just surprised. But then you and Ben were always pardners one way or another."

"You might say that."

"Could there be somethin' in all this for me?" asked Strand. "Seems like I might be useful."

Luke looked at the sunny sky, the mountains stretching gaunt and stark, minus their shading of the morning or afternoon. "It's a nice day. Too nice for buryin'."

Strand took the hint, inhaled, blew out smoke. "I could buy you a drink."

"And me on duty?" Luke cocked an eyebrow. "I'm guarding' the outside. Got a lad in there with a quick gun watchin' him."

"Quick gun?"

"Buckshot," Luke said. "Not your kind of quick gun."

Strand shifted position. "Matt Buxton's confabin' with four tough riders over yonder. What do you figure?"

"Lots of augurin'. No action."

"The lady, now. Mrs. Van Orden. She really the ma of the dead whore?"

Luke said, "Cole, you want to play a little cards?"

"You always beat me. Remember the time you cleaned me complete in Denver?"

"Just before you downed John Slater. Tell you what. I could rig up a monte game in the office. Just to pass the time. Two bits limit."

"Two bits agin you is my speed," Strand said cheerfully. "You about the only square dealer ever could beat me, doggone you."

They went into the office. Strand looked at the big door leading to the cells, at the locked gunrack, at the general neatness and efficiency of the layout, nodded and said, "Ben always was hell for a clean shack."

"And caution," Luke told him. "Ben's real careful. Anybody tries to break that punk out will catch hell."

"Just the three of you?"

Luke produced a miniature monte layout and a box of tiny red, white and blue chips. "Always carry a set, just in case. You think we need more people around here?"

Strand met his steady, suddenly unhooded, cold gaze. He took out some money and put it on the desk. "Four white chips for a dollar?"

"That's the game." Luke's good humor returned to him. "Reds are four bits, blues a buck."

"Run 'em," said Strand. He leaned back, his mouth slightly twisted in a grin, his eyes amused, paying attention to the layout which built under the deft, swift fingers of the gambler.

The grave of Buck Buchanan was already mounded among other plots across the width of the cemetery which had succeeded the old Boot Hill of Cobre. The group around the yawning hole in the corner close to the flower-covered graves of the Latin community was silent. Becky and Abe Getz were there and Jeb Truman and Jerry Kay. Speedy Jackson stood belligerently beside Mrs. Jay and the girls from the house — excepting Cora, who was absent.

Hancock held tight to Laurie's arm. Brewster ranged solidly on her left. She stood erect beneath the hot sun, her flesh cool to the touch.

Hancock whispered, "I'm rotten sorry about that lick-spittle preacher, Laurie."

"She never knew a preacher," said Laurie. She was tearless. "She doesn't need anything now."

A carriage came at an indecorous pace, braked to a stop. Jim Madison, Monty Dipple and Tomas Rosario jumped down and hurried to the graveside, removing their hats. They bowed to Laurie, then edged toward Mrs. Jay and her flock. Two Mexicans leaned on shovels under direction of Con Boyd, apart from the small crowd. The coffin lay on two ropes, covered with flowers. It grew hotter on the high plain.

Laurie said, "Can't we get on with it?"

Jeb Truman, black hat stuffed under his arm, stepped forward, clearing his throat. He glared at Mrs. Jay and the girls, handled a small, leatherbound Bible in his big hands. He spoke in a rumbling, subdued bass.

"It ain't fitten' nobody should say nothin' at a time like o' this. Me, I done spoke out plenty agin — about — well, ne'mine that. On t'other hand, the religious hands didn't have the gumption to come here and put the little gal away right. I don't hold with that." He lifted the Bible. "Mebbe the lady would like to hear somethin' read out?"

Laurie's voice caught but she managed to say, "Thank you, sir. The Twenty-Third Psalm, perhaps?"

180

Truman opened the book, fumbled for steel spectacles, perched them on his broad nose. The men bowed their heads. Hancock found himself staring at the coffin.

His grip tightened on Laurie's arm. He was remembering the laughter of the girl, the turmoil of dark nights at Mrs. Jay's, her eagerness for contact as though she were searching wildly for something barely beyond her grasp. Then he heard in his mind her last outcry, the scream before Jed Buxton shot her, the fear of death in her voice. He seemed to see her through the pine board of the coffin, defenseless, all the laughter gone at last.

" 'The Lord is my shepherd, I shall not want . . . ' "

Hancock turned his head from the coffin, suffering. Out of the corner of his eye he saw Linda Darr. She was accompanied by Dan Melvin. She seemed to be watching Laurie and her face was stone-cold. He could not sustain any thought of this woman who had been close to him. He could think only of the dead girl — and of her mother beside him standing so rigid and strong in her grief.

Truman finished the reading. There was silence as he bent and picked a blossom from the casket. Con Boyd directed the laborers and the well-greased ropes let the last remains of Maureen Pomfret slip down into the hole in the earth.

"Ashes to ashes, dust to dust . . . May God have mercy on her soul."

It was not precisely worded but it would serve. Laurie stayed firm in place while dirt fell solidly,

181

emptily upon the coffin. In a moment, however, the sound, the heavy perfume of the blossoms, the heat struck at her and she faltered, leaning heavily upon Hancock. Brewster helped support her to the carriage.

She said with infinite sadness, "Ben, I think I want to drive back alone. With Brewster."

"Should I stop by later?"

"Yes, please. Later."

He helped her into the buggy. Brewster drove with his hands held high, like a coachman Hancock had seen in New York in the olden times. He could not drag himself out of all the yesterdays. He shook his head to dispel the past as Jerry Kay creakingly mounted his dogcart and waved as he drove toward town. Speedy Jackson was herding Mrs. Jay and the girls to a carryall where Chompy waited. The whores were all the family Speedy had, Hancock thought.

All the others were gone now. He started, wondering if he would have to walk to town, realized that it did not matter, that he had use for time by himself. There were many subjects on which he should ponder, including his immediate future. He needed some opportunity to get hold of himself.

Then he saw that Linda and Dan Melvin were waiting for him beside the newspaperman's equipage, an old spring wagon drawn by a chestnut which Melvin used to get around the countryside on his reporting expeditions. Hancock walked toward them, still able to hear the dirt being thrown into the hole containing the body of the slain girl, still haunted, knowing he could not evade the trip to Cobre with the couple, wishing he could think of an excuse not to join them.

He assured himself sternly that the girl herself was not there, underground, that she was gone out of that shell to another world, that nothing of her was left — excepting her mother.

Linda did not speak, merely nodded. Dan Melvin had a wad of notepaper and a pencil; his air was didactic, as though he had grown in importance overnight.

"Surprised not to see you at Buck's funeral," Melvin said. "Sad day, very sad day."

"Sad, yes. Buck had the preachers, the council, Candlestick, everybody. Daisy only had us." Hancock's voice was harsh.

Linda stirred, looked away. Melvin poised his pencil, something he was not known to do ever before, pursed his lips, was stern and demanding.

"We'll be getting out an extra edition tomorrow. During this — uh — trouble, we will print whenever there is news. Now, about Mrs. Van Orden."

"You'll have to ask her anything you want to know."

"She is an old friend of yours."

"Who says?"

"It is obvious, Marshal. She is also the mother of the — ah — unfortunate Cyprienne."

"Cyprienne? What is this, Dan? You gone hifalutin' for fair."

"An expression, merely an expression. I merely want to report the news."

"Nothing to report," Hancock told him.

"I think we'd better get out of the sun and back to town," Linda said in flat accents.

"Well, of course." Melvin was slightly daunted.

They piled into the front seat, which was a close fit for three. Hancock was uncomfortably aware of Linda too close to his side.

Melvin said, "I have to report the double funeral, who was there, all that."

"It wasn't a double," Hancock pointed out. "It was two single ones."

Ignoring this, the newsman went on, "I need the facts. Mrs. Van Orden, a lady of means. Mrs. Jay, the connection between them."

"No connection, they never been introduced." Hancock was recovering the power of anger.

"Sheriff and prostitute, interred the same day."

"Ah, go soak your head," Hancock told him. "Shut up or I'll get down and walk."

Linda spoke for the first time. "It's not nice to squabble at a time like this."

"Reynolds is due any minute, may be in town now. The railroad is all-important. How will Reynolds react? These matters mean something to you, Marshal."

"Do tell." He stared straight ahead, containing himself. Suddenly the railroad didn't matter to him at all. Cobre, which he had designated as his town, was a place where he held a badge, like any cowtown of the past.

"Everything depends on how the — ah — situation is handled," said Melvin. "I'd like a statement from you."

"Get it at the hearing tomorrow."

"Are you going to run for sheriff?"

"Probably not."

Linda started, quickly turned to stare at him. Hancock did not return the glance. The woman was a stranger, the newsman an annoyance.

"You're being uncooperative," Melvin complained. "You need backing, Ben, you ought to know it."

"I'll take what I have now. My job, my deputies."

"Then make a statement. Don't underestimate the power of the press. Let everyone know where you stand."

"You heard of anyone with doubts?"

"I'm thinking of Santa Fe. El Paso, Denver, Tucson, San Francisco. New York."

"You got subscribers in all those places?"

"We have exchanges. A story like this, it will go all around the country."

Hancock pretended concern. "Shoot, now. I'd hate to think the President was upset about me. What with Korea and everything."

"No need for sarcasm." Melvin fell sullen and silent. Everyone in Cobre was changing by the minute.

They drew in at Linda's shop. She barely accepted Hancock's aid in descending.

Melvin said, "You're going to be sorry about this. Everybody needs to make himself clear on a subject of this importance."

"Just say I haven't got a position. Only the job. It's enough. And say talk won't help. Fact is, talk will hurt. That's all, Dan."

The buggy pulled off toward the livery stable. Linda had her back turned.

"Sad day," Hancock said vaguely, as to a stranger.

"Dan was right. You're going to need friends. I warn you, they'll be hard to find." She went into the shop and closed the door.

Hancock went across the street. Cole Strand and Luke were at the desk with the monte layout between them.

"Well, Cole," Ben said. "Been a long time."

"About time you got back. He's into me for eighteen dollars at two bits per chip. Howdy, Marshal?"

They shook hands as old acquaintances, firmly but without warmth.

"You can imagine how it is around here."

"I heard."

"Sure you did. How's with you? We hear, once in awhile."

"Yep, people do talk. Tall talk, lots of times."

Luke said, "It's those duds, Cole. People remember."

"Fine talk from a dude like you," chided Strand. "Reckon the game's over. Here's your unlawful gains."

Luke put away the paraphernalia. "Every little bit helps. Beatin' a notorious gunslinger like you, that's a risky business. Makes me feel right brave."

"Give a dog a bad name." Strand made a comical face.

"People know you, it helps sometimes," said Hancock. He felt urgent need of a drink. The light conversation held only part of his attention. He took the whiskey out of the drawer. "Luke wouldn't offer

186

you one, he's scared you might think he was takin' advantage."

"Which I don't need nohow," Luke said, producing the three glasses, going for cold water.

"Which is true," assented Strand. "You right about bein' known. Too many punks try to kill a man."

"Not so much any more." Luke returned and Hancock poured. "Things get quiet."

"You're sayin' that?" Strand's brows went up. "Here and now?"

"Murder," Hancock replied. "Different thing altogether. Wouldn't you say?"

Strand did not smile. "Yeah. That I'd say."

"Sure. A gun fighter, he's square," Luke said blithely. "Like a good dealer. He's got the edge but he's square."

Strand seemed mollified. "Anyways, you boys got trouble, seems like."

"Maybe."

"We've got Judge Grey, too," Luke said. "Almost sent you up over that Mesilla business, didn't he, Cole?"

"He tried. But you know I never stole a horse."

"Unless you needed one right smart?"

Strand laughed. "Like Ogallala? I sent him back, remember?"

"It was my horse," retorted Luke. "I mind it good."

"Well, that damn sheriff had no respect," said Strand. "He knew that tinhorn was sharpin' me — what was his name?"

"Sanders. A piss poor dealer," Luke said. "Trouble is, you don't know how to handle that kind."

"Nope. Had to shoot him and run."

"He drawed first," Luke said to Hancock. "I was there. Sanders was fast."

"Spoiled my best suit," Strand remembered. "I was askin' Luke here, could you use another hand in this hoorah?"

Hancock said, "Decent of you, Cole. We're all right for now. Matt's trying law and thinkin' of maybe some other ways, but we're all right."

"I may stick around. Wanted to ask you, what about the lady, Mrs. Van Orden?"

"Friend of ours." Hancock kept his voice easy.

"Saw her in Lordsburg. Real lady," said Strand. "What did happen with the daughter?"

"Got herself shot by Jed Buxton."

"Oh. Well, sure." Strand finished his drink. "I'll be moseyin' along. Maybe try what I learned from Luke down at Madison's place. See you later for a touch?"

"Any time."

He walked down the street. He had a slight swagger, a way of carrying himself which Hancock had noted among men of his kind. Luke exhaled, poured another drink.

"You reckon Buxton sent for him?"

"He didn't have to. He's got the nose for trouble. Smells it a mile away."

"He's awful quick. Don't care who he downs, neither."

"He's bad news, *amigo*. Any time, any place, he's real bad news."

Luke said, "You hear things."

"Plenty you don't hear with men like him."

"You could've pinned a badge on him."

"Not on him. Not never."

"See what you mean. Although I never did actually know of him back-shootin' anybody," Luke said carefully. "Not for sure."

"Not my kind," Hancock said. "Not Matt's kind either, but Matt's desperate about now."

Luke said, "He'll move. It's a question of when. Think I could go grab some grub?"

"Go ahead. Take your time. I'll be here."

The sun had shifted and the shadows were purple and the sky laden with fleecy clouds of all shapes, as of fish or elephants or cattle or birds. Today he had no eye for beauty in nature, again he felt the strangeness of the town. He stared at Linda's place, then went inside and checked Neddy and the prisoner, then went into the dwelling quarters and removed his dark clothing and lay down on the bed, hands beneath his head.

The way it had been with Daisy tormented him. His skin felt itchy and loose on him. His mind shifted from one subject to the other, paused briefly on the gray snake of the man called Cole Strand, went to Candlestick, to Judge Grey, to the city council and its chintzy fearfulness. Everything was complicated, uncertain. Events were not proceeding straight ahead, they were spinning in a circle. There were deep shadows where there had been cheery light.

The killing of the girl and the arrival of Laurie had been shocking developments in the simple world he had inhabited for so long. He knew he had to get straight in his mind and choose a careful course and

189

follow it with everything he had learned and all he could muster. It was almost impossible for the moment.

He heard Doc Farrar in the office and arose and went to meet him. The whiskey was at hand, they poured.

Doc said, "The inquest papers. You don't have anything to add, I take it."

"Want to read 'em?"

Farrar read off the eyewitness reports. When he had finished, Hancock said, "That's the way it was. I came in after the shot and took away the gun."

Farrar wrote in a neat, legible hand. "You didn't see him shoot her?"

"No. I arrested him."

"All right. Sign here." Farrar picked up his whiskey glass. "I think Judge will hold him, all right."

"You think?"

"The railroad, Ben."

"The judge wants him held, rails or high heaven. Or hell either, for that matter."

"There's still the governor. I don't know. And then — there's Matt."

"And the city council."

"Taggart wanted you to let him escape," Farrar stated. "Hell of a thing. Ben, if the thing goes wrong I'm leaving town."

"Save a place for me."

"Oh, you'll probably be full of holes. I'll stay long enough to do what I can for you. But Cobre is finished unless this all works out."

"Like how, Doc?"

Farrar shrugged. "It's not that clear."

"It's clear enough for me. Jed gets a trial. He goes to jail or he hangs. The hell with the rest."

"I thought you'd come to that. Land or no land, rails or no rails, eh?"

"You could say that."

"Maybe you're a fool. Maybe you're a hero. Maybe you're just a man doing a job. Any way it goes, you're right, deplorably. Cobre needs many things, a hospital, for one. I'm tired of working without tools — without a nurse, a younger man to help out. The rails would bring just about everything a frontier town could have. If something goes wrong, looks bad for us, we're finished. And I'll leave, I assure you."

"I know what you mean."

"Reynolds drove in awhile ago. Said he'd like to see you privately, in the hotel."

"Everybody wants to see me. Never was that important before," Hancock said.

"Well, I'll turn this over to the judge." Farrar took the inquest papers, hesitated at the door. "Damn few people are with you, Ben. Count me in."

"Never doubted it. Thanks, Doc."

He went to the wall peg and put on his gun belt. He slid the Colts gingerly in and out to make sure of the slickness of the leather, then tried a fast draw. He felt foolish. He had never been too fast, now he was far out of practice. Cole Strand would kill him before he cleared his weapon, he thought, chagrined.

He walked across the quiet Sunday street to the hotel. The lobby scene was unchanged, Matt front and

191

center, the riders finding their places around the walls. The difference was in their attitude. They seemed secretly pleased, complacent. They grinned at Hancock without speaking. Johnny Hunter came scuttling, motioning to Hancock to follow him. They went up the stairs and to a room at the rear of the building. Reynolds answered the knock.

Prentice Reynolds was a big man who wore rough clothing at all times, like a uniform. He was a combination of eastern businessman and construction engineer. He was in touch with powerful politicians all the way to the White House; he liked to think of himself as relating to all walks of life. He was a sharp-faced man with deep-set dark eyes and a slightly prognathous jaw. Hancock resented him and distrusted him but admired his drive and strength.

Reynolds said, "Ben, how are you? No, don't answer. I can guess."

They shook hands and Hancock sat on a straight chair. Reynolds continued to stand, staring out the window at the scene, looking toward the Burro Mountains.

"Things could be worse and probably will," Hancock told him. It was no use to compromise with Reynolds, the railroad had spies everywhere, knew all.

Reynolds said, "They must not be worse."

"Tell it to Matt Buxton."

"Matt Buxton has land that we need. He has been an ally of the railroad. Something must be done to make him see the light."

"Uh-huh. Good notion. Have you tried?"

"I've tried. He sits there like a frog on a pond lily and grins at me. Have you any notion of what he intends?"

"Tonight or tomorrow after the hearing he will try to get his brother out of Cobre. He won't make it without killing me and possibly my two deputies," said Hancock bluntly. "I don't think he can do it."

"I'm going over to Centro today," Reynolds said. "The decision on the route must be made this week."

Hancock sighed. "A couple days ago that would have upset me some."

"You mean you don't care whether we come here or not?"

"You know I care. But first things come first. Do I have to lay that out for you?" Anger was again rising in Hancock.

"That's not a good attitude, Ben. We've worked together on this, we want to come here. But with this violence pending, the people in the East will veto our plan."

"Will they, now? Then they should come out here and stop Matt and let the law take its course."

"I don't understand you," Reynolds said, thrusting out his prominent chin. A tap on the door distracted him; he opened it to admit Judge Grey.

"Good morning, Ben — Prentice," said the jurist. He squinted at them. "I see you're at it already."

"Reynolds seems to think I can arrange everything to suit him," Hancock snapped.

"I merely want matters — cleared up. Clarified." This seemed to please Reynolds, as though he had stated an understandable position. "I want Buxton to sell us his right of way. I want this town peaceful. We cannot proceed if there is a town war plus a property fight."

"Wantin' ain't gettin'," said Hancock. "Threats don't cut any ice with me."

"Threats? Did you say threats?"

"It sounds damn like threats!"

Judge Grey said, "I think the marshal interprets pretty well, Prentice. May I add that no power except the will of the people may interpret the law? There is a matter of crime here, the most heinous crime, murder. The law is being enforced as of now. I know you and your people would rather see Jed Buxton smuggled away, forgotten . . ."

"I did not say any such thing!"

"Your people have sent veiled messages to that effect," Judge Grey said. "Matt has inundated the capital with pleas and threats. This is statewide now, and will become a national story no doubt."

"I too have been in touch — with Washington," said Reynolds. "Frankly, I have carte blanche so far as this track is concerned. And I want peace, I want a solid, business community for this station."

"You're going to get what the law allows," Judge Grey told him. "Isn't that what you should want?"

"There are ramifications in this situation . . ."

Hancock said to the jurist, "He wants Jed turned loose or at least charged with second-degree murder, can't you see that? Matt's downstairs grinnin' like a fat cat. Either we go easy on Jed or the railroad goes to Centro."

194

Reynolds was silent. The judge arose from his chair and went to the door. Hancock followed him.

Judge Grey said, "There is a conflict here. There may be violence. The city council agrees with you, with the railroad. I do not say I can't understand your position, Reynolds, although I find it specious. But believe me, Cobre would be the wrong place if you and the others who agree with you had your way. Good day, sir."

They went out of the room, leaving the railroad man standing at the window, controlled anger making his body rigid. There was no give to the man, both knew. They went downstairs, past Matt and the Candlestick riders, into the bar. They ordered a drink and stood close together.

Hancock said, "There goes the railroad."

"That may be." Judge Grey seemed older, wearier.

"It makes some kind of sense to let Jed off — at least let him go to prison," said Hancock tentatively.

"It does, doesn't it?"

"Fact is, he probably wouldn't live out his sentence. He's not tough," Hancock probed further.

"True."

"Cole Strand is in town."

"You think Matt sent for him?" asked Judge Grey.

"Matt's got somethin' to be happy about. Thing is, Strand's for sale any time. A few hundred and we could turn Jed loose and he'd be dead the next day."

"You're being realistic today."

"Just touchin' all the bases," said Hancock. "Shall we talk?"

"Not necessary, my friend," said Judge Grey. He drank his whiskey. "The hearing will be at ten tomorrow."

He left the bar without further words. Hancock lingered over his drink. He wondered what made Matt so self-satisfied. If he knew that, he would be ready for the next circumstance, he thought. If he knew whether Matt had sent for Strand it would be helpful also.

Brewster touched his elbow. Hancock started, then smiled and said, "Have a drink?"

"Oh, no, sir. It's Mrs. Van Orden. She wants to talk to you."

"Why, sure." He put down the glass and followed the big man up the stairs. The lobby was empty of Candlestick men and he wondered where Matt was attacking now. He went into the converted sitting room but Brewster gestured toward Laurie's bedroom. Hancock took a deep breath and went through the door. Brewster closed it gently behind him.

The shades were drawn but enough sunlight filtered through to enable him to see her. She was in bed, propped against pillows. There was a bottle of brandy on the table near her elbow and she poured two small drinks into goblets which had never been provided by the hotel. The air was redolent with the odor of the liquor and of the woman.

He put his hat on a chair, hesitated. She hitched away from the edge of the bed and said, "Ben. Come here, where I can see you."

He perched alongside her, his gun belt uncomfortable, his mind whirling again, back to that other time when they had made of the bed a wondrous playing field. He held the tiny brandy snifter in his fingers, remembering how she had served it then, in that other time and place. He had never been so uneasy, so mixed up in the head, he thought. He could find no words for her. She took his hand and held it tight and he returned the pressure and looked at her. She was incredibly young and beautiful in the half light.

She said, "Ben, the worst is over. But there is a stone inside me."

"Why, Laurie, you got a right."

"I'll accept my responsibility. But he murdered her, didn't he, that young man?"

"He shot her in the back."

"Yes. Maybe I'm evil. But he must hang."

"The odds are that he will do that."

"There's nothing I can do, nothing. Only make him pay. That's not Christian but until he does, I'll never be close to complete again. Perhaps that won't help. But I want my pound of flesh, Ben, I want it."

Her vehemence made him a trifle more uncomfortable, he tugged at the gun belt, finally released her hand and removed it, apologizing, "It's a nuisance most times."

She said, "I love to see it on you. I love the fact that you're guarding the killer. It's a dramatic circle — you're here, I need you."

"I'm glad you feel that way." He reached for a way to say what was in him, faltered. "It's the greatest thing to have you here since — since we were together in New York."

197

"I should have followed you then." She sipped the brandy rather faster than she had taught him to imbibe it. "Ben, it's true. Everything was a compromise after you left. I didn't know it — as I didn't know anything about myself or — anything else in those days."

"I had to come back home. What good was I in that place? What could I do?" It had been more than that. It had been carelessness, lack of knowledge of what she had meant to him. It had been a lot of things.

"I could have supported us." She broke off, smiling. "How foolish. Not even for love."

"Love," he said. It was a word he had never used.

"We knew it, then." She again seized his hand. "Did you ever know anything like we had? Did you?"

"No," he said. "No, Laurie, honest."

She said, "When this is straightened out — this terrible deed — when it is avenged we will talk."

"Yes." He struggled for words, found none.

"I'll be here. I won't leave your country, I promise."

He could see too much of her. Memory of the old days and what it had been like drove him away from her. He stood up, trembling. "We'll work it out." The thought of Daisy — Maureen — impinged upon him. "Better get some sleep. I'll see you later."

"I can sleep now. I had to talk with you. Tell Brewster I'll take a nap."

"Do that, now, you hear?"

She blew him a kiss as he found the gun belt and backed awkwardly out of the door. Brewster was not in the sitting room, but in a moment he came out into the hall.

Hancock said, "Take care of her, Brewster. I don't want her bothered by anybody."

"I'll be here, sir." In his shirt sleeves the muscles rippled in his big arms. He peered anxiously at Ben. "Is she sleeping?"

"She'll sleep, now."

"She puts great confidence in you, sir."

"And in you."

"I hope so."

"I'll be around," Hancock said. There was something in Brewster's voice he did not quite understand, but when he thought of the Britisher, with her every day, week in and week out, he could make a guess. Brewster was a puzzle, out of Hancock's experience, but he was a man, no doubt of that.

He hesitated, turned. "There's a man named Strand."

"I know about him." Brewster was grim.

"He's a fast man with his gun. Look out for him."

Brewster's face broke into humorous lines. "I am a fast man with my fists."

"Then stay close to him," Hancock warned. "Yell for help. It's no disgrace, against Strand."

"I understand." Brewster lifted a clenched hand. "Thank you, Marshal."

The lobby, surprisingly, was empty. Hancock went into the street. It was still a peaceful, if restless, Sunday in Cobre. Three people spoke to him on the way to the office, all rather bemused. Luke was reading his book.

"Awful quiet," Hancock said.

"This here Ferret." Luke held up the volume. "He mixed up with some mugs like we knew in New York. Awful bunch of junk, though. Fella keeps puttin' on and takin' off a beard to fool people. And guns — this fella don't know doodley-squat about guns."

Hancock suggested, "Deal me some monte for that two-bit limit. It'll pass some time, anyway."

Luke brightened, digging after his layout. "Four bits for reds, a dollar for blues, right? You reckon Buxton's goin' to start anything tonight?"

"I wouldn't know. Deal 'em, gambler." But he was thinking about the woman and about the dead girl. He would have to get the girl out of his mind completely before he could get straight with the woman, he knew.

And they were going to tell it in court how he had been to bed with Daisy, the whore . . .

The office of Jim Madison seemed crowded and too hot. Dave Pitts leaned against the wall, Muley Ward blocked the door. Matt Buxton sat behind a bundle of cash and a bank draft and waited. Madison wiped his upper lip.

"It ain't right."

"It's business," Buxton told him.

"It would be a runout."

"Not nohow. Your saloon is worth maybe five thousand, maybe less if the railroad don't come. I'm offerin' you ten. You take Dipple with you and leave tonight."

Madison reached for a tablet, swallowed it with water. "I can't make Monty do anything he don't wanta do."

Dave Pitts shifted and grinned. "He'll go."

"Monty ain't scared of you," Madison told him. "He's a shotgun man."

"Nobody's scared of no one," Matt Buxton said. "This is a deal I'm makin' you."

"I keep thinkin' of the dead gal," muttered Madison. "And I keep thinkin' of Ben. You're gonna have to kill Ben to get Jed outa there."

"That's just what I don't want to do," Matt told him.

"You can't buy all the witnesses. Cole Strand's out there in the bar right now — and you tell me you ain't aimin' to start killin'?"

"I work with the law," Matt said.

"And your money." Still, Madison stared at the cash and the empty bank draft which was as good as gold in California when signed by Matt Buxton.

Pitts said, "Why go through all this, boss? If you say Dipple and this one goes — they go."

"Outside," said Matt, showing anger for the first time. "Both of you. And don't start anything, you hear me?"

Sullen, the riders went out of the office. Matt regained his smile, touching the cash on the desk.

Madison said, "I don't like it, Matt."

"I dunno where you got those hifalutin' ideas. A dead whore, you can't bring her back. Ben? He's goin' to be mud when it's told how the whore was his favorite gal. You know about towns, how they are.

Where you gonna be when all this comes out? The railroad people ain't about to stand by anybody mixed up in this here mess."

Madison said, "That ain't it."

"You scared people will say you run out."

"I don't want to run out."

"But cash talks. Real loud." Matt slowly gathered up the bills and the draft. "I'll be at the hotel. You think it over. You got till the mornin' stage, the early one, afore the hearing."

Madison said, "I just don't like it."

"I don't like Jed settin' in that jail, fearin' he's gonna hang, neither," Matt Buxton told him. "I don't like that at all."

He went out into the bar. Cole Strand was casually bucking the faro table. Muley and Dave were at the bar with beers. Nothing changed when he walked through, no one even looked at him. He knew them all, had known their kind since he was a boy. He cared nothing for them. He cared only for what was his and this he meant to hang onto, one way or the other.

Virgie was lying down on the bed in the hotel room. Matt kissed her and lowered himself onto a straight chair. He kicked a foot under the bed where they had stacked the guns and ammunition and felt strong and confident.

She said, "They get Daisy buried?"

"Sure. Don't you feel good, honey?"

"I can't feel good," she said drearily. "The guns, the way you take on, everything."

"It'll work out. I think I got Madison on the run. Reynolds wants it quieted down. Worst can happen is Jed goes to prison. I can get him out through Santa Fe."

"You can do that," she acknowledged. "If that's the way it goes, you can."

"You think they'll hang him, don't you?"

"I think he deserves it."

"I'm sorry about that. I truly am. I just won't have it."

"But you're not going to try and break him out."

"I won't say that. The boys — they want to try it. I'm studyin' on it."

"You can't start a fight in town. Anyone might get killed. Our friends — you can't do it."

"I thought on that."

"Candlestick is ours. We built it. Somethin' goes wrong, how can we stay here? Why should we go down with Jed?"

"He's my brother." But he was uncertain. He patted her shoulder. "I always listen to you, don't I?"

"Of all times, listen to me now."

He wondered about Madison. If the barkeeper sold out, if Cora Jones testified as Finnegan had coached her, if Hancock could be discredited — too many ifs, he thought. Still, he did not want to kill anyone. Virgie was right.

It was one time he could not hold the reins tight and direct the course of action. He had to play it loose. There had to be some way to get Jed away from Cobre. The guns were hidden in the room, he wanted to leave them there. But he knew the men, they were close to Jed, they were proud, they now hated the marshal and Monty Dipple and Madison. Larson had been beaten by Hancock. It would take only a spark to ignite all this powder.

He sat like a large lump, thinking, worrying, while Virgie lay on her back and stared at the ceiling.

There were moments when Cole Strand felt the power. It was pure inspiration, it came without pondering, out of the blue, an answer to unspoken questions. He said from his place at the end of the bar in Madison's saloon, "Larson, I got a notion."

"Who cares?" Larson had trouble speaking in his normal accents, he was drinking whiskey with beer chasers.

"I got a notion how to break Jed loose and make a pot of money at the same time," Strand said. He looked at Monty Dipple at the other end of the bar. "You want to go some place and talk?"

"The hell with you," Larson told him. "You're bad news."

Strand shrugged and began to walk toward the swinging doors. He felt the eyes of Muley Ward and Sandy Farr upon him. Dave Pitts, the fast gun, was surly but it was he who gestured to the others, so that when Strand was on Buxton Street they followed, keeping to the shadows. All had been drinking heavily. Muley and Dave smarted from the rebuke administered by Matt in Madison's office. All had been riding with Jed long enough to have lost many scruples.

Dave Pitts asked, "Money? What you got in mind about money?"

"If Jed gets loose, Matt won't come through with much," Strand told him. "It can never be the same, don't you see that? You're Jed's boys. No matter what happens, you're in the soup. Jed'll have to leave town. What happens to you-all?"

"Jed leave town? Why?"

"He shot the whore in the back."

"Yeah," breathed Dave Pitts. "He did, at that."

"So?"

"We spring him and grab some loot and make for the hills?" Pitts inhaled. "I dunno."

"Not just a little loot. The biggest haul you ever heard of. Bigger than anything ever pulled before," Strand told them, building it in his mind as he went along.

"Just how big is that?"

"Fifty thousand dollars apiece."

"Fifty — you're plain loco."

"Then you don't want to listen." He had them now, he thought.

"What about Larson?" asked Dave Pitts.

"He's Matt's foreman, Matt's man."

"What about Jed?"

"He's in."

"How you aimin' to go about this, Strand?"

"You really want to talk?"

"We want to listen. Right?"

They all agreed, their mouths open. They had never dreamed of owning even fifty hundred dollars apiece.

205

Pitts said, "Matt's too hard without Jed around. Never did cotton to Larson much, tell the truth. Further and more if it's Hancock, I'll take care of him when the time comes. Talk some, Strand."

They began walking in leisurely fashion to a place in the open where they could not be overheard. Strand's mind was working like a well-oiled grandfather's clock, he thought with exultation; it was all coming clear.

Book Three

EXPIATION

CHAPTER
ONE

Hancock woke up with a start, vague dreams driving him. There was a bad taste in his mouth. He drank from the iced pitcher, shook himself. The sun was high, it was time to convey the prisoner to the courtroom at city hall. He undressed, washed with a rag, donned a clean white shirt, his dark Sunday pants and coat, knotting a string tie, reaching for his rolled brim black hat. He buckled on his gun belt, rolled the barrel of his Colt and tried it in and out a few times.

All the time his mind ran over the one fact: Today it would be revealed to Laurie that he had slept with her daughter, Daisy the little whore. There was danger to face, there were machinations to avoid, there were legal points to keep in mind, but only one thing stabbed at him, brought him down, tortured him. If Laurie were to hate him, leave him, he would be shattered, he knew. The moment he had seen her the realization had pierced his heart; she had been on the edge of his consciousness for all these years. He had been lulled into accepting a substitute, he would have gone the rest of his life with this small cloud nudging him perhaps. But the sight of her and the feel of her had been like a bolt of bright lightning in a summer storm.

He braced himself against the world and went out into his office. Luke was sitting behind the desk, calm and unruffled, oiling a Colt .45, a shotgun athwart his knees.

"Mornin', Marshal," said the gambler. "Everything's in shape around this here joint."

"Mornin', Luke." He reached for the coffeepot. "Had breakfast?"

"Yep. Everybody's et but you."

"I don't feel hungry. Better get Neddy out here. I slept uneasy and a mite too long."

He opened the big door and Neddy, fresh and grinning, came into the office, stuffing the little blue book into his pocket. Hancock unhitched two rifles and a cartridge belt from the rack and locked the shotgun Neddy had been carrying into its place.

"You know what to do, now."

"On the roof of the hotel," said Neddy. "Watch every which of a way."

"High gun," Luke said. "The town can't make a move you don't know it."

"Only one thing," said Neddy.

"Yeah. I know. You wouldn't want to hit the wrong person. Just holler when action starts. They'll clear the streets. Bear down on Jed if you can."

"I'll do that. If they try it, I'll make sure of him."

"And don't let anybody see you making it to that roof."

"I'll try," Neddy said. "Back stairs, up through the trap door, I know how."

210

"Better get going," Hancock told him. "Down the alley and across the back lots. People will be looking to see Jed make his march to city hall."

Luke said, "I'll get him."

Virgie had brought in a dark coat and clean shirt and light trousers for the prisoner. He was manacled hand and foot, not to keep him from running away but to prevent would-be rescuers from affording him a horse he could mount. He was complaining as usual but Luke hustled him through the office and onto the verandah.

"See you later," said Neddy, and ducked out the side door into the alley between the jail and the *Copper Bulletin* building.

There were too many people in town, Hancock thought, but it was unavoidable. Many miners had taken the day off, farmers had driven in with their families, all the small ranchers were there secretly pleased to see Candlestick in trouble. The members of the city council were waiting at city hall, where the hearing would take place. Men, women and children thronged Buxton Street.

"A damn circus show," Jed was expostulating. "You oughta have a carriage to take me down there. How'm I gonna walk in these damn leg irons?"

"Crawl if you must," Luke told him. "Let's get goin'."

It was a walk as long and excruciating for Hancock as it was for Jed Buxton. Luke led the way, the marshal trailing. The prisoner's boot heels clicked and his chains clanked as he took short steps between the men wearing the stars. A lane opened along the boards at

211

the end of which was the city hall. Women murmured, one said aloud, "He's so young, why do they chain him like o' that?" Hancock wanted to shout that he was a killer, that he had murdered a girl, but he knew better than that, people saw only what was before their eyes, they did not think, they only looked and blurted.

Abe Getz stood in the doorway of his store and watched without comment. Young Johnny Hunter had climbed to the rail of the hotel porch and almost fell into the crowd as the three men went slowly by. It was, Hancock knew, a test of the town, of himself, of the process of law.

The Candlestick men rode their horses down the middle of the street, scattering quondam pedestrians. Larson was in the lead, his nose still in splints. They came to the trio and formed a picket line, reining in like an escort in a parade. A couple of soldiers from Bayard set up a cheer — they were the pair who had been rousted by Hancock. Some few others joined in. Candlestick was powerful, the influence of Matt Buxton ran deep in the countryside among certain elements both envious and loyal. Every rancher wanted in his heart to be a Buxton, Hancock thought.

They plodded along. It seemed a long distance to walk in this fashion but Hancock had feared a runaway horse stampeded by accident or design. If an attempt at delivery of the prisoner was to be made he preferred to face it afoot with both hands free and Luke to back him up. He really did not expect such action now, not before the hearing, but Matt and the riders had seemed smug and secretive and it was certain they had plans.

212

He saw Linda Darr across the street, noted that Madison's place was closed tight, imagined that Madison was communing with his stomach and his headache and wishing he need not testify — then wondered how the saloonkeeper would stand up under Finnegan's questioning. He saw Linda caught up in a swirl of people, saw Cole Strand go to her aid and elbow a path for her, wondered if Strand was shifting his attention to Linda and conjectured what might be his reasons, knowing the gunslinger did nothing without reasons.

He could see the city hall now, where Matt Buxton waited outside the locked door with Lawyer Finnegan and Virgie. Mayor Taggart was inside with the city council, awaiting the arrival of the prisoner. Jeb Truman stood with his arms folded, apart from the others, and behind him were Mrs. Jay and Chompy and the whores. The women of Cobre did not so much as glance that way, but the men peeked, shuffled their feet, talked behind the backs of their hands in whispers. Preacher Doer and Father Donner were like black shadows in the bright sunshine against the adobe wall. The entire county was represented; there were more people in Cobre than Hancock liked to see upon this occasion. As the crowd thickened, pouring toward the city hall, Hancock was grateful for the Candlestick horsemen, who cleared the way.

Upon sighting Matt and the lawyer, Jed Buxton's head came up and his mouth went to work again. "Now you'll see. You damn no-good bastards, you'll larn what it is to try and run on Candlestick. Now you'll see."

213

Hancock pushed him from behind and he stumbled up the steps, where Taggart was opening the door. At the last possible moment he unlocked the manacles and turned the prisoner over to Finnegan as an officer of the court. They went inside in a wave of polite but determined humanity as the elite took precedence over the run-of-the-mine citizens without protestations.

Laurie Van Orden came from around the corner of the building. Brewster's bulk preceded her and Hancock was waiting. They went immediately to the chamber which had been converted into a courtroom. He led her down the aisle and Luke was waiting, as prearranged, with seats in the front row. A few people glared but Hancock ignored them, whispering reassurance to Laurie, then mounted the dais.

When he turned around he saw that Cole Strand had somehow managed to make a place for himself and Linda Darr next to Laurie and Brewster. Again he felt the twitch of annoyance, the warning signal of danger ahead. He looked for the Candlestick riders and saw them against the far wall, standing in a row, apparently unarmed.

Two tables had been arranged, one for the defense, one for the prosecution, and Mr. Edward Evans of Santa Fe and points east was already in his place. He was a lean man with a prominent nose and a long jaw, and eyes which could be blank as drawn window shades or sharp as daggers. At the other table, Finnegan sat Jed Buxton down and pulled up chairs for Virgie and Matt. Luke remained at the rear of the room, where he could command a full view.

Judge Grey entered, wearing a robe he had brought West with him. Hancock made a motion of his hand and everyone stood up excepting Jed. The prisoner slouched, sneering as always, until Finnegan reached out and snatched him to his feet, with a belated assist from Matt, who growled fiercely into his brother's ear.

"This district court of the Territory of New Mexico is now in order," said the judge.

Everyone sat down. Hancock counted noses — and was aware of a gap in the picture he had projected in his mind. Jim Madison and Monty Dipple were not in the courtroom. Cora was there, in the back of the room near the Candlestick riders against the wall. Dr. Farrar was down front. But the two main witnesses for the prosecution were absent.

This, then, was the cause for satisfaction among the Buxton crowd. They had somehow rid themselves of the saloonkeeper and his bartender. Cora was suborned. The riders would certainly not testify against Jed. Hancock had not seen the actual killing — and he well knew the plan they had for discrediting him.

He inhaled deeply, concealing his concern as best he might. He looked at Luke, who spread his hands in disgust. The preliminary reading of the report of the coroner's jury by Doc Farrar seemed meaningless. He stared out the window. There was a crowd of holiday proportions waiting to hear what happened. Many of them believed that Jed would not be held for trial, some hoped he would not, others demanded justice. Again he thought that it was a crowd which could become a mob at any untoward instant.

Reynolds was not on hand either. He was probably in Centro, making arrangements to clean up the town for the coming of the railroad which Cobre seemed to have lost. It was, at this moment, a complete debacle, with the worst yet to come when Finnegan cross-examined.

Into the maze of his thoughts the voice of Mr. Edward Evans penetrated, incisive, precise, low-pitched. "May we have the testimony of the arresting officer, your Honor?"

"Marshal Ben Hancock, take the stand."

Taggart was acting as bailiff, holding the stiff, new Bible purchased by the Woman's Auxiliary of I. O. O. F. and presented to the town. Hancock put his right hand upon it and tried not to tremble, tried not to look down at Laurie. He sat on a straight chair at the end of the dais. There was a problem with his hands; they seemed in the way, he did not know what to do with them, finally folded them in his lap, never more uncomfortable in his life.

"If you will just tell us what happened, in your own words, Marshal?" asked the prosecutor.

He told it as it had happened, his voice gaining resonance as he went along. When he had finished, Evans seemed satisfied but Finnegan now arose and addressed the court.

"Let it be noted, your Honor, that this witness did not actually see a crime committed."

"It is so noted," said Judge Grey. "Do you wish to cross-examine?"

216

"Only one small question, may it please the court," said Finnegan. He strode forward, thrust out his jaw and spoke directly, loudly to Hancock.

"This victim, this dead woman, she was an inmate of the house of prostitution operated by one Mrs. Jay?"

"Objection," said Evans. "Immaterial."

"Granted," said Judge Grey.

Hancock breathed in relief, but Finnegan was not finished.

"And were you not a customer of this house of ill repute, and was not the whore, Daisy, your favorite partner?"

"Objection," said Evans without altering his voice.

"Granted. You will confine yourself to the facts of the alleged crime," Judge Grey said to Finnegan. "This is an arraignment, not a trial."

Finnegan bowed and said, smirking, "Certainly, your Honor. No further questions."

Hancock hesitated, then arose and resumed his position at the edge of the dais. He had seen the shock on the face of Laurie, he had seen her change color, seen Brewster frown, seen Linda Darr smile thinly, seen Cole Strand grin from ear to ear. The damage had been done.

Oddly, he was now truly relieved. It had happened quickly, it was over. His mind cleared, he listened intently to the evidence as it was presented, detached, deeply interested but no longer concerned about himself. He kept his thoughts away from Laurie with dogged determination; that could wait until later.

217

He heard Linda Darr say coolly that she had really seen nothing, had only heard a scream and a shot, had found that Daisy was dead and had then retreated in search of Dr. Farrar. He heard Cora deny everything, including the fact that she had been in Madison's when Daisy was killed. He heard the Candlestick men repeat one after the other that they had been minding their own affairs and had heard nothing they could remember and had seen even less.

From the beginning it was apparent that Finnegan had one chance of gaining a dismissal, and only one. If no one had actually witnessed the killing, had seen the gun fired, there could be a tiny element of doubt. The worst that could happen might be admission to bail.

Without Madison and Dipple, the Territory had no eyewitnesses to the murder. Hancock wondered if they had been scared out of town or bought off by Matt. Either way, it was tremendously damaging and his mind leaped ahead to the consequences, to Laurie's reaction, to the burning anger of Mrs. Jay and others who detested Jed Buxton.

Then there were the others, openly relieved. Mayor Taggart was close to smiling outright. The city council would love to have Jed released and banished from Cobre. It might well solve the problem of the railroad, at least so they thought.

Oddly, Cole Strand was scowling, bending forward slightly as Finnegan began making his plea for this "poor, misunderstood young man who has been brutally mistreated by the law in this town of Cobre in the great Territory of New Mexico . . ."

Hancock put this attitude of Strand's away in his mind. Luke was easing down the crowded side aisle and he bent down from the dais to listen.

"Looks like we lost our little pigeon."

"Hell, everyone knows he did it," whispered Hancock. "We'll have him in the cage again. But he might get bail out of Santa Fe connections."

"You reckon?"

"Matt swings a lot of lead up there and they don't know anything excepting what Judge Grey's been able to tell them on the wire."

"You think Jed'll live to get out of the country?"

"That's another matter. Watch out that other window, will you?"

"For Madison?"

"I didn't think he'd run out like a chicken. And Dipple is tough. Maybe they're holdin' them someplace."

Luke looked across the courtroom. "They're all here, seems like."

"Matt's got twenty men on the range. Keep lookin' and check on Neddy if you can."

"I'll duck out," said Luke. "Be right back."

He edged back among the crowd, slid the door open and vanished. Finnegan was still rolling out his lawyer talk, a mixture of oratory and downright lies. Judge Grey looked as though he'd swallowed a lemon. Edward Evans was apparently not listening, leaning back, staring at the ceiling.

Finnegan was winding up. "And, your Honor, I ask this court to dismiss the charge against my client as unproven."

"Denied," said Judge Grey without hesitation. "Circumstantial evidence points to the fact that the dead girl was shot in the back with a bullet from the gun of the defendant."

"Exception," said Finnegan. He took a step toward the bench, all confidence. "Then, your Honor, may we speak of bail for this boy, that he might rejoin the bosom of his fine family and begin his life anew as a worthy citizen?"

Judge Grey looked gloomily at Edward Evans, who continued to stare at the ceiling. "You have no further witnesses, Counselor?"

Before the state's attorney could answer there was a stir in the audience. Laurie Van Orden stood up. Hancock looked at her, his heart contracting. She was dressed in gray, with a scarf about her bright hair, her face was pale and taut. Her voice was that of the practiced performer, scaled low, persuasive, emotional, pleading.

"Your Honor, may I address the court?"

"It is somewhat unusual, Mrs. Van Orden. However, in view of the — er — circumstances, you may speak."

"Objection," snapped Finnegan. "This lady was not in town when the killing occurred."

"This lady is the mother of the unfortunate girl," Judge Grey said. "I will hear her."

"Thank you." Laurie drew herself up, her voice rang out. "I, too, object. I object to bail for this murderer."

A wave of sound ran through the hall. Judge Grey rapped for order. Laurie went on, her words rushing from her.

"I have been here long enough to know that this man is a criminal. Yes, a known criminal, who breaks the law with impunity. His wealthy brother protects him. But he is a foul murderer who shoots girls in the back . . ."

Judge Grey rapped again. "Not proven, Mrs. Van Orden."

"Not proven? Why, then, who did murder my daughter? Those men?" She pointed a dramatic finger at the Candlestick riders. "That poor girl, Cora Jones? The missing witnesses? Tell me, who else was present when she died?"

"The law," began Finnegan at the top of his lungs. "The law . . ."

"The law is to protect the innocent and convict the guilty," Laurie cried. "Turn that killer loose on bail and allow him to intimidate or murder anyone who might testify against him? Is that justice? Is that your law?"

"I object," Finnegan was shouting.

Edward Evans, however, had awakened. He was now standing, resting his knuckles on the table, an imposing figure. He rapped out, "I concur in what the lady is saying, your Honor. I believe this man should be kept in jail until all possible attempts have been made to locate the missing witnesses."

From the back of the hall Luke Post's voice said, "It won't be necessary."

Everyone snapped around at full attention. Luke was inside the door. Coming through the portal were Jim

221

Madison and Monty Dipple. Behind them was Neddy Truman with his rifle sloped and his star shining in the morning light. For a moment there was bedlam in the courtroom.

Hancock, although startled, maintained a watch on the Candlestick people. He saw Matt's chin drop, saw Virgie touch her husband with compassion. He saw the riders stiffen, then exchange glances, shrugging, not looking at Matt. He saw Cole Strand smile and wondered at this.

He saw Laurie turn, recognize the situation, saw her hard smile, saw her seat herself, composed, satisfied but watchful. She did not look toward him nor in any way recognize that he was present.

Mr. Edward Evans did not resume his seat as he awaited the witnesses. It was as though someone had handed an unarmed man a gun, Hancock thought, that he might fight his battle against the enemy. The tall lawyer had Madison on the stand in a jiffy and was talking with him in even tones, smiling, encouraging the nervous saloonkeeper.

"You did not intend leaving town, did you, Mr. Madison? You did not intend to forget your duty to the court?"

"Well, no, sir," said Madison. "And then again — a man's tempted."

"Tempted by fear, sir?"

"Yep." Madison looked apologetically at Hancock. "I was scared. I'm scared right now." His gaze went to Matt Buxton. "But I seen it. I seen the girl die right on my floor."

"Ah, you saw it?" Evans spoke slowly, quietly. "Will you tell the court what you saw?"

"I seen them, Daisy and Jed. I seen them argufyin'. Laughin', she was. He cursed her. Then he slapped her. Then she ran and screamed — God, how she screamed. Then he shot her."

"Jed Buxton shot Daisy, otherwise Maureen Pomfret?"

"Daisy, she was. That's all I know. A little girl, a strange one. He shot her."

Finnegan said, "I object to the manner of this testimony."

"Overruled," said Judge Grey. "Cross-examine?"

Finnegan said sullenly, "No, sir."

"You may step down if there is no further evidence."

Madison said, "Yes, sir. That was it. That's what I saw."

Mr. Evans said, "That's enough. Mr. Monty Dipple."

Hancock was strung like piano wire as Monty told his story. The riders were closer together, excepting Larson, who seemed outside their periphery now, nursing his nose with one large hand, brooding. Matt and Jed sat low in their chairs, Virgie's face plainly showed her weariness and sorrow. Laurie was bright-eyed with attention.

Dipple was saying, "I seen it like Jim did. I pulled down on Candlestick when the marshal come in alone and without his gun. Jed, he kilt her. That's for real. No matter what anybody says, he kilt her."

"Cross-examine?"

Finnegan gathered himself, arose. "Mr. Dipple, may I ask why you were late to this hearing?"

"I object," said Evans.

"I'll allow the question," Judge Grey said.

Dipple hesitated, then he said, "Your Honor, I'll tell you. Testifyin' against Candlestick ain't healthy in this town. It took some thinkin'. We was still talkin', Jim and me, when Neddy Truman came at us with a rifle . . ."

"Objection!" cried Evans, his face angry.

Judge Grey said, "Sustained. We are going astray from the case."

Now Finnegan was raving. "It was just stated under oath that a deputy employed by this town brought these witnesses here under a gun, by force. Was there a warrant issued? Did he have authority to subject two citizens to force? I demand an explanation."

Dipple said blandly, "Oh, we was comin' in anyway. Neddy didn't know it, but we just made up our minds. Bein' scared of Candlestick is one thing, a dead little hoor, that's another."

The outcries came from several sources. Hancock poised, ready for action. There seemed no cause for action. Judge Grey merely pounded away with his gavel; soon there was quiet.

"If there are no further witnesses I will render a decision in this case instanter. Mr. Finnegan?"

Finnegan was talking in Matt's ear. Jed Buxton was lounging, contemptuous of the proceedings now, not caring, looking at his riders, winking at them.

Finnegan faced the bench and said, "It is obvious, your Honor, that we cannot set up a defense at this hearing. We will need time. I ask for a continuation . . ."

"Denied."

"Then I ask that trial be postponed until we can gather further evidence and bring in authorities who might alter the disposition of the case."

"Denied."

"Then we respectfully take exception. We have no witnesses at present." Finnegan sat down.

Judge Grey said, "It is the decision of this court that Jed Buxton be remanded to the custody of the town marshal in lieu of the sheriff and be detained in prison until one week from today, when a jury will be impaneled and trial held in the case of the Territory versus same Jed Buxton. Court is adjourned."

He gathered his robes about him and walked swiftly from the room. Hancock went forward. Luke came in from the rear of the hall and Neddy held his rifle ready on the periphery of the crowd. Taggart tremblingly opened the door and people began to file out. As the news spread swiftly among the assembled people, the noise began again.

Hancock went directly to the prisoner, the chains dangling in his hands. Matt said nothing, his face hard and stark, taking Virgie's arm, going up the aisle. The Candlestick men watched and then Hancock saw that Laurie and Brewster and Linda Darr and Cole Strand had not left and were also watching. He affixed the manacles.

225

Jed said, "You goddam bully lawman bastard. And you, brother, what good are you and your dumb lawyer? Law! Law! Damn the law to hell!"

Hancock said, "Out, Jed. Walk easy, boy. There are people around who'll get you if we don't watch out."

They walked out the door, Luke and Neddy trailing, guns ready, watching the crowd with all its many faces turned at them, all kinds of faces mirroring all kinds of feelings. They went back to the jail. Hancock's heart seemed to be beating in time with their slow march.

Laurie had not looked at him from the time he had been on the stand and Finnegan had made his accusation.

CHAPTER
TWO

Hancock walked Buxton Street beneath a moon which dimmed the oil lamps on their standards, lighting every nook and cranny in ghostly fashion. Madison's was open and the miners and cowboys and small farmers were talking among themselves and every man Jack of them, he felt, wondered what Matt would do now that a trial was certain and the verdict predictable. He paused outside the hotel and looked into the lobby.

Matt sat in his big chair as he had since the killing. Virgie sat behind him. Larson was nearby but the other riders were not in evidence. Everything seemed to have a meaning and Hancock was worried, far more concerned than he had been at any time until now. He looked up at the windows of the three rooms taken by Laurie and worried some more.

Luke and Neddy were on the job but he should have another deputy, he thought. Monty Dipple would have his shotgun ready but there was Madison, who could be picked off by a rifleman if he showed himself upon the street.

Hancock went in the side door and to Madison's office. The saloonkeeper sat at his desk, belching, taking powders, passing a hand over his forehead in curious fashion, his long nose appearing pink and damp.

"Ben."

"Jim. How you makin' it?"

"The hard way. I told a lie, you know."

"You were pullin' out?"

"Monty was agin it. Monty's got more guts than me, but I always knew that. Then Neddy come down with the rifle and I knew it was no dice. I had to testify."

"You sure you were goin' to pull out?"

Madison groaned. "I dunno. I dunno nothin'. Matt come in here and offered me plenty to get out. Wanted to buy the place — twice what it's worth. A man can only go so far, seems like."

"If I was you," Hancock told him, "I wouldn't mention Matt to anybody else. It might save your bacon."

"If he wants to take me, he can do it a dozen ways. Just didn't see where it would do any good to tell on him," Madison said. "I'm stayin' close. But if he wants me, he'll get me. You know it."

"Matt's no killer."

"No. But them riders. Dave Pitts and them. They set great store by their boy Jed. Don't worry about it, Ben. I nearly cracked up. I didn't. If they get me, the hell with it. I didn't want to pull out. I knew Monty was right. So I told. It's enough."

"Stay close until it's over," Hancock advised him. "Don't have any truck at all with Candlestick."

"You don't have to tell me. My stomach tells me."

Hancock said, "Well, reckon we don't have to worry about the railroad any more."

"Matt offered me plenty, said he'd see to it the town got the rails, make everybody happy. It was somethin' to think on, Ben. It was truly somethin' to study."

"Done some studyin' myself," Hancock assured him. "Thing is, we saw the gal on the floor. We heard the big mouth of Jed Buxton. It was too much."

"I never was a brave man," Madison told him. "I never counted myself too much. I dunno why I'm here. Monty, maybe; Monty can shame a fella. The gal, all that blood. Matt tellin' it nice and smooth, how he'd take care of everything and you know no man can take care of everything."

Hancock said, "You testified. It's all written down by Doc Farrar. No matter what happens, you did it."

"I did it." Madison sighed and took another powder.

Hancock got up and went to the door. "I'll do what I can if they go against you. Stay tight."

"No other way."

Hancock went through the bar and out the side door. Even the alleyway was full of moonlight. People did strange things in the full of the moon, he thought. Anything could happen tonight of all nights. Yet he did not know which way to look for the trouble.

He saw tall Jerry Kay at the door of the bank and they waved, then Hancock walked past the hotel again and spoke. "You thinking the same way I am?"

"I mind a time some boys wanted somethin' and they hit the bank first. Just to get attention. They got ten thousand dollars, too."

"I remember someone started a fire. Talked to Moriarty earlier, he's got volunteers ready."

"I'll sleep here tonight," the banker said. "If it comes trouble in town, I want in."

"There'll be trouble," Hancock assured him. "Thing is, I don't know from which way."

"Matt don't reckon to hurt people."

"I'm countin' on that."

"Set tight in the saddle," Kay said. "The hell with the railroad."

"Thanks." Hancock went on toward the jail.

From a hotel window across the street, Cole Strand watched and grinned skull-like. The room seemed too full of bodies. He turned and held up a key.

"Courtesy of young Johnny Hunter. He takes bribes. Nasty little bastard. But this will get your guns for you."

Dave Pitts nodded. The other two were young and uncertain but now they followed Pitts as they had followed Jed Buxton.

Strand said, "You two boys go down and just help yourselves. Mr. and Mrs. Buxton are safe in the lobby, eatin' out their hearts, doin' nothin'."

Sandy said weakly, "Matt promised her there'd be no killin' or nothin'."

"Right. No killing. I told you, over and over. We're helping Matt whether he likes it or not. This job don't call for killing. This here is a dream job. Nobody ever thought up anything like this job. Not in this country."

Dave Pitts ordered harshly, "Do like he says. Ain't you got a lick o' sense amongst you?"

"Wrap them in blankets." Strand stripped his bed. "Here, take these. No noise, understand?"

"But the horses," Sandy Farr objected. "What about horses? Jeb Truman is a rough old man, y'know."

"The horses will be attended to," Strand said. "Will you just do what I ask? It's for Jed and for Matt and the whole town so far's that is concerned."

Dave Pitts said, "Go git them guns."

They folded up the bedclothes and eased out into the hall. Strand squinted at Dave Pitts.

"What about those boys?"

"They will come along."

"All the way?"

Dave Pitts grinned. "Once in, how they goin' to get out?"

"You got brains," Strand said with satisfaction. "You see this whole rangdoodle."

"I see it good."

"South America," Strand said. "Sunshine and bananas. I been there."

"Women and booze."

"Beautiful," Strand told him. "And plentiful. Now remember, don't kill anybody. You got that straight?"

"I ain't got that itch," said Dave Pitts. "I'm a fast gun, sure, mebbe as fast as you. But I ain't cut down on anybody in over a year. Then it was to save Jed."

"I heard. So long as you remember. It's important. Kill the wrong one and we lose the loot."

"And our necks," said Pitts.

"No chance," Strand said. "You got all the details worked out? Timing, that's the knack of it. It's got to be timed to the instant, you understand."

"You done told me. About ten times."

"All right." There was a tap at the door and the riders came in staggering under the weight of rifles, short guns and ammunition. Strand had them arrange it all on the bed while each chose a weapon. He said, "The back stairs must remain clear. Sandy, you handle that. Anybody gets in our way you buffalo them. No noise."

"You bet no noise. Matt'd really be sore if he knew about this."

"Matt'll be the happiest fat man in the country when we pull it off," Strand said. "Keep that thought with you."

Farr went down the hall on tiptoe. Strand drew a deep breath and beckoned to the others. They left the room, leaving the door unlocked. They went toward the front of the hotel. They could see Sandy at the head of the stairs at the rear. Strand stopped in front of the door to Laurie Van Orden's makeshift sitting room and motioned the others to an exact position. He was counting heavily on the fact that Brewster disliked him and was not afraid of him. This portion of the scheme depended entirely on that, but he seldom made mistakes about his relations with people. He knew what they thought of him, Hancock and Matt and Luke and the rest of them. He did not care very much, he wanted only to take advantage.

He tapped upon the door, not too loud but with some decisiveness. After a moment Brewster opened up. Strand stepped back into the hall, drawing Brewster toward him. This put the Candlestick duo behind the Britisher.

Brewster said, "Really, sir, can't you learn that madam does not wish to see you?"

Strand kept his voice low. "Oh, she'll see me, all right."

The two riders had their guns drawn. There was a small oil lamp in a bracket upon the wall to give them light enough for their deed. They struck with the muzzles, one from each side. Brewster choked and fell forward and Strand hit him again at the nape of the neck.

"That'll do it." He took a coil of wire from his pocket. "Tie him good, boys, then bring him into the room."

He went through the door, paused, checked the room to the right, found it empty. Then he smiled most unpleasantly and went to the opposite door and opened it without ceremony.

Laurie was sitting up in bed wearing a nightgown and a silk wrapper. She opened her mouth to speak, saw the gun in Strand's hand, stared round-eyed.

He whispered, "Just get out of the bed. Put on something. Anything, but it better be good for a little journey."

"Are you mad?"

"Don't raise your voice. Don't talk at all," he commanded in the same sinister whisper. "I don't want to hurt you. Far from it. Get up, I tell you."

She put bare feet on the floor. There was no resistance in her; the cold steel of the gun, her knowledge of the character of the man were enough to make her obey. She reached for her gray traveling suit and he laughed a little. Realizing that it matched his costume, she rejected it, selecting a divided skirt and a blouse. He did not take his eyes from her.

There was a shuffle of slight sound, the grunts of men bearing a load in the room behind him. He saw the woman's eyes widen in horror and pain. He kicked the door shut and whispered, "Brewster is not dead because I don't want him dead. Just go ahead and dress and no tricks."

He sensed a difference in her. She had inwardly thrown off the shock and the fear. She opened a drawer and he said, "Steady, now. I'll kill you if I have to."

She removed a camisole and a pair of lacy drawers and long stockings and a small garter belt. She placed them alongside the skirt and took out a linen blouse. She deliberately, too deliberately, bent down to find a pair of riding boots. Then she faced him, standing near the open bureau drawer.

She removed the dressing gown. She was covered with only the most diaphanous material. Staring at him, she reached down and pulled the night garment gracefully and slowly over her head.

His throat caught as the drive struck him. For a split second his eyes filmed with desire. Then he leaped forward, striking with his bare fist.

She was dipping into the bureau drawer. He hit her as she grasped the butt of a small-calibered pistol. The blow caught her at the base of the jaw and drove her to her knees, semiconscious, fighting for breath.

"Very good," he whispered. "You tried. You got a sample of what you'll get if you try again. Now get dressed, fancy lady."

Numbly she donned the garments, found a serge jacket and a French beret she had brought from abroad. Her shoulders were bowed but he was not misled, he had seen the fire in her, the fire he had imagined upon first view of her back in Lordsburg.

He said, "You are a beautiful lady. Now we will take a walk. Down the back stairs, my dear."

He motioned with the gun and she went ahead of him. She faltered at the trussed and gagged body of Brewster, unconscious on the floor, but he nudged her sharply in the lower vertebrae and she moved again according to his wishes, going out the rear way of the hotel without incident.

Sandy Farr covered them as they went down the alley.

"It's a little notion I got. 'Course I've wanted to be alone with you since I first laid eyes on you. But this is business, purely business. Next time you get nekkid will depend on how the business goes. It'll be the choice of your old pardner, Ben Hancock."

She said, "You're mad."

"Not me." He chuckled. "Jed, now, that boy may be loco. He's got all the earmarks. It's him you'll have to watch out for."

"Jed Buxton?" Now she was astounded.

235

"Couldn't be helped. I found out he knows a hidey place in the hills. And I needed his boys and the onliest way to get 'em was to turn him loose."

"You'll get us all killed!"

"Now that would be a shame. You're too prime to be butchered just yet, lady. Keep that in mind, because I'm dependin' on you to make it all clear to Hancock, who ain't possessed of the purest brain."

"Make what clear?"

"That all will be fine and dandy if everyone does like I say. Worked it all out in my mind and I'm the one got the brains. You'll catch on."

They walked to Buxton Street. It was late enough for the streets to be nearly cleared of casual pedestrians. From the alley next to the *Copper Bulletin* came Dave Pitts, who gave a wave of the hand to indicate that all was clear. They came together and Dave said hoarsely, "Hancock's in his office. Luke's sleepin'. The kid's in the cells."

"Follow me close and take Luke. Leave Sandy outside. Has Muley gone for the horses?"

"He's bringin' up the back way. Stole two dandies right off the hitchin' rack; couple of waddies stone drunk and won't miss 'em until mornin'."

"Okay," said Strand. "Now, Mrs. Van Orden, shall we make a pleasant call? Remember, this gun hangs on a hair. It goes off loud and clear. Wouldn't be much left of your chest if it exploded like."

She said, "Ben will surely get you. Don't you know that?"

"He'll sure try, one day," Strand said. "Right now, he won't do anything but yell uncle. Nice and easy, please, dear lady."

He thrust the gun against her hard enough to make her wince, knowing that she would recognize force, that she was intelligent, aware — and dangerous until the plan was completed. They went up the stairs and into the office.

Hancock looked up. Seeing Laurie, he grinned widely and came to his feet in anticipation. Strand leaned against the wall, the gun trained upon Laurie's back, and growled, "Easy does it, Ben."

Hancock started, half spun, then realized the danger was to the woman rather than to him. "What's this, Cole?"

Dave Pitts came in, rolling on bowed legs. He went past Hancock and into the bedroom, his Colt in his fist. Hancock's head spun, he began to see what was happening. He leaned against the wall, gathering all his forces.

Strand said, "Little notion of mine. This lady, she said where people could hear, has got a million dollars. Too much money even for a beauty."

"You think so?"

"That's my notion."

Luke, bootless and sleepy-eyed, came into the office, Dave Pitts behind him. "What the hell's all this nonsense?"

"It ain't funny," Strand told him. "First, we're going to get Jed boy out of here. Then we're going to take a nice ride to a safe little place."

237

"That's a big order," Hancock told him.

"It would be. 'Ceptin' we're taking Mrs. Van Orden along with us for safekeeping. Safe for everybody."

Hancock licked his lips. "There's got to be more of it."

"The money. Cash. It'll be a bargain for youall," Strand assured him. "Two hundred and fifty thousand. Only a quarter of a million. Leavin' the lady plenty of loot. And the town, it gets rid of Jed boy. A nice clean deal."

"And how do you get this money from the lady?"

"Brewster will know," said Strand. "We left the limey nice and comfortable. The lady will sign a paper."

"Why should she?"

It was going well, Strand thought, with everything laid out and with Hancock extremely aware of the gun trained on the woman. Nothing else mattered. Everything would work out if the threat was centered upon her.

Dave Pitts growled, "Let's get outa here. The horses will be along and somebody might get nosy."

Hancock said, "So you're taking the lady along?"

"For safekeeping. Now will you please open that big door, makin' sure your shotgun boy don't get brave or somethin'?"

Hancock said, "Just a minute, Cole. About deliverin' this money, saying we can get it. What about that?"

Strand said, "Later, Ben, later. Now get that damn door open before something mean happens. You been around, you know when you're hamstrung. Act smart for once!"

238

Hancock said slowly, "Yes. I see it plain enough. Open the door, Luke. Call out, tell Neddy to put down his gun. It'll only hurt for a little while."

"It's hurtin' pretty good," Luke replied. "I don't take this kindly, Cole. Want you to augur on that."

"I already said my prayers," Strand told him.

Luke took the key from a hook. He went to the door, cracked it, said, "Neddy, put down the gun and come on out."

Neddy asked, "Are you crazy — 'put down the gun'? This gun has grown to be part of me. Have to amputate it."

Hancock said, "Put it down, Neddy."

"I don't understand." He came into the office empty-handed, stared, saw the revolvers in the hands of Strand and Pitts, saw Laurie's predicament. "Oh, that's it."

Strand said, showing the first sign of strain, "Dave, you get Jed out of there. Now, everybody keep real still, or the lady will get her bosom blown off."

He had to make it move swiftly, he realized. One slip and there would be a massacre. He could kill the woman without compunction but once the deed was accomplished he would not survive her for more than seconds. He had not the least desire for killing now, that would come later, he supposed, when things became tighter and the complications which he had foreseen from the inception of his plan became evident. He stood firm, managing a smile as Pitts took the big key and went into the cells.

Hancock said, "If you hurt her in any way, Cole, it'll be the last time for you."

"Wouldn't harm her for the world. It's the money we want," Strand said. "We'll let you know where to leave it. No bills bigger than a hundred. Make a nice package for us. When we get the money, you get her back."

"Supposing something prevents us from getting the money?"

Strand produced a stiff piece of paper. "This here is legal like. Gives Brewster power of attorney. Writ it myself. Get out your pen and ink there. The lady will sign it."

Laurie said, "I'll sign it, Ben." Her voice was harsh and steady. "Do as he says, for now."

Hancock pushed a penholder with a steel point and a tiny vial of black ink toward the front edge of his desk. Laurie signed the paper without reading it. Strand watched as Hancock sanded the signature and put the paper in his top drawer, ready for any overt move, sighing with relief as the marshal stepped away empty-handed.

Jed Buxton, rubbing his eyes, shaking sleep from himself, came into the office. His dull intelligence was scarcely equal to the moment. Strand commanded him sharply.

"Get outside. The horses are coming down the street. Mount and be ready to ride."

"Wh-where's Matt? Where's my brother?"

Hancock said, "Matt's not in this. He wouldn't be."

Strand snapped, "Matt'll be with us later. Get goin'!"

240

Jed went out the door onto the verandah. Strand balanced himself, holding the revolver on the woman.

Pitts said, "You take her along. I got these jaspers. They make a move, I'll cut all three of 'em down."

"Are you that fast?" Hancock asked him. "I wonder."

Strand knew what he had to do. He produced another small roll of wire. "Tie their hands. You'd better hold still, gents. I want a start, you can see that. It's hold still or be knocked in the head."

Pitts holstered his revolver and for a moment Strand thought Hancock would make his move. He stuck the revolver hard against the head of the woman. Hancock relaxed.

In a moment the three men were tied. Handcuffs were available in the cabinet; Pitts attached them to their ankles, most painfully.

Strand said, "Get a sheet and gag them." He went to the gun cabinet and smashed the locks of the weapons, one by one, against the edge of the big jail door. He picked Hancock's gun belt from the wooden peg and draped it over his arm. He searched for more weapons and found Luke's .32 and stuck it in a pocket. All this time he managed to keep his own Colt handy and one eye upon Laurie. He said, "Guess I'll be pretty unpopular around here after this. But then you lawmen never did care much for me."

Outside there was the sound of hoofs and creaking saddle leather and the low tones of Muley and Sandy telling Jed to keep quiet and mind orders. The three representatives of the law lay on the floor in an uncomfortable row.

Strand said, "I could put you in the cells. But time and tide awaits no man, my pappy always said. Make sure of that cash now, make damn sure of it."

He stared hard at them and saw that they realized every facet of the situation, which was all he could ask at the moment. He waved his gun at the woman. She was staring at Ben Hancock, utter compassion in her. But not fear. He exulted in that. He had been right about her from the first, she had no fear. There would be no hysterics. She would go — and she would pay the money.

He prodded her out into the street. A few people were staring, it was time to make haste. He put her on a horse and saw that she was at ease in the saddle — she knew how to ride, another boon. It was all nice and neat, he thought.

They mounted and rode without haste, going south on Buxton Street toward Broad, where they turned decorously westward, as though to take the Gary Road to the Buxton Ranch. They had put a hat on Jed and pulled it down over his eyes hoping no stray witness might identify him too soon. They put the horses to a trot on Broad Street to confuse prying eyes further.

But they were not going to the ranch. Strand would not have attempted this scheme without a hiding place. And for this he needed Jed and the riders. He needed them now, he amended, just until the money was turned over to him. After that — well, everyone to his own.

And the woman — he would have to study on the woman.

CHAPTER
THREE

Linda Darr sat behind her drawn curtain and fought with her sense of guilt. She heard the last jingle of bridle diminish up Broad Street toward Gary Road. She shuddered, wondering what had happened which she had not been able to see from her window.

There was guilt and a sort of triumph, also. Ben had rejected her. He was paying. The woman was gone, a captive in the hands of Jed Buxton and Cole Strand.

But she had contributed, she now knew. A bowl of chile at the Mexican's, some kind words from the man in the gray habiliments, a bit of flattery which she had seized as though it were a lifeline, and she had talked. She had opened her big mouth and told all — or almost all. She had imagined things about the woman and Ben in New York and she had made fun of him, the country boy, and the woman, the lady millionaire. She had answered all the questions and volunteered some answers of her own.

Now she sat doubled over, stomach muscles cramped, wondering if the blank front of the jail concealed corpses. Had she been the partner of murderers, she and her talk? Was Ben Hancock weltering in his blood, as had the little girl on the floor of Madison's?

She managed to straighten up and went through the shop to her bedroom. She struck a match and the sulphur odor choked her and she remembered a poor whore in Montana who had committed suicide by swallowing a packet of such matches and the odor of death smothered her, so that she cried out. When the lamp was finally lit she raised it, staring at her haggard features in the mirror which had so recently given her back a roseate reflection. Did she hate Hancock that much?

In panic she began to throw on clothing, careless of the selection, careless of everything excepting her haste to go somewhere and tell someone. If she had a close friend — but she did not, she realized now, of a sudden. She had never made friends. Her one goal had been marriage.

She ran out the rear door and up the alley, remembering Hancock and Larson fighting in the street. She started across toward the jail but found that she had not the courage to look for herself at the damage. She started down the street, her steps uncertain. At the hotel she wavered, seeing Matt Buxton and Virgie and the foreman still sitting in a tight circle. Then she went in, crying, "There's trouble at the jail, bad trouble!"

They came up as one and Matt demanded, "What trouble? Is Jed all right?"

"They took him out," she said. "Strand and your men. I saw them ride out. They had a woman with them. It must have been Mrs. Van Orden."

244

Matt said, "Larson, get down there." He spoke gently to his wife. "Want to go up and check on the lady?"

Virgie said, "Cole Strand? God help us all."

Matt said, "Better rouse the judge, too. He'll know what to do. Steady now, girl."

He went out after Larson. From behind the desk the mousy Mrs. Hunter crept to Linda and patted her arm.

"You look faint like, Miss Darr."

"I've never fainted," she said. "Never."

Then the blackness came down and Mrs. Hunter, a woman who had never patronized her, who had scarcely exchanged words with her, supported her gently to the chair, and soothed her with small sounds of sympathy.

The taste of soiled sheet was only part of the poison that ran through the nightmare of Ben Hancock. He lay still, refusing to fight against the wire cutting into his wrists. He wished he could tell Neddy not to torture himself by threshing about in an attempt to be free. The wormwood was deep enough but the gall would come with their discovery — the lawmen of Cobre trussed up like pigs for the sticking.

Much deeper was his fear for Laurie, his rage against Cole Strand. He lay there with pictures running through his mind, knowing the carnality of the gunslinger. Five of them, including the vile youth, Jed Buxton, would have her at their mercy — what mercy? He knew her vitality, her inner toughness, but it was no consolation to him.

He shut his eyes and tried to think of solutions. None came to him, not a single one. Strand had them to rights, he had the woman, they all had to reckon with that one fact. There was nothing to do but pay off — if that were possible — and then race Strand to the nearest port of departure. The gunman would not dare stay in the country, Hancock estimated. Too many people would rise up in anger at the kidnapping of a woman — any woman.

Saliva choked him, he swallowed with great difficulty, feeling as though he were drowning and smothering at the same time. The utter helplessness of his position was shattering, he had never before been bound hand and foot. He made himself think of the actual happening, going over it from the moment he had seen the gun pointed at Laurie. Had there been a moment when one of them might have acted? Would it have been better to attack, try and knock away Strand's Colt, take a chance? Would Laurie have been better off?

He knew the answer. Life was precious, life was everything. One could endure. Only the snuffing out of the lights was final, eternal. If they did not kill her or cripple her, she was better off alive. It all depended now upon Strand, of all people. Jed Buxton was bestial, a freak, he would commit any act to satisfy his impulses. The riders were ordinary men, excepting perhaps Dave Pitts, but they were no match for either Jed or Strand.

He tensed every muscle, fighting to control himself. Someone would come along. It was surprising that someone had not checked before now. He had lost track of time but knew it was not yet midnight. The moon still shone boldly on Buxton Street and again Neddy was struggling to get loose.

Then Larson was staring down at him. The foreman of Candlestick had come in on tiptoe, wary, suspicious. There was a flicker of pleasure in his eyes, but it evaporated as he stared around and took in the entire scene.

Larson knelt and removed the gag. "Pincers?"

"In the lower drawer," Hancock choked.

The foreman found the cutting pliers and snipped the wires. Hancock sat up and rubbed his wrists. There was blood on them, but Neddy's were worse. Luke seemed better off. Larson propped them all against the wall and looked into the empty cell block.

"Strand, the lady said. Linda Darr. She saw 'em ride out."

"That was an hour ago," Hancock blurted, then was silent. Linda had taken her time, all right, but she had given the alarm and that would have to be enough.

Luke said, "That Cole, he don't miss much. He took our keys. He busted the guns. He's got Laurie."

"All three riders?" asked Larson.

"All three."

The foreman's face darkened, his mouth twisted. "Damn pukin' fools."

"Not so foolish," said Hancock. He saw Matt Buxton come rolling in and nodded to him. "Mind getting Jeb Truman? He'll have to cut these cuffs loose."

Matt stood foursquare, staring down. "Cole Strand and my three riders, eh?"

"And Jed."

Matt said, "You know I wasn't in on it."

"You wouldn't take a woman. They want two hundred and fifty thousand dollars."

Matt said, "Haven't got a chance to raise that much cash. Don't think the town could raise it."

"Strand's counting on Mrs. Van Orden. Take a look at the paper there on the desk."

Matt looked, nodded. "May work. Virgie's checkin' at the hotel. Hell of a thing, Ben."

"You could put it even stronger."

"Strand. Should've run him outa town."

"He wasn't breaking any law."

"Might know he would, though. Had a notion," said Matt. "Gave him a hint he didn't take. Damn it to hell."

"Your brother's loose," Hancock said wearily. "That's what you wanted."

"Not thisaway," Matt said dully. "Larson, better saddle up."

"No," said Hancock.

"What do you mean, no?"

"The woman," Hancock said. "We'll have to wait for notice of where to put the money. We'll have to get hold of the money. Send a posse out and they'll kill the woman before you can get to them."

Larson said, "I be damned if I'll ride out, Matt. I don't know the woman nohow, but Hancock's right."

"You think Strand won't kill Jed? You know how it is with Jed? You know he won't take orders."

"Strand may kill him," Hancock said. "And the woman. And the Candlestick boys. Strand's real handy at it. But nobody rides after them until we see how it goes."

Matt started to say something, then his eyes hooded. He grunted, "Get yourself fixed up and come see me." He lumbered out of the office. Larson hesitated, then remained. Blood was trickling from the wrists of Neddy. Larson went to the water pitcher, found a soft cloth and knelt beside the youth, awkwardly bathing the wounds caused by the wire.

The foreman mumbled, "Hope y'all know how I feel about this. My own men and all."

Hancock said, "Not your fault."

"Cole Strand," Luke said. "Always thinkin' up something. Almost smart."

"He's got all the cards this time." Hancock made a terrific effort to keep his voice calm. "We can't make a move until he says so."

"Sure. He's got the cards. Let's see him play them."

Larson asked, still uncertain as to his welcome, "You reckon Jed'll cross him, don't you?"

"It plain don't interest me," Hancock told him.

"He'll sure as hell kill Jed if he crosses him," Larson continued. "Matt'll hurt bad if that happens."

Hancock's attention came to a sharp point. "It would be interestin' to know where they'll hole up. Strand wouldn't know any place; this country's not his."

"Lots of places in the hills, since he knows we can't go out after him," Larson said quickly.

"I mind Jed and the boys had a place," Hancock said. "Nobody could find them. Old Buck looked and looked, had a couple Apache friendlies lookin'."

"You mean the time of the Mex gal trouble?"

"You remember," Hancock told him.

"Wasn't with 'em," Larson answered. "Matt had things for me to 'tend to."

"That's right." Hancock shifted the subject. "Funny thing. Dave Pitts had a gun. They busted our long guns but they never did look in the closet for the ones you and them checked with Luke."

Larson straightened up with his basin of bloodstained water, went to the door, emptied it carefully off the end of the verandah, walked back inside. He said, "I work for Matt Buxton. Him and me, we didn't have anything to do with taking the lady. Nor with breakin' Jed outa here. Anything else you want to know, ask Matt. I'll be goin' along now."

"Larson," Hancock said.

The big foreman stopped. "Yeah?"

"The closet at the end of the gunrack. Your Colt's in there."

Larson said stolidly, "I'll pick it up when Matt says so." He tromped out of the office and went down the street toward the hotel.

Luke remarked, "That straw boss ain't happy about anything right now."

"He knows something," Hancock said.

"Could be."

Neddy said, "The way they did it. With the lady. I never did hear of anything like it."

"Cole Strand," Luke said. "It'll be his last rangdoodle. He's got no way outa this one. He gets his hands on that money he'll grow wings and fly away if he can manage it."

Meantime, Laurie was in his hands, Hancock thought. Worse, there was no way to get at him and his companions. The clank of tools announced the arrival of Jeb Truman, all concern and indignation.

Truman said, "Dangedest thing I ever heard of. Doc is takin' care of the Britisher. They buffaloed him pretty bad, seems like. Lemme get those irons off you."

Hancock listened to the talk, the explanations, the exclamations, the execrations. All he could think of was Laurie. A raging ball of fire was building in his guts; he felt the nerve-strain down to his toes. He had to get to Brewster, arrange for the ransom, have it delivered as per Strand's instructions wherever and whenever designated.

Then he wanted action.

CHAPTER
FOUR

She had ridden astride before, the western saddle was a boon, the moonlight was so bright that she had no problem among the rocks and slippery terrain of the mountain. The numbness had been banished by fear, then the deep strength of her had taken firm command. Now her intelligence was working. Her knowledge of men came to her defense. She maintained silence throughout the diatribe of Jed Buxton, his recriminations, his mouthing of obscenities directed at her and at the dead Maureen — Daisy, of course, because no one in Cobre had known Maureen, not even Ben Hancock.

Rescue, she realized at once, was out of the question. No one would dare ride to save her because of the danger to her life. If she had doubt that Cole Strand would kill her, which was reasonable, certainly Jed would commit the act without compunction, without a second thought.

They had gone down the Gary Road to the ranch and Dave Pitts had vanished, then reappeared leading a pack horse laden with provisions appropriated from the store at Candlestick. Then they had circled, she realized, doubling back toward Cobre but mounting high into the hills. Now they were in the Burro

Mountains, she thought, remembering that Ben had named them for her and Brewster en route to the cemetery. Not that it mattered, they were riding single file on a narrow ledge of rocky trail, ascending, it seemed in the brilliant night, to the top of a mountain peak. It was a barren trail, without vegetation, but below there was an *arroyo* filled with pines which grew smaller as they climbed.

They were, she thought, not so far from town as the crow might fly, but in a most inaccessible position. They came abruptly to a plateau and there was the sound of water trickling as Jed Buxton threw up a hand, important, the leader, halting them. She saw the dark mouth of a cave in the wall, and here grew yucca and some tangled brush.

"This here is it. Found it all by myself. Hid out here when things got too mucked up."

Strand rode from behind Laurie, pulling up beside Jed but apart from him. His voice was an octave lower than that of the youth and crisp with command.

"Boys, you mind unpacking? The lady's bound to be wore out. We make a fire tonight. Some hot coffee, grub will help us all. Got a lantern, Dave?"

"Yeah," said Pitts. "I been here before. Cave's right deep."

"We can make a fire in there," Jed said, trying to recapture the leadership. "Homemade flue, right through the ceilin'. Smoke goes driftin' down the canyon yonder."

Strand ignored him. "Mrs. Van Orden, if you care to dismount, we'll make you as comfortable as possible."

Jed snarled, "Make her comfy, make her comfy. The hell with her. Mother of a whore!"

Strand slid to the ground and looked up at the youth. "Mouthy, ain't you, Jed? All mouth. Well, I'll admire for you to keep it shut awhile."

"Who made you boss of this outfit?" Jed swung down lightly, whirled around, spreading his arms. "This here is my hidey place. These here are my boys. How'd you get so uppity of a sudden?"

Strand let the words hang in the air a moment, then spoke to Pitts, who was standing by as Muley and Sandy removed the pack from the lead horse. "Tell him."

"Cole figured this out," Pitts said. "We agreed to let him run it."

"You did what? You work for Candlestick. I rep Candlestick here."

"Reckon we don't work for Candlestick now," Pitts said. "Fifty thousand apiece, that's what we're workin' for. Kindness of Cole and this here lady."

"I be damn if anyone's gonna boss me." Jed's voice was too high, Laurie thought; he was on the verge of hysteria. "I been in that jail and I don't like it. I don't know where everybody was when I was in that jail."

"You ain't makin' any sense, Jed," Pitts told him. "Cole figured how to get you out. Why don't you simmer down?"

"Muley? Sandy?" The voice became a whine. "What kind of rangdoodle is this here?"

Muley Ward said, "We voted. You wouldn't be here if we didn't agree."

Now Strand became conciliatory. "It's all right, Jed. You're among friends. Just take it easy and we'll all be rich."

"I'm already rich! I'm Matt's brother. Whereat is my brother, anyways?"

Strand shook his head sadly, again turned to Pitts. He was playing it carefully, Laurie saw, building his leadership step by step without seeming to use power.

Pitts said, "Uh, now, Matt ain't in on this. You know he wouldn't go for it, Jed. He got Virgie to bring in the guns, sure. But he wouldn't let us have 'em."

"You mean him and Larson are agin this?" demanded Jed.

"We didn't rightly give 'em notice."

"Matt was goin' to leave me to stand trial?"

"We didn't wait to ask. Fifty thousand apiece, that ain't exactly straw for the cowbarn."

Jed walked in a small circle, his hands flapping at the ends of his long arms. He was confused. He stopped to peer at Laurie. "The whore's mother. She's got all that money?"

"Watch your language, Jed," Strand said. "She's got it."

"And we got her." Jed was looking her up and down in the light of the moon. A grin stretched his loose features. "Hey! How about that? You done good, boys. You done real good."

Muley Ward and Sandy Farr had finished unpacking and were now attending to the horses. Dave Pitts went to lend them a hand. Cole Strand never took his eyes from Jed, speaking slowly and distinctly.

"You won't lay a hand on Mrs. Van Orden. Understand?"

"Ha!" said Jed. "We got her, ain't we? There's no dames in jail, y'know. I been a week without. She's old, but she don't look so bad."

Patiently, Strand said, "You heard me. No dice."

"Wait'll the boys have been here a few days," Jed jeered at him. "We'll see about the old dame."

"You don't know me very well," Strand said ruminatively, standing hipshot. "I keep forgettin' you don't listen very much and you don't read anything. I keep forgettin'."

He made a move Laurie never did quite follow, a gun barrel flashed, several shots echoed among the high rocks, giving off echoes that bounded back and forth among the precipices and their walls. Splinters flew from the sheer wall close to the opening of the cave.

Strand said, "Take a look, boy. If you find one you can't cover with your hand, I'll buy you a new hat."

There had been five bullets fired. They had grouped together inside the diameter of a playing card, a quintet of scars in the stone face of the cliff. Laurie watched Jed, saw the strong effect such swift marksmanship had upon the youth, recognized fear in the boy who had killed her daughter. Her mind was working normally now. Nebulous plans began to take form. Strand was showing his teeth, bowing to her.

"Hope I didn't startle you, ma'am."

"I am startled. And impressed," she said. His tone had altered; he was, in his manner, wooing her. He was balancing the whole endeavor, playing it out step by

256

step, she thought. He wanted the money — and he wanted her.

Dave Pitts was looking at Strand, walking back to where Jed was all apart again, wagging his hands, wordless. The Candlestick rider drew his own gun and fired five times.

The result was not so neat as the pattern made by Strand, but it was good enough. Now conditions had subtly altered, Laurie thought.

Pitts observed, "This here scheme, it's yours, Strand. But don't try and scare anybody."

"I wouldn't think of it," Strand told him. "Just tryin' to keep your boy in line. You doubt he needs it?"

"Could be. Only we know him good. We rode with him. Maybe we ain't Candlestick no more. We want him out of reach of the hangman."

"I'm giving you a chance. See that you play it with all the cards on the table," Strand said.

Now the two gunmen were face to face. Laurie hugged herself. One false move and her life would be forfeit, she thought. If the cowboys opened fire on Strand, he had no chance. She would prefer to be caught in the barrage rather than be alive at the mercy of Jed Buxton. She had no real fear of the others, only of Jed. Her body had been a vessel for men whom she did not love, she could endure indignity if necessary to gain a point. But the thought of being forced by the killer of Maureen was too much. She closed her eyes.

Strand said, "Fifty thousand dollars. South America. *Señoritas*. I'm givin' all that to you."

257

In the background Sandy Farr breathed, "Yeah. What's the use of fussin'? Let's get the money. How do we go about it, Cole?"

"When Jed boy settles down, we'll talk about that."

Dave Pitts said, "Just so everybody understands everything."

"Fifty thousand," Jed echoed. "Okay, Strand. Okay."

The moment of danger was past — averted for the time being, Laurie amended. She managed a tremulous, "I'm very weary. Could I lie down, please?"

Strand was all good manners. "The boys have your blankets all ready. There'll be food right soon."

He led her into the low-ceilinged but deep cave, a freak of the ice age, angled slightly to the north, wide enough to accommodate a span of four oxen. On previous occasions the Candlestick men had brought up pine boughs to make rude sleeping nests and it was in one of these, moved far apart from the others, deep around the bend of the cave that Laurie's blankets had been arranged. She lowered herself onto the springy makeshift bed and was surprised at its resilience.

Strand said, "Nobody's goin' to harm you, Mrs. Van Orden. I'll want a small note about the money." He produced a tablet and a pencil. "You might be thinkin' on what to say."

"The money — that is nothing." She lowered her voice. "Allowing Jed Buxton to escape — that's everything."

A small fire, ignited by Pitts, flared up, and she saw the man's strange eyes alter, go bleak. For a moment

258

she thought he was going to make a proposition about Jed, but he shook his head.

"Them boys stick together. Not saying they won't be caught before they get out of the country."

"That's not good enough for me. I'd pay to have him brought to trial."

"Not a chance, ma'am. Sorry."

"You're not sorry. I'm sorry." She turned her face away from him and rested against the rough blanket. She was sore from the ride but not disabled. She put her mind resolutely to work.

Astounding, she thought, but she had not yet had time to con her deepest disturbance. She had deliberately put it aside. She had, even before the entry of Strand, attempted not to dwell upon pictures of what had happened between Maureen and Hancock . . .

Now it was absolutely not the time to think about it, about Ben and what he meant to her. Now was the time to use every ruse, every device to remain alive and whole and to seek the downfall of Jed Buxton.

Hancock's sleep had been a continuous nightmare. He came into the office and sat for a long time staring at the big oaken door behind which he had failed to keep Jed Buxton. There were footsteps on the verandah and he spun around to see Prentice Reynolds entering. He did not arise.

"Reynolds."

"Well, Marshal. Not a good morning for you."

"No."

"Thought you might like to have some good news. We ran into something at Centro. It seems the town is the distributing point for the Mexican weed that's been causing trouble there — and here and other places. Unless it's cleaned up, Centro is out."

"The railroad's the lawgiver, huh?"

"Whatever you want to call it." Reynolds stiffened. "You're not very friendly."

"No. I'm not friendly."

"The kidnapping, now that's another matter."

"Sure. It's fine Jed got away but the rest of it is just something to toss to the hogs."

"I understand the lady's a friend of yours. I'm sorry."

"Sorry, my left hind foot. You and the railroad and this goddam town," said Hancock. "You can go to hell."

"That attitude will not get you anyplace, you know."

"It'll get me out of here when I get Mrs. Van Orden away from your friend Jed and that nice Cole Strand," Hancock told him. "Just don't bother me, will you, Reynolds? Just go and make palaver with Mayor Taggart and them."

"Indeed, I shall do just that." The railroad man wheeled around. At the door he said, "Of course you won't be running for sheriff."

"I wouldn't run for dog catcher in this burg. Goodbye, Reynolds. I hope you choke."

The door slammed. It had not been politic nor even very satisfactory to lay it on the line for the man, but Hancock felt a little better. He looked at his watch. It was almost time for the stage. If he was correct, the message from Strand would come in with the driver.

Easiest way would be to stop the stagecoach and use it for that purpose. With all the cards in the deck in his possession Strand would take the simplest way, he thought.

Luke Post came in. The dapper little gambler had never looked so hacked, depressed and angered, Hancock thought.

"Hear anything?" he asked.

"Not a word," said Luke. "Only a bunch of gas around town. Madison is still scared. Matt Buxton sits in the lobby of the hotel and looks glum."

"Matt wasn't too happy about it."

"Strikes me kinda funny. I figured he'd be the kind wouldn't care about Laurie too much. Just so's his damn brother got free."

"A man like Matt, he ain't bad. I keep sayin' that. Sure, he'd bust Jed out if he saw a clear way to do it. This is a horse from a different stable."

"I'd give two bits to know what he's thinkin'," said Luke moodily. "I'd give a lot more to know where they got Laurie cached."

Hancock walked out of the office and onto the boardwalk. Luke followed, still scowling, looked at the mountains as the marshal spread his hands.

"You see 'em? Everywhere you look. They got a bunk up there, God knows where. They got high gun on us, Luke. The dirty rotten buzzard-bastards. Even if we knew, what good? They got high gun."

Luke said, "I know it. I hate to admit it but I know it."

"I better see how it is with Brewster," Hancock said. He had trouble with his hands when Laurie and her captors were mentioned, they seemed to shake a lot. "Doc says he ought to make sense this morning."

"I'll be waiting." Luke went up the steps. He seemed diminished, as Hancock felt diminished. Neddy Truman was home in bed with a fever and Hancock thought he knew the cause of that too. Cole Strand had put them down, he had bested them. The fire started in his gut again and he walked faster to keep it from exploding.

People went about their business as usual in Cobre. It seemed to Hancock that their step was lighter, their expressions smug. Prentice Reynolds had unquestionably given the partial good news to Taggart, who had spread it thick on the town. The railroad was a cinch now, all was well in the world.

Speedy Jackson popped out to say, "Stage is late. Reckon you're right, there'll be news."

"Bad news. No other kind," Hancock answered, going on to Dr. Farrar's office, where Brewster was being cared for in the back room which served as an emergency hospital.

"Give him a couple of hours," suggested the doctor. "He suffered a bad concussion. He's very strong, however."

"You wouldn't know how much chance there is of him getting two hundred and fifty thousand dollars together, would you, Doc?"

"I'd say it was difficult." He peered at the marshal. "You're under too much strain, Ben. Let me give you a sedative."

"Who, me?" Hancock recoiled. "Stuff like that's for women and Jim Madison. You lay off me. I'll be back when the stage gets in."

He plodded into the bank and sought Jerry Kay. In the small, stuffy private office at the rear he asked again, "How can anybody get a quarter million in cash together?"

"I can't," Kay said sadly. "Matt can't. Between us, we can't raise it."

"Matt?"

"He'd put it up if he had it. Responsibility is a two-way road, Ben. Jed's with the gang that got the lady."

"Should've thought of that," Hancock acknowledged. "Give 'em the money, get Laurie back, then see what we can do."

"T'aint likely to be easy," warned Kay. "Strand is a smart donkey. He'll hamstring you as good as he can."

"He's got to get flat outa the country," Hancock said. "After we get her back I'm takin' off after him."

"He's got the capital to make a good run, if we can raise his purse. There's enough of 'em to make a stand any old place."

"There could be a hundred of 'em, I'll be after 'em."

The ex-cowman regarded Ben kindly. "You all tightened up, friend. Reckon what they're sayin' about you and the lady is true, eh?"

"My business, Jerry."

"Right. Well, don't get yourself kilt now. Anything I can do, you come to me."

Hancock went into the bank. Gus Mueller and Mayor Taggart were making deposits, talking briskly and happily together. He ignored their greeting, striding past them to the street. The stage was coming in. He hastened his steps, running to the Wells Fargo office.

Reb Johnson swung down before Mitch could bring the stage to a stop. He ran to Hancock and thrust an envelope at him. "Thought it was a damn holdup, then we seen it was Dave Pitts. He gimme this and said take it to you pronto. What the hell's goin' on?"

"Trouble," Hancock told him. "Speedy'll tell you all about it. He's fairly busting with it."

He walked down to the office with the envelope in his hand. Luke was waiting for him. He sat down behind the desk and stared at the epistle.

"Know how you feel," Luke said.

"Sick and scared," Hancock admitted.

"Might's well open it."

"Yeah. Might's well." He slit the envelope with his clasp knife. He took out a folded sheet of paper covered with careful, round handwriting. He began to read aloud:

Dear Ben:
    Two hundred and fifty thousand, remember? Nothing over a hundred-dollar bill. I'm givin' you time seeing I am in such good company, ha, ha.

His hands shook again and Luke took the paper from him and went on:

When you get the money you go out to the graveyard and build a fire can be seen from up high. In this here country that is a cinch way of doing. Then you go to my room and get my things and pack them good. I'm careful, like we said, about my duds. Put the money in carpetbags. You hire a rig and drive out alone to the place on Gary Road where the wire is cut. You remember, where Buck was scalped? Then you get back to town. Three hours later come and get the lady, alone again, no tricks. We got a way to know. You better do this like I say, Ben, because I will otherwise turn the lady over to Jed. You know me. What I say goes. All I want is a start with the loot, you better give it to me. Yours very truly, Cole Strand.

Hancock stared at the wall. Luke put down the paper as though it was burning his fingers.

"He's got it figured to the nubbin."

"Three hours. They'll be a long piece down the road."

"Let's get the money, if we can," Luke said. "Don't dwell on it."

"I got to think how to get them."

"They got a watch, wherever they are. Better give in to 'em, get on the trail when she's back with us."

"I'll talk to Brewster. To everybody we know."

Luke said kindly, "You got to loosen up. You need some sleep."

Hancock picked up the paper and replaced it with care and put the envelope in his pocket. "Thanks, Luke. Do me a favor, get hold of Taggart and tell him to call a town meetin' this afternoon."

"Maybe I better spread the word like?"

"You do that."

He went out again onto Buxton Street, where he had walked so often among friends, the keeper of law and order. Ignoring all else, he plodded down to Dr. Farrar's office. The sun was rising high, bestowing its glare upon the town, removing the generous shadows and the reflections of color. There was not, he thought, two hundred and fifty thousand dollars in cash in all of New Mexico. Only Brewster could possibly produce such a sum and even then it would take time — time while Laurie was in the hands of Cole Strand — and Jed.

Luke was right, he needed sleep, he had to get hold of himself. His guts were watery, dirty pictures formed in his mind asleep or awake. He was not a man who thought evil but this was something new and different. He was in the grip of revulsion and rage such as he had never before experienced.

He went into the doctor's office and was startled to see Linda Darr seated behind the desk reading a newspaper. He said, "Well, mornin', Linda."

"Ben." She was nervous, putting down the paper, rising. "I'm — Doc had to make a call. I've been helping with Brewster."

"Well, fine. How is he? Brewster, I mean?"

"Doc says you can talk to him. But not for long." She went to the door leading to the hospital room, paused, did not turn. "Ben?"

"Yes?"

"That Cole Strand. He asked questions. I answered him."

"Yeah. I saw you at the hearing."

"I'm sorry, Ben. I was — upset. I talked too much."

He said, "Linda, it don't matter. Man like Cole, he'd learn what he wanted to know. He fed coins to little Johnny Hunter. He's one of those hombres who can learn things."

She turned to him then and her face was pale and drawn. "I keep seeing Daisy. On the floor. I wake up screaming."

Her agitation calmed him, oddly, alleviating his own fears. "No use to think on it. We do what we can is all."

"The town," she went on distractedly. "The town just don't care. Mr. Reynolds is saying the railroad is coming. That's all they talk about."

"Human nature is a critter." He found himself trying to calm her. "They don't know Laurie. They only know Jed's off their hands. They don't know we got to raise a quarter-million dollars to get Laurie back."

"A quarter million — that's impossible!"

"I think I better see Brewster now." It was, he thought, impossible all right. It was something only the Britisher could answer. He went past her into the antiseptic white-painted room.

Brewster's head was encased in bandages, propped upon two feather pillows. His color was bad but his eyes were clear. He stared at Hancock in complete despair.

"Have you any news, sir? I mean — Marshal; she asked me not to say 'sir,' you know."

Hancock said, "Bad news. They want money. We can't get at them because they'd sure kill her if we did."

"How much money?"

"Two hundred and fifty thousand dollars."

Brewster said, "My God in heaven, they are mad!"

"She told Matt she had a million."

"Of course. More than that. But English estates take months, years to be settled," Brewster replied. "There were details we neglected when news came of the child's disappearance. What cash she has is her own. I doubt there's ten thousand of it left. No more, certainly."

"It figured," Hancock said.

"Marshal, what can you do?"

"Try to raise the money," said Hancock dully. "I got a few friends."

"I must get up from here," Brewster said, twisting on the pillows. "The doctor forbids me. But I must."

"Take your time, do what Doc says. I'll be working on it, believe me."

"I know you will. She thinks the world of you, Marshal." Brewster's face resumed its normal calmness, he looked straight at Hancock. "She believes in you."

"We'll get her loose from them, one way or another. You take it easy now. May need you later."

"I am very strong." Brewster touched the bandages. "They struck me several times, you see."

"Yes. With gun barrels," Hancock said. "You'll get your shot at them. I promise it."

"I, too, believe in you," said the Britisher. "God go with you, Marshal."

"Thank you." No one had mentioned God before, Hancock thought dryly, going out into the office. Linda was sitting at the desk again.

She said, "I'm praying for her, Ben."

"You and Brewster," he told her. "Thanks."

God wasn't much thought about on the frontier, he knew. He walked toward the bank. The preachers in Cobre were spineless, poor descendants of the padres, of Jedediah Smith and his Protestant Bible, nothing compared to the Mormons over in Utah. Religion took form and lost allure, but when he was a small boy he had gone to Sunday School and to church. His father had been a praying man, tough as shoe leather but humble before God. If it would save Laurie, he would say a few prayers himself.

CHAPTER
FIVE

The afternoon was waning. Dave Pitts had returned
and was now seated on a rocky promontory, only his
hat showing, keeping watch through binoculars. Cole
Strand sat near Laurie's niche, now and then regarding
her with amusement — and desire. Jed Buxton stalked
about, strutting, completely taken with Strand's coup,
bragging about what he would do with his share of the
money, occasionally sneering at Laurie, not sure
enough of himself to indulge in further abuse, ordering
Muley and Sandy to perform trivial tasks from time to
time. The cowhands obeyed, shrugging, accustomed to
him, keeping the peace in their own fashion, she
imagined.

There was no doubt who was in charge and who was
second in command. Strand handled them in an
offhand manner which forbade discussion. Dave Pitts
and his gun were totally removed from his former
companions, dedicated to the leader. She had remained
quiescent, accepted the coarse food with thanks,
keeping her eyes open and her mind active.

No one was more aware than she that the money
would not be forthcoming from her purse. That part of
it depended upon Hancock, she knew. If he failed she

270

was lost. She had no illusions about that part of it —
rape and, hopefully, a quick bullet in the head.

If it were only the cowboys, she might have managed,
she thought. They were polite, even bashful in her
presence. Pitts did not seem to be a rapist; he was a
killer, a lover of whores whom he could buy at will. It
was Jed she had to fear — and Strand in a different
fashion.

They were, in her mind, simple men. She had known
many with brains and imagination to spare. Even Cole
Strand should know it was impossible to raise a
quarter-million dollars in New Mexico in the time
allotted him and his followers. However, they were
dangerous, she was completely in their power — and
everything depended upon Ben Hancock.

Strand asked her, "How long you reckon it will take
for your Britisher to get the money?"

"There is the telegraph," she temporized. "It will
take time. And I am afraid of Jed Buxton."

"You needn't be."

"He killed my daughter."

"He won't kill you. And you ain't scared of him. You
just purely hate him."

"Of course. And I'm also frightened."

"Can't blame you. Under the circumstances." His
attitude was ingratiating. He hitched closer, lowered his
voice. "Fact is, I been thinkin'."

"Good. I know you're a thinking man."

"You know I can't turn you loose until we're clean
away and on the run."

"Yes. I know that."

"On the other foot, I got to turn you loose sooner or later."

"So?"

"Well, look at it this way. We'll be headin' for the border. Quickest way. Now I'll make you a deal."

"Yes?"

"You ride along, no trouble. You stay with me in a place I know, real quiet and secret for awhile. I'll kill Jed for you."

"Kill him now," she said. "Start a quarrel, it'll be easy."

Strand said, "With his boys watchin'? Oh, no."

"Pitts will take your side on account of the money." Then she realized she had gone too far. She saw his face close in.

"You're not so smart, at that. Come a fight, I need those boys. Even Jed. No, it won't do. You'll have to take your chances. And don't be foolish like. Because I can always turn you over to Jed."

He got up and abruptly left her. But she knew he would not turn her over to Jed. He wanted her for himself, she had seen it in him, she had known it since Lordsburg. He would take daring chances in order to have his way. The problem was how to use him.

She dreaded the night. In daytime she could conquer the fear, try to use her brains. She knew the plan, she had heard them discuss it openly. She knew there would be a night watch for the bonfire at the cemetery, she knew how they intended to pick up the money and make the run for Mexico. But she could think of no way to obstruct their scheme.

She saw Jed leering at her from the mouth of the cave and knew what he was thinking of for later in the operation. He was dangerous no matter what Strand thought. He was somewhat deranged, she believed. Strand was quicker and smarter, but the actions of a person like Jed Buxton could not be predetermined.

She dreaded nightfall.

Again the town hall was filled, but there were no standees this time. The council was present and Jerry Kay and some others. Hancock felt ill at ease at the lectern in the center of the dais. He knew what he had to say but he felt the coolness of the crowd.

The door opened and Virgie Buxton came in, followed by Matt. They sat down on a rear bench and were very still, looking straight ahead. There was a rustle in the audience.

Hancock said, "You all know why we're here. Cole Strand and some others got a lady captive in the hills. There is no way to get at them without harmin' the lady. Jed Buxton is with 'em and he's wanted by the law."

The door opened again. Brewster came in on the arm of Linda Darr, swaying a bit, his head bandaged still, but determined, holding the back of the bench, then sinking down to sit straight and tall.

Hancock went on, "They want more money than any of us ever seen. They want a quarter-million dollars to turn loose the lady."

Gus Mueller called, "But not Jed, just the lady already?"

"Just the lady."

"The mamma of Daisy the whore?" continued Mueller.

"Mrs. Van Orden, a lady I know well."

"Humph," said Mueller. "So vat?"

"So Jerry Kay promised twenty-five thousand. Abe Getz will put up five thousand." Hancock consulted a list. His hand was shaking and sweaty.

"*Ein bissel verrückt,*" Mueller grunted.

Matt Buxton arose in the rear of the hall and said, "I can scrape twenty thousand together quick and more later."

Now every head spun around.

Matt said, "Kidnappin' a woman. Jesus! If I could get holt of more I'd pay it all."

"But Jed gets away," Mayor Taggart said boldly, then sank back, appalled at his own outbreak.

Hancock interposed, "We don't figure any of 'em to get clean away. We aim to get them and the money after they turn the lady loose."

"What about her?" demanded Mueller. "She got a million, she says."

Brewster managed to get to his feet. His voice was shaky but clear. "I assure you that every cent of the money will be repaid if anything goes wrong. I have Mrs. Van Orden's power of attorney. Her money is entangled in an estate in England but it will be available in time."

"If she's dead?" demanded Mueller.

Brewster's face grew even whiter. "I must admit that I cannot answer that question."

"*Ja,*" nodded Mueller. "Tell them, Mayor, what we decided."

Taggart arose. He was nervous but determined. "The council has met and decided that this is not our business. Jed Buxton is wanted by the law. Let the law recapture him. The lady is no part of our business. We feel we should remain out of it entirely."

"Not even good luck to us?" It was Jerry Kay, rising to face them. "You and the mineowners. Citizens. Come to our country to take what you can get. Give nothin'. I know youall. I told the marshal. Amongst us all we might could raise this money, thanks to Matt Buxton and a few others. It could be done. But you ain't goin' to do it and I knowed it. Sheepherders!"

He walked out, his back very straight. Matt and Virgie Buxton followed him. Hancock came down from the platform knowing he had failed. Luke caught up with him and they moved together, ignoring the council, the mining people. Jeb Truman joined them at the door and they stood a moment in a group with Abe Getz and his wife.

Truman said, "I got a few dollars. Miz Jay, she told me she'd pony up four, five thousand. Can't we make it up amongst us?"

"No," said Hancock. "We can't. It's too damn much."

Luke said, "I could sell some property but it wouldn't be soon enough. There's no way."

"Jim Madison has got some," Truman continued stubbornly. "I bet the hoors have got stockin's with cash in 'em. Count it all up, Ben."

"No use," Jerry Kay said. "I counted every dime and I'm an old countin'-up man. Right now I'm countin' up on this town." He sighed. "But now the railroad's comin' with all their fooforaw, reckon I'll soon be retired and out of it."

"The hell with the railroad," Hancock said bitterly. "Judge Grey went to Reynolds and got turned down. They want Jed away and don't care about anything else."

Brewster leaned heavily still upon Linda Darr. "What can we do? If we only knew where they are hiding, I would go there."

"They'd kill her first," said Luke.

"My lady would rather die," said Brewster calmly. "If the murderer is punished, she would die willingly."

There was a pungent silence among the men of Cobre. Then they silently went their way, each with his own thoughts. Hancock and Luke started down Buxton Street toward the office. Ben's head was spinning, his stomach was in knots. He had not eaten that day nor did he feel hunger.

"*Amigo,*" said Luke, "the world is always a couple drinks short. Let us get a bottle and start usin' our brains."

"There's no alley without a dead end," Hancock said in despair. "I been up and down 'em all."

"There's got to be somethin'," Luke insisted. "Strand ain't all that smart. We've not been thinkin' clear."

They were passing the hotel. A voice called.

"Ben. Matt would like to see you, please."

It was Virgie Buxton. She beckoned to them. "Bring your friend."

They went into the hotel and up the stairs to the Buxton suite. Matt was sitting on the bed. His bulky frame seemed empty, his hands supported him. He waved them to a table where there were glasses and a bottle. Virgie anticipated them, pouring straight and hefty, including one for herself.

Matt said, "Virgie's been after me. God knows she's plumb right."

"I don't know what you can do, Matt," said Hancock.

Virgie went to the big man's side and put a bony hand upon his shoulder. "You hush, Ben. Let him talk."

"He never was no good," Matt said painfully. "He was ornery from the time he was borned. Used to think it was cute. Things he did, stealin' pies from the cook, all that. He could ride anything that wore hide, kinda misled us, I reckon. Boy that can ride, you think he must be somethin' like a man. Caught him usin' a spade bit once, thrashed him bloody. But he kin ride. And that's all."

"He never sassed me — much," Virgie said.

"Didn't dare. Thrashed him for that, too," Matt said. "No, my fault or not, he's no good, never was any good."

There was a tap on the door and Johnny Hunter piped, "The paper, Mr. Buxton, Miz Buxton."

Virgie dug out a coin, opened the door. She took the *Bulletin,* shooed the ever-inquisitive boy away. The odor of printer's ink was redolent in the room. Dan Melvin had outdone himself with black headlines:

Mother Of 'Daisy' Abducted . . . Gang Frees Jed Buxton . . . Huge Ransom Demanded . . . Marshal At Complete Loss . . . Matt Buxton Refuses To Talk . . . Mrs. Van Orden In Dire Danger.

"Talk to Melvin? What good would it do?" Matt went on. "Newspapers, stirrin' up trouble. Never was much for book larnin'. Mebbe I shoulda been." He was suffering, Hancock saw, as though he wore a bullet somewhere inside him.

Virgie said, "Tell them, Matt darlin'."

Matt said simply, "I know where they are."

"It won't help," Hancock said. Then he paused and stared hard at Matt. "You know how to get at 'em?"

"When that mess with the Mex gal was on they took to the hills, Jed and the boys. Nobody knew whereat, not even Larson. It didn't set good on me. People forget, I was a rider and a tracker and a fighter. When somethin' gets at me I do whatever. I went out and scouted 'em."

Virgie said, "Like to wear him to a frazzle but he found 'em."

"The Burros," Matt said. "A natural cave."

"Can we get some people up there?"

"No way. They got high gun. They can see miles in this country, 'course."

Hancock said, "You're talkin' around somethin', Matt."

"One thing."

"Like what?"

"They ain't atop the mountain."

"How much time to get above 'em?" He saw it at once; any veteran of the country would see it.

"Take a couple days."

"We've got a couple days. They know that money couldn't be raised in less. They don't know we can't put the money together."

"They don't know I can find 'em," Matt said.

"How many you figure we can take up there?"

Matt shook his head. "You know how it is. More we take, the less chance."

The adrenalin was pumping within Hancock. "Luke Post. Neddy Truman."

"And me."

"You?"

"Told you, didn't I? I do whatever." He sat there blinking up at Hancock, miserable, tortured, determined.

"But Matt . . ."

"He goes," Virgie said. "Or he don't tell you where they're at."

After a brief moment Hancock said, "Yeah. I see how it is. Reckon there'll be one more."

"Brewster, the limey," Matt agreed. "He's got a right."

Hancock's mind raced ahead. "We'll have the fire lighted at the time we expect to be there. That'll split 'em. We'll pick up the messenger. How far?"

Matt said, "They ain't five miles away from the spot."

"When can you start?"

279

"When my hoss gets here. Larson's bringin' him in. Got to have a big brute, y'know."

"Larson and Jeb Truman can handle the town end," Hancock said. "Two days. I wish it was quicker."

"Got to go around the long way so they don't spot us."

"Yeah. I know." Still there were the nights with Laurie among that crowd. He shivered and knew Matt was watching.

Matt said, "Know how you feel. Ain't no other way."

"Cole Strand. I want him."

"Better take a rifle."

"I know he's faster than me. But I want him."

"No sense gettin' kilt. Way I see it, we'll be lucky if they don't get to the lady. It's tetchy, Ben."

"If there was another way. But there ain't."

Virgie said, "I was you, Ben, I'd take another big swig and lay down for an hour."

"I'll do that, ma'am." He went to the door. "Matt, I wish you wouldn't go. It might be real bad for you."

"They'll fight," said Buxton. "Expect it. Howsomever. The lady lost her daughter. We all got to lose. What is there besides six feet of earth?"

"Just what goes on in between," Hancock agreed. "Thanks, Matt."

He went down to the lobby and out onto Buxton Street. They had named it after a good man, he thought, good enough in the tight. He walked to the office, got out a pint bottle and poured.

He said, "Now I reckon to get in one hour of sleep. Get things ready, will you, *amigo?*"

280

"Truman got a good horse for me?"

"Check him, he's got a buckskin'll take you there. Get Neddy. I dunno about Brewster but he deserves a chance. He and Truman could handle this end with Larson, mebbe."

"Which I misdoubt." Luke was on his way. "Get that nap, pardner. Two days in them hills ain't a picnic."

Hancock swallowed the liquor. "It'll be a picnic to me."

It was cold in the high cave. There could be no fire and small things crawled in the darkness. The woman lay huddled in her bower but did not sleep, Cole Strand knew. He was learning more about her each hour and the animal he kept contained within him stirred too often. She was entirely desirable in every possible way. The more he observed her the more she aroused him. Under other circumstances he would have forced the issue without ceremony; he would have laid hands upon her one way or another.

Now he had to be careful because of Jed Buxton. He was sick to death of the talk, the posturing, the constant whining, but he knew he had to have the support of all the Candlestick riders and he knew Jed had the hold on them so common among the cowboys and their simple code.

He had thought of killing Jed. It would be easy during the night watch — he kept the man with him always so that he might watch his actions — a simple knock on the head and a push down onto the pine trees far below the mountain eyrie. It would precipitate trouble, he feared. Dave Pitts was avid of the ransom money but he was also a Candlestick man and he had a certain amount of perspicacity.

No, the way to go was to play it straight until the time was ripe. It was not easy to be so close to her and control himself but he could manage it, he believed.

He should be sleeping but he could not. He arose, took one more look at the woman. She regarded him with large round eyes and he shook himself and went to the mouth of the cave. Jed and the two younger men lay in a row like slumbering boys, saddles for their pillows. He had nothing but contempt for them, thirty a month and found slaves to a Matt Buxton, hardhanded and hardheaded, stupid workmen. What was their future? Once broken and unable to labor, where did they go? He spat and climbed up to the lookout point where Dave Pitts hunched upon a square rock formation, a folded blanket beneath him.

Pitts said, "You leavin' Jed with that woman?"

Strand put out a hand above the natural chimney through which even now a small heat emanated. "Makes a nice peephole, hadn't you noticed?"

"Ain't much for peekin'," Pitts answered.

"You can hear through it too." His gray clothing was rumpled and the chill night air struck at his bones. "You're worryin' about Jed, too, are you?"

"Not much for worryin'," Pitts said.

The view from the promontory was gorgeous beneath the moon. Clouds played lazy tricks around Mount Cooper miles away to the southeast. The lights of Cobre were tiny, landlocked stars. Behind them the mountain loomed steep and serrated, rocky and forlorn. Below them were the piny valleys.

Strand said, "When we spot the fire the horses must be ready to go."

"Yep."

"The woman rides with us."

"You say."

"You don't like it?"

"Nope."

"But you'll go along."

"Until we get the cash I'm your man."

"And then?"

"We ride south. The woman is yours. We ain't waitin' on her nohow."

"Okay. Now if Jed starts something with the woman . . ."

There was a small scream from below, echoing through the aperture in the rocks. Pitts did not move. Strand scrambled down the face of the rock, past the two riders trying to disentangle themselves from their blankets. The glow from the tiny fire blended with reflected moonlight to throw strange shadows around the corner of the elbow of the cavern.

Jed Buxton had the woman by the throat. She was kicking at him but her efforts were becoming feeble as he shut off her wind. He had ripped the stuff of her blouse to the waist. He was making sounds in his throat like a rutting beast.

Strand went past them. He was wary of the ricochet of lead if he had to shoot and he was not a man to close with an adversary. He held the gun low, seeing the riders confused in the background.

"Get away from her," he commanded.

The woman made a last convulsive movement and the youth fell away, staggering, loose-lipped, eyes glaring hatred. "Damn you! Damn all of you! A whore's mother, what are y'all waitin' for? Nothin' but meat, you hear me? Meat!"

"You looking to die right here?" Strand asked casually.

Jed wiped a sleeve across his lips. "You some damn outlaw, you are. You some kind of damn steer, are you? You been deballed?"

Without altering his tone, Strand said, "Get up on the watch, Jed. Take your rifle and go on, now."

"I damn likely to use that gun," said the oddly shrill young man. "I damn likely to kill you and that slob woman before this is over."

Behind him the riders moved uneasily and one of them said softly, "C'mon, Jed. Remember all that money."

"Yes, remember the money," Strand said. "Now, go on and do like I ask you."

The woman had regained her strength. She came toward him, one hand outstretched, her bosom bare in the strange light.

"Kill him," she insisted in harsh accents. "Kill him now. He's worse than a snake. He should die."

She almost walked between them, into the line of fire. Strand put his left arm around her, feeling the silk of her flesh, gritting his teeth.

"Just take it easy. Jed, you go on."

Down the flue the voice of Dave Pitts echoed, booming, fierce. "Yeah, Jed. You come up here. Don't you get your nose in the way of this job. You hear me?"

Jed picked up his rifle and Strand's finger trembled on the trigger of his Colt. There was a moment, then it was past and Jed, still mumbling, was gone from the scene.

Sandy Farr said, "This here ain't right, Strand. I don't like it nohow."

"Speak to your friend," Strand said. "Now go and get your sleep."

They went but there was unrest in them, he knew. He became aware of the softness of the woman in his arm as he reholstered his revolver. She turned away from him and his hand felt hot, electric, where it had touched her. The two primal instincts by which he lived struggled in him. He could take her now, he thought, one way or the other, but he dared not because of the others. He breathed deeply and led her to the bower of branches. She sank down and stared up at him.

"You missed your chance," she told him, her voice still low and unnatural.

"It'll come to pass again," he promised her. "It'll work out."

"Will it?" She sank back, covering herself. "I have grave doubts. You missed."

He had to leave her. It was essential that he stand the same watch as Jed. He walked slowly through the cave to the entrance, where the two riders were again in their blankets. He looked at the moon, then down upon

Cobre. Never in his life had he wanted so badly to see the signal fire which would set the scheme in motion again. Never had he been so shaken. On the other hand, never had he been so determined.

On the second night of the ride around the Burro Mountains they began the ascent. Matt rode a huge hammerhead buckskin and Brewster a good enough hack from Truman's corral. Hancock worried about them both, big men for varied reasons unfit for the rarefied ozone. He was himself worn to a frazzle with worriment, lack of sleep and the cold food of the past two days.

They were climbing a narrow trail with Matt in the lead and Brewster in the middle. The sound of the shod horses was startlingly loud against canyon walls, another source of worriment. But Matt doggedly urged his big horse up and around the sharp corners, grunting, cursing and sweating despite the cold night air.

There was a sudden break in the cliff wall, a place where a stunted growth of pine struggled for life. Matt swung heavily down from the saddle and muttered, "This here is it."

Hancock sat and stared. The trail they had been traversing suddenly ended. Horrible suspicion struck him.

"It's a dead end."

"Yep," said Matt. He had insisted upon leaving Luke and Neddy at the appointed rendezvous in case anything went wrong in the Burros. He had said that no more than two men should try the high place, and only reluctantly consented to have Brewster try it, doubting that the Britisher could make it all the way in his weakened condition.

"If this is a trick, sir, I shall kill you," Brewster said thickly through his weariness.

"Fella learns quick," sighed Matt. "Just about got here, already he's on the prod. Well, folks like us settled the damn country, what kin I say?"

Hancock dismounted. "Talk some more."

"You didn't think we was gonna ride down and politely ask 'em to surrender, did you?" The fat man sat on a round rock. The moon seemed close enough to take a dipperful at arm's length. Stars sparkled across the sky. "Haven't been up here in many a day. Nice, ain't it?"

Hancock said, "Keep talking."

"Dunno if we can all three make it," Matt pursued. "Figure one of us with a rifle might. But they could still kill the lady. Anyway, figure the fire'll be set and they'll see it and start down for the money. Right?"

"We agreed on that."

"No other way to get at 'em and not see the lady hurt. Might not make it thisaway," Matt went on. "Told you that too."

"You mean we make a climb from here? Afoot?"

"Hand and foot, you might say." He jerked a thumb over his shoulder. "Injun trail."

Hancock walked to the spot indicated. There was mountain brush and beyond it a handhold, above it another. He knew at once that Apaches had at some time retreated from an enemy and had constructed this precarious way upward.

He asked, "How close does this bring us to their cave?"

"Close enough."

"I'd rather not tote a rifle," Hancock mused. "Man needs all his toes and fingers up yonder."

Brewster, mollified, came to peer. "I've some experience in this. The Alps, y'know. The Master was for it when he was younger."

"Good. You can carry me," said Hancock. He was sick at heart, he was almost beyond feeling. "I never had mountain goat in me."

Matt said, "I made it a couple years back. Gonna make it again. Figure we might rest an hour or so."

Hancock looked at his watch. "That's drawin' it pretty fine. But you're right."

He removed the saddles as the others sank to earth, big men who had overextended themselves without complaint. He knew their worth but he did not know their value under the circumstances. He stretched his tarp and lay down with his head on the saddle, trying to relax against the task ahead.

Matt was rumbling along. "Reason I told y'all to wear soft shoes, you see? Now the ropes, we need the ropes."

"As I said, sir. Ropes." Brewster was dead tired, his voice was slow and thin.

"Got to be quiet. Remember that. They'll have a strong lookout. Oh, sure, they'll have the rifle ready. Strand and Pitts, they're old hands. Jed, he don't know nothin'. Never could teach him. Tried and tried." The voice trailed off.

Matt was worse off than he would admit, Hancock thought. With the worst of the trip ahead, his bulk was already telling upon him. There was no question now of his integrity; he had promised to lead them and he would do it. When it came to the fight — well, there was no way of knowing what he would do.

Again his thoughts went to Laurie and again he managed to turn them off. He slept and then he awakened and the moon was higher and it was time.

The two big men were snoring. Hancock looked at them and thought of leaving them, going on ahead by himself. The ride up the high plain and around the neck of the Burros and up the western slope had been terrible for Brewster, whose injury was serious. Matt was as vulnerable, with the extra weight he carried.

They had come along, however. They had deep concern. They were involved. To leave them would be a bad thing, Hancock decided, uncoiling a lariat, looking up in the moonlight to the protuberance of rock which must be their first aid in the climb. He had once been good with the rope but it was a long time ago. He made a tentative cast and missed.

Matt Buxton awakened and said, "Let me try."

"Take it easy." Hancock set himself, tried again. The wide loop settled over the angle of the rock and he pulled it tight, testing. It held. "One at a time. I'll bring the other ropes."

Brewster shook himself and said, "We should tie ourselves together, y'know. That is the way it is done."

"Not on this climb," Hancock told him. "You go first. We back you up."

"It's not the proper manner."

"It's the way we go."

Matt said, "Ben's right. But I'll go first. I been over these hills afoot in the old days. Gimme a rope. I ain't that old or that fat."

It was better not to argue with him, Hancock thought. They each took a spare rope. Matt slung a rifle, but Hancock thought this was no good, that a rifle shot might be the signal for them to kill Laurie. He said nothing, unwilling to cross Matt at this time.

He watched the owner of Candlestick begin the perpendicular climb. It was amazing how agile, how powerful he was beneath the rolls of fat. There was no sound except the crackle of leather shoes on loose surface shale. In a few moments Matt had reached the place where the rope was secured and made his cast for the next goal, a stunted but sturdy tree upon a small shelf.

Brewster said, "I say, he is amazing."

"How's your head?"

"Quite all right. I shall be there with you."

"Go ahead, then."

Matt was already essaying the next climb up the almost sheer side of the mountain. The Apaches had left tiny indentations for footholds but they were difficult to find. Brewster took hold of the rope and in a moment Hancock saw that he knew what he was doing, that he really had experience and that his determination might well carry him all the way.

He removed the bridles from the horses and took them one by one to the downward trail and slapped them on the flank. They were hungry enough to go clattering toward home. He went back to the base of the cliff and tightened his belt. The holster was a nuisance, his hands were clammy as he gazed toward the sky. All his life he had suffered from a fear of heights.

He thought of Laurie and drew on rawhide gloves. He took hold of the rope and began to climb.

The first step was a breathless scamper which he made without drawing a breath. Then, panting, he resolutely did not look backward or downward, releasing the lariat, coiling it, adjusting it on his shoulder. He took hold of the second rope and sought a toehold, made three of the small Apache steps, which brought him halfway to the next position.

Then he missed with his toe. He hung there, suspended, soft from city dwelling, spinning on the rope. He gasped for air and clung to the lasso, trying again and again to find a place to set his foot, to arrest his panic.

From above, Brewster's voice came softly. "Drop back. Let yourself down."

His brain began to work again. He slid down the rope to where he had found the previous step. He made it by light of the moon and braced himself there, regaining strength, searching for the spot he had missed. He found it and began to climb again. This time his toe caught in the crevice.

He gave himself only a moment's respite, then began to clamber again. This time they had reached a small plateau where all three sat and drew what oxygen they could at the dizzying altitude.

Matt warned, "Worst is yet to come."

"Wasn't for Brewster I wouldn't be this far," Hancock said.

"It is something I know about," Brewster said mildly. "Should we not press on?"

"Yeah. Press on," said Matt.

They arose and studied the next step, which would take them to a trail leading over the peak of the mountain. Brewster was containing himself almost too well, Hancock thought. His insistence upon making the trek had been evidence enough of the depth of his rage, but he was taking it one step at a time, without display of passion. The ugly pictures began to unreel again in his mind and his hands to shake again and he said, "Press on, then."

As the two big men began their slow, painful ascent, he forced his mind back to the take-off and the people who had been kind. Jerry Kay, the Getzes and Virgie with her package of cold food, and Jeb Truman. And Luke and Neddy who wanted to come along, maybe should have, since Neddy at least was younger and stronger excepting for his bandaged wrists. But he had thought it better for them to remain with the fake carpetbags at the meeting place until the fire was set and then to use their judgment if no one appeared to collect the ransom. He was not sure of his judgment but he had to play it the way the card fell, with Strand dealing. He remembered Linda Darr and her feeling of guilt and how Judge Grey had spoken quietly of the law. He remembered very well about the judge and he knew that his job was to bring in Jed Buxton for trial, although he doubted this would ever come to pass. It was not a spot for taking prisoners and if anything did happen to Laurie, the lives of those responsible would not be worth a plugged two-bit piece, not so long as he held a gun nor so long as Brewster, he added, was able to swing a weapon.

Brewster went up out of sight on the steepest climb yet. Hancock took hold of the end of the rope and thought of the others who had stood aside, Taggart and Mueller and the council and those who wanted the railroad so bad and Reynolds who secretly wished they would all be done away with so that the town might be left to the power of the company. There was bile in his throat as he began to pull himself up, knowing now that the Apaches, shorter of stature, had made their little toeholds closer together than he would have liked in his haste.

There were two more complete hitches. His arms ached, his lungs seemed about to burst, his mouth was dry, his feet were sore from digging into the little places. He never knew whether it was his anger against the town of Cobre or his love for Laurie that got him, at agonized last, to the summit of the mountain peak.

He coiled the last rope and as he came to the end which had been part of the loop, it broke in his hands, frayed through. He shivered once and tossed it aside. The three looked at one another, their clothing

293

tattered, their boots worn thin, their faces and bodies bruised. Hancock managed a short laugh and the others joined him, then were silent as he looked at his watch and repeated, "Shall we press on?"

Matt asked, "You thought on Truman and the fire? How there's some might stop him?"

"I thought about those others. Jerry Kay. The judge. Virgie."

Matt said, "Press on."

Moonlight bathed an entire world of jagged peaks and high clouds and shadows of a thousand grotesques here atop the mountain, but they had not time to admire it, they had only to make a perilous way downward one third of the distance to Cobre, where the hideout was, and with no utter certainty that it was the place, a matter none mentioned. They made their way in silence and with pain. It was steep enough to try their remaining strength but not so precipitous as to require the ropes, although Hancock retained one, just in case.

Then finally there was a straightening out, like a huge lip thrust forth. Matt stopped them.

He whispered, "Down below there. No sound, now, none!"

Hancock nodded, held up a hand in sign, began squirming down toward the edge of the lip. He removed his hat, crawling on his belly, inching his way. After a moment he returned, gathered the other two, spoke in their ears.

"Looks like Farr and Ward. One watchin' for the fire. The other watchin' this direction."

"Figures," said Matt.

"When Truman lights that fire, we go down," Hancock said. "They're bound to stare at it. It's a mighty big chance but there's no other way."

"We'd never take them comin' up the trail, you see?" Matt was anxious to have proven himself correct.

"You were right all the way," Hancock told him. "Now we crawl close in there and wait."

"How's the time?"

"It shouldn't be long now."

They got to their knees and edged their way down to the protruding lip of the mountain and lay there, cold and weary, waiting for the signal. Matt lay on his rifle, Hancock removed his revolver and warmed it in his hands. Brewster took from his pocket a curious device which he slipped upon his left hand and it was a moment before Hancock remembered from New York City the knuckle-dusters which were the favorite weapon of the slum gangs.

It was impossible now not to think of Laurie, down in the cave which Matt had described. It seemed ominous that the two cowboys should be on watch while the gunslinger Pitts, Cole Strand and Jed Buxton should be below. Hancock's pulse beat like a railroad watch, his blood ran hot and violent in his arteries. There was nothing to do but wait, at a time when what he desired above all was action.

He turned his watch to the moon which had served them so well on the journey and which he now wished would vanish from the sky to give them the protecting mantle of darkness. It was after midnight. Truman was late with the fire and he thought about Matt's comment and wondered if there was a battle in Cobre. He could see the town only vaguely at this hour, with the lights extinguished. He sank back, trying to conserve energy, to be ready for what was to come.

Then there was a faint glow, a promise of more at approximately where the cemetery should be. The two Candlestick riders exclaimed, the one watching the high place turned. Hancock held up a hand in warning. The bonfire burst into a high, pale flame topped with a wisp of smoke which hung over the town.

One of the riders below them yipped. Both started to move. Hancock went racing over rock in his soft boots, his revolver poised. Behind him came Brewster, stumbling a bit but making remarkable speed. Matt was a poor third in the race.

Hancock hit Muley Ward behind the ear, caught him as he fell, hit him again. Brewster's heavy arm came around in a perfect arc and almost knocked Sandy Farr off the promontory. He then snagged him with his right hand and dragged him back. Matt came lumbering up to disarm the pair and take a position where he could command the scene below as Hancock and Brewster went piling down.

They were all out staring at the fire. Only Cole Strand spun around and in that instant Hancock saw that Laurie was with them, outside the cave, in a most dangerous position. Hancock ran forward but Brewster, spinning from the force of his effort, rammed into him.

Matt said, "No, Cole. Not this time."

Strand's hand rested on the butt of the revolver. He stared up at Matt, at the rifle trained upon him. There was a moment in suspension, then Dave Pitts made his draw. Brewster, still off balance from the collision, drove into him, a fury of a man. Pitts fired, but Brewster hit him with the brass knuckles and the Candlestick gunslinger went down as though shot by a cannon.

Jed Buxton found the moment to act. He seized Laurie around the waist, using her as a shield, his six-gun drawn and ready.

"You don't get me," he screamed. "I'll kill her. I might's well be hung for two as one!"

The one thing Hancock had dreaded was now a fact.

Cole Strand, still with his hand on his gun, drawled, "Well, what do you know? A Mexican standoff."

Brewster was down, hit by a .45 slug. Even then he did not utter a sound, breathing hard, lying on one hip, supporting himself with one thick arm.

Hancock said, "You move a finger, Cole. Just one finger."

Strand took his hand away from his gun butt. "Why should I?"

Jed was still yelling. "Damn you all. You damn fat brother, comin' to hang me. I got her now. I'm goin' down and get that money. You can't stop me. I'll kill her if you try. You understand that?"

"Don't do it, boy," Matt said. His voice was slow and sad. "Don't try it."

Jed stabbed the gun into Laurie's side so that she cried out in pain. "Ha, fat brother! Gotcha this time. All my life you been boss. Now I'm boss."

"You won't live it out, nohow. Mayhap I can get you off hangin'. But you won't live this out." Matt was begging now.

Strand said, "Don't listen, Jed, move. Take her down to the horses. Saddle up three of them, chase the others. We've got it made, just do like I say."

Hancock said, "Matt?"

"Yeah, Ben."

"I'll take Strand. You cover Jed?"

"Like you say, Ben." The fat man held the rifle steady. "Lady, I can shoot. I can pick him off any time. You might get hurt. Is that okay?"

"It is." Her face was white but she did not flinch.

"There's your standoff," Hancock said to Strand.

"You wouldn't take a free shot, would you, Ben?" The gunman laughed. "Put up your iron there. I'll gamble with you."

Hancock returned the smile. "I'm wearing tin, remember? I don't have to give a kidnapper an even break. Look, this is over. Put down your guns, you're all under arrest."

"Spoken like a nice little lawman," jeered Strand. "Way I see it, Matt won't shoot his little brother. He's bluffin', you're bluffin'. Jed — start walkin' backward with the lady."

Jed was raving on. "I know what I'm doin'. I got all you damn people by the balls . . ."

298

Brewster came to his feet. Blood ran from him but he put down his head and charged straight at Laurie and Jed. There was no thought, no reason, he was in shock from the impact of the bullet. He merely reacted to the dangerous position of the woman.

Jed hesitated a split moment, then fired one shot.

Cole Strand went for his gun. Hancock, alarmed and distracted by Brewster's ill-timed move, barely had time to wheel around toward the gunslinger. Their weapons went off almost as one.

Hancock felt a twinge in his right elbow. He fired once more. Strand, not five paces away, went over backward, his gray-clad feet flying up over his head.

Hancock came around in the other direction. Brewster had reached Laurie and was tearing her away from the open-mouthed, confused Jed Buxton.

Hancock called, "Stand still, Jed. Very still."

In complete panic, Jed turned and ran clattering down the rocky trail toward the horses. Matt lifted his rifle, then lowered it. Hancock triggered off two cartridges, aiming high. Jed continued his wild pace downgrade.

Hancock called, "Let him go, Matt. Let him go."

The fat rancher wiped a hand across his face. His voice was wild and bitter and self-accusing. "I couldn't do it, Ben. I just couldn't do it."

Hancock said, "No reason for it. Luke and Neddy are waiting for him."

But he went down the trail behind the fleeing figure and used two more bullets to put Jed on a horse and prevent him from stampeding the others. Then he went back to where Laurie knelt over Brewster, tearing apart her clothing to make bandages.

Matt came down from the promontory, sweating, contrite. "The Britisher, he tried real hard. I'm damn sorry. I shoulda done better."

Hancock knelt beside Laurie. "Tie up Muley and Farr, will you? They can walk in. I'll get Brewster down there. He's alive."

"Will he live?" Laurie asked. "Has he a chance?"

"Only if we stop the bleedin' and get him to Doc." They worked then, using Hancock's shirt and her shirtwaist and whatever they could rip and stuff into the wounds. The first one was the worst, Jed's had gone through the fleshy part of the thigh. Brewster was mercifully unconscious.

"The horses," Hancock said. "Bring one up here."

Matt obeyed without hesitation. They managed to get the heavy form tied to the most docile of the animals.

Hancock looked at Laurie for the first time. "Can you ride alongside and help support him?"

"I can."

Hancock said, "Matt, you bring the boys in. We'll go on ahead. Okay?"

"You sure about Luke and Neddy?"

There were shots down below, then silence.

Hancock said, "We want him alive, Matt. Let's hope we got him that way."

Matt said, "You truly do want him alive. Yeah. The hell with the town, huh?"

"Judge Grey said it right," Hancock told him. "Sometimes the town don't know what's right for it. Reynolds and the railroad don't make everything peaches and cream. Money's fine but this is a country needs more'n prosperity. You agree with that?"

Matt said, "I dunno. I purely dunno." He walked heavily up to secure the Candlestick men. He paused and called back, "I'm glad we didn't kill him, Ben. I'm purely glad it wasn't us."

Hancock mounted a horse, steadied Brewster in the saddle. Laurie came around to the other side and they rode slowly down the rocky side of the Burro Mountains.

CHAPTER
SIX

Hancock came out of his sleeping quarters shaved and bathed and dressed in fresh clothing. Luke and Neddy were at his desk, the monte layout between them.

"Shame," said Hancock.

"You think I'd take the boy's money?" Luke was injured. "After the way he snaked that Jed off his horse? Reached right up and snatched him. And Jed shootin' like a Fourth of July celebration."

"He's teachin' me the game," Neddy explained.

"When you think you've learned — don't bet on it," Hancock advised. He went to the big door and unlocked it and peered within. Jed Buxton, somewhat battered, sat on the edge of the cot and stared at him numbly.

"I want to see my brother," he muttered.

"Sure you do."

Hancock locked the door and hung up the key. The players were deep in their game, Luke lecturing on the odds. Hancock went out onto Buxton Street. There were many errands to perform this day.

Melvin came bustling from the newspaper office. "Oh, Ben, have you got a minute? There are several items I would like to check with you."

"Later," Hancock told him. "And maybe, just maybe."

He went on to where Abe Getz waited. The little man's face was glum.

"Marshal, it's a bad day, no?"

"You don't worry about it. You stick in there."

"The mayor, the council — *oy veh!* Are they crazy mad!"

"They don't dare say so out loud. So why worry?"

"But they say you will quit, that you told them last night you were quitting."

Hancock said, "First time they got things straight in a long time. See you later, Abe."

Speedy Jackson intercepted him. "Ben, just got some news. Damnedest thing you ever heard."

"Like what?"

"Reynolds is fired. They're sendin' in another man. No decision on the railroad. We won't know for months, the judge told me when he heard about it."

"Couldn't be less interested," Hancock told him.

"People is real upset about Jed comin' to trial and all."

"Some people, you mean."

"Yeah." Speedy winked. "Some people!"

Hancock walked on, past Gus Mueller, who did everything but spit at him, into the alley to the redolent odors emanating from Ching Hoo's domain. The aged Chinese popped out of the door and said, "No got. All out. So solly."

Hancock said, "Word does get around in this burg."

"No unnastand."

"You get six pints of the best over to my place and make it fast. I haven't left town yet. You savvy?" He thrust his chin at the old bootlegger.

"Me savvy, me savvy." Ching Hoo retreated.

Hancock went on to Pass Avenue, waved to Jeb Truman and cut through to the house of Mrs. Jay. Chompy opened the door and actually grinned.

"Hey there, Marshal."

"I hear there were gals on the street again. You're going to get your ears pinned back, you know that?"

"They 'scaped me," said the pimp contritely. "I gave them a — I yelled hard at them for it."

Mrs. Jay came into the parlor. "You're no good, Chompy. If I could find me a real man. Now, Mr. Hancock, if you'd care for the job . . . ?"

"People get real smart when they know a man's leavin' town," said Hancock. "Real smart."

"You mean I can't joke with you?"

"Sure you can. Got a message for you." He handed her an envelope. "Mrs. Van Orden says thanks."

"Thanks?" Mrs. Jay's eyes were wide and lost. "God help me that she should thank me."

"You were good to the kid."

"I — I never heard of such a thing. She was — Daisy was — kinda special, is all."

Hancock said, "You were decent. And you said somethin', you said everybody has rights. So long, Miz Jay."

He left her sitting with the envelope in her hand, for once without words.

He walked down the east side of Buxton Street and entered Jim Madison's place. Business was slow. Madison was in his office, glooming, taking pills.

"Mrs. Jay might buy you out," Hancock told him. "She just came into some money and she's a savin' woman anyway."

"I'll sell damn cheap. This town don't like me and I ain't exactly crazy about it."

"But you're going to testify at the trial?"

"Yes. Me and Monty. Then we'll pull out." Madison managed a weak smile. "It's time. Cobre's just another stop on the road. We always know that, me and Monty."

"Good luck," said Hancock. "Talk to Mrs. Jay, you hear?"

The next stop was Dr. Farrar's place. The office was empty but Brewster was ensconced in the back room. He was pallid and weak, he was missing a rib and lucky to be alive, but he was propped on pillows and Linda Darr was attending him.

Hancock said, "Any better today?"

"It will take some time," Brewster said resignedly. "It was foolish of me, y'know. You could have handled it. I was clumsy."

"You were shot," said Hancock. "I've seen men do crazier things."

Linda Darr said, "He frets too much. He thinks he will not be strong again."

Hancock regarded her. She flushed a bit, standing her ground.

She said, "I'm getting to be the town nurse. I don't mind. It's something to do that is helpful."

"Brewster appreciates it, don't you, Brewster?"

"Of course, Marshal."

"Well, press on," said Hancock. "Be seein' you later."

"Press on," said Brewster, grinning, looking more youthful, as though he had been relieved of a burden. "All will be well."

Hancock crossed Alamo Street, paying no attention to the curious stares of those who had marked each step of his progress. He went into the hotel where Matt sat in his big chair and Virgie perched beside him.

Matt said, "How's he this mornin'?"

"Same as before. Askin' for you." Hancock shook his head. "He's caved in."

"Pitts died, eh?"

"Fractured skull."

"I do thank you for lettin' me have Farr and Ward. The judge was real nice, knowin' we need 'em right now at the ranch."

"They'll be around to stand trial. But they'll tell the truth and it won't be too hard on them."

Matt said, "The truth. About Jed and all."

"It's got to be," said Hancock gently.

"You think they'll hang him?"

"I don't know."

Virgie said, "We hear you're quittin'."

"That's about it."

"Reynolds was fired," said Matt. "Town's goin' to need good people."

"The town don't want me," said Hancock. "You know it. Every time they think of the railroad they're goin' to want me a lot less."

"The rails might come next year, sometime."

"The rails will come when this has blown over. Me, I got other things to think about."

"Times change." Matt looked old and weary. "Virgie and me, we're goin' home tonight. I'll see Jed, then let Finnegan take it over. I seen it in the mountains t'other night, the last of it. You been a good law officer, Ben."

"I take that to be the best thing you could say," Hancock told him sincerely. "Goodbye, Virgie. Take care of your man."

He went upstairs. He tapped upon a door and Judge Grey bade him enter. The jurist was sitting at the window reading from a book.

"Marshal, good morning."

"Mornin', sir." Hancock did not seat himself.

"The trial will be on Monday. Evans is ready, Finnegan has no further recourse. Then you will be free to go."

Hancock said, "Yes. Everything is in order, Judge."

The older man hesitated, then said, "I have just been reading Lincoln's debate with Douglas, the one about principles. 'It is the eternal struggle between these two principles — right and wrong — throughout the world. They are the two principles that have stood face to face since the beginning of time and will ever continue to struggle . . . ' So he said. The difficulty is to determine which is right and which is wrong."

Hancock said slowly, "Well, as to that, a man makes up his own mind."

"According to his conscience?"

"Accordin' to who he is and where he is and what's goin' on," said Hancock.

"All right, Marshal. You've made up your mind, then."

"I have."

"I shall see you, then, in an hour?"

"I'll be obliged."

"I wish you luck."

"Thank you, Judge."

He went down the hall. The door to the sitting room of the suite occupied by Laurie was open. He went in and called her name.

She was wearing a loose white gown which swept in simple lines to the floor, unlike anything he had seen before. She came to him and rested her head on his chest for a moment, then stepped back, folding her hands.

"Darling."

He said, "Everything that happened, it's behind us."

"Yes." Her face was composed but there was agitation in her, he saw her hands tighten together.

He said, "Judge just was talkin' about right and wrong. It occurs to me, I don't know sometimes. I mean, what's what. So it's time to unpin the tin star."

"I noticed you weren't wearing it."

He took it from his vest pocket. "I'll keep it until after the trial."

"I wanted him shot down. Jed Buxton. I wanted him killed. That was wrong."

"Was it? Just another time I wouldn't know. Bein' the law, I had to bring him in alive if I could."

"Yes," she said. She brightened. "Then neither of us are perfect, are we?"

"You might say so," he drawled, grinning.

"And you can sleep, now?"

"What's past just ain't," he said. "It took some time to figure that out."

She looked out the window. The sun shone on Cobre. She said, "All right. I'm ready."

They went decorously down the stairs and across the street to Dr. Farrar's office. They went into the room where Brewster lay on his pillows with Linda Darr at his bedside. Luke Post came in, dressed in his Sunday finery. Then Doc entered, scowling, protesting he was too busy for unimportant affairs, not meaning it. The room seemed crowded with people when Judge Grey entered with a Bible in his hands.

Hancock looked at the lady. "You're right sure, now?"

She said, "I'm sure."

Hancock was suddenly flustered. "Well, everybody's here. Reckon we might as well get on with it, Judge."

"If you'll just stand there together. Who has the ring?" the judge asked.

Luke produced a gold band. "Compliments of Abe Getz. I'm ready if you are."

Everyone became very solemn. The judge began to read the simple ritual marriage service. Hancock held tight to himself. It had to be right, he thought, it had to be, if they could wipe out the past. He felt the return pressure of Laurie's fingers and knew it was as right as it could be.

William R. Cox was born in Peapack, New Jersey. His early career was in newspaper journalism. In the late 1930s he began writing sports, crime, and adventure stories for the magazine market, and he made his debut as a Western writer with "Night of the Blood Bucket Raid" in Dime Western in the January, 1941 issue. It is worth noting that his Western story debut was with the first of several stories to feature a series character, Terry Glenn. During the 1940s Cox created a number of other series characters for the magazine market, most notably the Whistler Kid who appeared regularly in 10 Story Western and Duke Bagley whose adventures usually were featured in Star Western. "The short story form was blissful until there were no markets," he once recalled. In the 1950s and 1960s Cox turned to television and wrote at least a hundred teleplays for such series as "Broken Arrow", "Dick Powell's Zane Grey Theatre," "The Virginian," and "Bonanza." He also won a host of readers writing original paperback Western novels, the best known of which are novels about the adventures of two series characters originally published by Fawcett Gold Medal: Cemetery Jones in a series published under his own byline and the Tom Buchanan series which appeared under the house name, Jonas Ward. Dale L. Walker in the second edition of TWENTIETH CENTURY WESTERN WRITERS (1991) commented that William R. Cox's Western "novels are noted for their 'page-turner' pace, realistic dialogue, and frequent Colt-and-Winchester gun play. The series of novels built around the strong West Texas character, Tom Buchanan, are very typical Cox Westerns." Among his non-series Western novels, among his most notable titles are COMANCHE MOON (1959), THE GUNSHARP (1965), and MOON AT COBRE (1969).

ISIS publish a wide range of books in large print, from fiction to biography. Any suggestions for books you would like to see in large print or audio are always welcome. Please send to the Editorial Department at:

ISIS Publishing Limited
7 Centremead
Osney Mead
Oxford OX2 0ES

A full list of titles is available free of charge from:

Ulverscroft Large Print Books Limited

(UK)
The Green
Bradgate Road, Anstey
Leicester LE7 7FU
Tel: (0116) 236 4325

(Australia)
P.O. Box 314
St Leonards
NSW 1590
Tel: (02) 9436 2622

(USA)
P.O. Box 1230
West Seneca
N.Y. 14224-1230
Tel: (716) 674 4270

(Canada)
P.O. Box 80038
Burlington
Ontario L7L 6B1
Tel: (905) 637 8734

(New Zealand)
P.O. Box 456
Feilding
Tel: (06) 323 6828

Details of **ISIS** complete and unabridged audio books are also available from these offices. Alternatively, contact your local library for details of their collection of **ISIS** large print and unabridged audio books.